PRAISE FOR
Sin of a Woman

"The latest addition to Roby's beloved Curtis Black series is satisfying and sinful...well-written, fast-paced."

—*RT Book Reviews*

"Roby's latest sizzles with scandal. A deliciously decadent beach read of temptation and the wages of sin."

—*Kirkus Reviews*

ACCLAIM FOR KIMBERLA LAWSON ROBY

"Roby writes with high-octane levels of emotion. She pushes characters hard, spotlighting their flaws, showcasing their weaknesses, drawing in the readers to be more than bystanders."

—*USA Today*

"Roby pulls you in until you're hooked."

—*Indianapolis Recorder*

"Roby has reached a pinnacle most writers only dream of."

—*Rockford Register Star*

"Roby's highly engaging prose offers edgy characters and intense drama."

—*Booklist*

"[Roby] knows how to give readers what they want."

—*Essence*

"Kimberla Lawson Roby weaves truth into fiction."

—*Indianapolis Star*

Also by Kimberla Lawson Roby

THE CURTIS BLACK SERIES

Sin of a Woman
A Sinful Calling
The Ultimate Betrayal
The Prodigal Son
A House Divided
The Reverend's Wife
Love, Honor, and Betray
Be Careful What You Pray For
The Best of Everything
Sin No More
Love & Lies
The Best-Kept Secret
Too Much of a Good Thing
Casting the First Stone

STANDALONE TITLES

Copycat
Best Friends Forever
A Christmas Prayer
The Perfect Marriage
Secret Obsession
A Deep Dark Secret
One in a Million
Changing Faces
A Taste of Reality
It's a Thin Line
Here and Now
Behind Closed Doors

Sin of a Woman

KIMBERLA LAWSON ROBY

GRAND CENTRAL
PUBLISHING

NEW YORK   BOSTON

Copyright © 2017 by Kimberla Lawson Roby
Reading group guide copyright © 2017 by Kimberla Lawson Roby and Hachette Book Group, Inc.
Cover design by Elizabeth Connor. Cover photo © gmutlu/Getty Images. Cover copyright © 2017 by Hachette Book Group, Inc.

Grand Central Publishing
Hachette Book Group
1290 Avenue of the Americas, New York, NY 10104
grandcentralpublishing.com
twitter.com/grandcentralpub

Originally published as a hardcover and ebook by Grand Central Publishing in June 2017
First trade paperback edition: January 2018

Grand Central Publishing is a division of Hachette Book Group, Inc. The Grand Central Publishing name and logo is a trademark of Hachette Book Group, Inc.

The Hachette Speakers Bureau provides a wide range of authors for speaking events. To find out more, go to www.hachettespeakersbureau.com or call (866) 376-6591.

Library of Congress Cataloging-in-Publication Data

Names: Roby, Kimberla Lawson, author.
Title: Sin of a woman / Kimberla Lawson Roby.
Description: First Edition. | New York ; Boston : Grand Central Publishing, 2017.
Identifiers: LCCN 2017003031 | ISBN 9781455569694 (hardback) |
ISBN 9781455571253 (large print) | ISBN 9781478967491 (audio download)
Subjects: LCSH: African American women--Fiction. | Urban fiction. | BISAC:
FICTION / Contemporary Women. | FICTION / African American / Contemporary
Women. | FICTION / African American / General.
Classification: LCC PS3568.O3189 S562 2017 | DDC 813/.54—dc23 LC record
available at https://lccn.loc.gov/2017003031

ISBNs: 978-1-4555-6968-7 (paperback), 978-1-4555-6970-0 (ebook)

Printed in the United States of America

LSC-C

10 9 8 7 6 5 4 3 2 1

For my two amazing brothers,
Willie Stapleton, Jr. & Michael Stapleton.
I love you both with all my heart.

Sin of a Woman

Chapter 1

Raven—Pastor Raven Jones Black, that is—scanned the interior of her massive second-floor office, smiled, and strolled closer to the large picture window. But as she gazed down at all the vehicles that were lined up in the church's parking lot, it was still hard to believe that everything had evolved so quickly. And in such perfect order, too. Yes, having a one-thousand-plus-member congregation was all that she'd hoped for, but she wasn't sure she'd expected to see her dreams come to pass in only two years. Of course, it hadn't hurt that nearly two hundred members from her ex-husband's former church had joined right away. Because had they not, she knew her ministry would have taken a lot longer to build.

Raven gazed around her office again, admiring her espresso-colored Italian leather sofa, matching loveseat, two oversized chairs, CEO-style mahogany desk, and executive chair. When they'd first purchased New Vision Christian Center and had moved into the building six months ago, the pastor's study had been only half the size it was now. But the more folks had joined the congregation and paid tithes and offerings on a regular basis, the more upgrades Raven had been able to make—both at the church and for herself. From tearing out a wall and doubling the size of her office to clearing out her closet at home and stepping up her wardrobe game, she'd made lots of changes for the better. To tell the truth, she'd always dressed in expensive clothing, even when she'd been married to that awful ex-husband of hers, Pastor Dillon Whitfield Black. But today she only wore suits that came from some of the highest-end stores people shopped at. In fact, the couture-style fuchsia jacket and skirt she wore now had come from Bergdorf Goodman in New York. She didn't get the opportunity to shop there often, what with her residing in Mitchell, Illinois, but whenever she did fly to New York for a ministry engagement, she never left before spending at least a little time at Bergdorf, Barneys, or Saks's flagship location. She did the same thing at the Neiman Marcus flagship store when she visited Dallas, and although some people might not understand her great desire to live well and have the best of everything, she knew it was only because they didn't know her story. Her childhood horror story. Her reason for deciding early on that when she became an adult, she would never go without any of the things she wanted, not if she could help it.

What was so amazing, though, was that regardless of how great her life seemed to be going, she still reflected on her blemished past. She certainly didn't want to, but no matter how hard she tried, she couldn't forget about her very public and very nasty divorce from Dillon. She couldn't pretend she hadn't spent time in prison for stealing a hundred thousand dollars from her former father-in-law, Reverend Curtis Black. She couldn't dismiss the fact that she'd once struggled with a very serious gambling addiction.

She hadn't even known Dillon back when she'd worked as CFO for his father's church, and now, she regretted the day she'd contacted him. But when she'd heard about the fallout between him and his dad, she'd decided to reach out to Dillon, letting him know that she understood his pain and that she could help him build a much larger church than the one Pastor Black had founded. This, of course, had secured Dillon's undivided attention, and not long after she'd been released from prison, they'd begun seeing each other and had gotten married. Raven had truly loved him, too, and she could tell he'd loved her—at least for a while. But then greed and power had become a lot more important to Dillon, and he'd commenced having an affair with another woman. And then a second one.

But of course, when Raven had lied and told Dillon that God had called her into the ministry and that she wanted to be named co-pastor, he hadn't liked it. He hadn't shared his feelings with her straight out, but she could easily tell that he wasn't happy. What he'd wanted instead was to continue running things all on his own, even though she'd always been the true brains behind the ministry. She'd taught him everything she knew, including all that she'd learned while working for his father, but Dillon hadn't cared about her love, commitment, and loyalty to him. So finally, when Raven had demanded that she be named not only co-pastor but also co-founder, Dillon's church had suddenly caught on fire and burned to the ground. Raven couldn't prove it, and thus far neither had the fire marshal, but she knew Dillon was the guilty party. There was no doubt in her mind that the sole reason he'd destroyed the church was because he would rather have no church at all than to have to share control of it with anyone. Although there was another reason, too, for his resorting to such drastic measures. If he hadn't burned down the church and had still refused to give Raven what she wanted, he'd known she was going to circulate that salacious sex tape she'd gotten possession of—the video that his first mistress, Porsha Harrington, had secretly recorded of the two of them and given Raven a copy of.

Raven shook her head and half laughed because who would've guessed that she and that same Porsha Harrington would become fast friends, and that Porsha was now NVCC's associate minister? Who in their wildest imagination would have foreseen the fact that Porsha would join forces with Raven by investing $250,000 for the ministry's start-up funding? Because it certainly wasn't the most common sort of thing, personally or professionally, that might happen between a wife and the woman who'd had an affair with her husband.

But with Raven and Porsha it *had* happened, and they were both benefitting greatly.

Raven left the window to sit behind her desk, but just as she did, someone knocked on her door.

"Yes, come in."

Porsha walked inside. She wore a black St. John suit that Raven hadn't seen before, and while it looked good on her, it wasn't nearly as nice as the black one Raven had purchased a few months ago.

"I know you're preparing for your sermon, so this will only take a minute," Porsha said.

"No, you're fine. Is everything okay?"

"Everything's great, but I've been doing a lot of soul-searching and God has been leading me toward being a little more active on Sunday mornings than I have been."

Raven wasn't sure she liked the sound of this, but she didn't show her apprehension. "Really?"

"Yes, so what I've decided to do is begin saying a few words to the congregation, right after praise and worship service. It would be just before you enter the sanctuary."

Porsha had spoken to the congregation many times before, and sometimes she even delivered the sermon if Raven was out of town, so Raven wondered why she'd specifically come to tell her about it today.

"You've done that before, and I think it's a great idea."

"Well, the only difference now is that I'm going to be doing it every Sunday. I'll be giving a short inspirational message, and I'd like to have this new segment printed in the weekly program. You know, make it a normal part of our service. But more than anything, I wanted to make sure you don't have any objections."

Raven couldn't say what she wanted to say, but of course she *did* have objections. Still, she smiled and said, "No, not at all, and will you be speaking for a certain amount of time?"

"Not more than five to seven minutes. It really will be brief, and it won't infringe on any of your sermons. I just want to say something that will encourage our members, right before you deliver your message. I mean, you already give them everything they need, but again, I believe God wants me to do this."

Raven smiled again but secretly cringed on the inside. "Not a problem. I think it'll be fine."

"I'm glad you're okay with it, and since praise and worship is just about over I'd better get going. I'll see you out there shortly."

Raven watched Porsha leave her office and shut the door behind her. This was so not the kind of news Raven wanted to hear, and more and more she wished she'd borrowed that $250,000 from a bank instead of accepting it as an investment from Porsha. Porsha's offer had seemed like a real blessing at the time, though, and Raven had seen no reason to take out a loan with interest when she had someone willing to invest the entire start-up capital. Not to mention, Porsha had agreed to a very nice deal. She'd only wanted one-half of her investment back, and that wasn't until the ministry had begun bringing in enough money to cover all expenses and pay the two of them more than ten thousand dollars per month. She then wanted to continue receiving 50 percent of all proceeds minus all expenses. They were very careful not to use the word *profit* out loud since they were referring to church income, but they'd also figured out a legal way to compensate themselves with healthy salaries. They did so by taking a percentage of what was actually considered *profit* on each previous month's financial statement.

In the beginning, they'd each earned about eight thousand a month, but by the start of year two, the ministry had grown tremendously, particularly because of Raven's online contributors, and they now *each* received checks for just over fifty thousand dollars—every single month. Porsha was already wealthy and didn't need the money the way Raven did, but Raven was ecstatic to be earning more than a half million dollars annually from the ministry. This also didn't include the generous honorariums she received when she gave sermons at various churches and large religious conferences. She was doing exceptionally well, but this new idea from *Minister* Harrington made her a bit nervous. Especially since, as of late, Porsha had been offering opinions and unasked-for advice much more than usual. She'd begun suggesting lots of new programs and other planning points that she expected to be incorporated. It was true that Raven was the sole founder of the ministry, but again, Porsha had invested the initial dollars and felt as though she had the right to offer input and make crucial decisions. Thus far, Raven and Porsha hadn't had any major disagreements, but for the last several months Raven had noticed a few looming in the background. As a matter of fact, the only reason they likely hadn't exchanged angry words was because Raven had purposely held her tongue to keep peace between them. She hadn't wanted to make any waves and cause problems for the ministry, and she hoped that this could continue to be the case. And it would as long as Porsha didn't try to control Raven or interrupt the way she ran NVCC.

Raven leaned back in her chair and sighed, but now someone else knocked on her door.

"Come in."

Michelle, Raven's assistant, walked in. "It took me a little longer than I thought, but here's your revised copy."

Raven reached for her sermon notes. "Thank you so much, Michelle. I know I always have last-minute changes, and I'm not sure what we would do without you. Porsha and I really appreciate everything you do for us."

"I love working for both of you. It's really a joy for me."

"Well, thank you again."

"Okay then, if you don't need anything else I'm going to head out to the sanctuary."

"No, I think I'm good to go."

Michelle smiled. "You're always so prepared anyway, but I still wanted to ask."

"I feel like I have to be. Not everyone believes a woman should be senior pastor of a church, and some don't feel a woman is capable of being a minister at all. So that's why, from the very beginning, I've always done the same thing. I begin writing my sermons on Thursdays, I review and edit them on Fridays, and then I verbally practice them on Saturday evenings. I also practice once more on Sunday mornings before I get dressed."

"I knew you wrote them on Thursday and practiced on

Saturday, but I didn't know you practiced on Sunday morning as well."

"Yes, but again, it's mostly because I feel like I have to."

"Well, you always do an amazing job."

"I appreciate that."

"Okay, I'm heading out now, but I'll see you soon."

Raven smiled again, and Michelle left on her way. She truly was the best executive assistant ever. She was precise and knowledgeable, and she went over and above to get things right. She'd only been working for Raven and Porsha for six months, but she'd attended New Vision for more than a year. She also wasn't your normal executive assistant, as she'd completed a double major in college in marketing and finance, and she was now working on her MBA through an online university program. Not many MBA candidates would even consider working as an assistant, but Raven knew it had been important for them to hire someone who had clerical skills and so much more. What they'd needed was someone who could speak for them when they weren't available and keep them abreast of anything new, business- and social media–wise. It was the reason they paid Michelle accordingly, to the tune of eighty thousand dollars per year. Although, in all honesty, it was mostly Raven who Michelle worked for. She handled a few items for Porsha, but it wasn't daily or even weekly, because Porsha didn't have nearly as much going on as Raven.

Raven flipped through her pages of notes one last time and took a deep breath. She closed her eyes as she prepared to calm her thinking so she could meditate. At first, her thoughts wandered back to Porsha and this new weekly message she wanted to deliver. But in a matter of seconds she pushed Porsha and everything else from her mind. She sat quietly, taking more deep breaths, in and out, praying and waiting until it was time to leave her office—and hoping that more people joined the congregation today, and that NVCC received more tithes and offerings than ever.

Chapter 2

*R*aven stood in the side hallway with her eyes closed, waiting for one of the church elders to announce her entrance into the sanctuary. When he did, a female usher opened the door, and Raven walked inside, smiling and waving to her members. Their high-spirited applause and standing ovation never ceased to amaze her, and it always sent her adrenaline into overdrive.

She absolutely loved the incredible way her congregation welcomed her every Sunday morning, and she couldn't imagine them *not* doing it. She knew this wasn't the norm—a pastor being formally announced and then making a grand entrance into the sanctuary—but from the first service she'd held, this had been the way they'd greeted her. They'd done it without her even expecting them to, and it had motivated and inspired her so much that she'd decided to make her special introduction permanent. Kane, her significant other of one year, thought her "celebrity-style" intro showed no humility and wasn't appropriate for a pastor, and she could tell that Porsha basically felt the same. But Raven paid no attention to either of them—not when she believed that all pastors, especially founders of churches, deserved to be treated with unique honor and praise.

She stepped up the pulpit stairs and then behind the glass podium. "Thank you all so very much. Thank you for being the blessing that you are and for showing me more kindness and love than any pastor could ask for."

The applause continued, but soon Raven raised both her hands, gently motioning for everyone to take their seats. Then she subtly checked beneath the podium, making sure the hospitality staff had poured ice water in her favorite crystal glass and set it on a small sterling silver platter, alongside her lace-trimmed handkerchiefs. Last week, they'd used some other glass that she'd never seen before, and for a few seconds, their reckless mistake had thrown off her concentration. From the very beginning, though, she'd made it clear to everyone who worked for New Vision Christian Center and New Vision Ministries, Inc., that she had pretty high expectations. She'd warned that certain errors wouldn't be tolerated. So, thankfully, the hospitality staff had gotten things right this time.

As she did at the beginning of every service, Raven scanned the congregation and recited Romans 8:30–31 from memory. "Moreover whom he did predestinate, them he also called: and whom he called, them he also justified: and whom he justified, them he also glorified. What shall we then say to these things? If God be for us, who can be against us?"

"Amen," everyone responded.

"It is certainly wonderful to see all of you here today, and as I look out at all your beautiful faces and think about the way you have continued to support me as your pastor and the ministry as a whole, my heart overflows with joy. This is the reason I love Romans eight, thirty through thirty-one so very much. It confirms my calling from God not just to become a minister but to become a pastor. It solidifies my reason for answering His call, even though there were a lot of naysayers. Even though many folks right here in the city don't believe a woman should organize a church or serve as its leader. But more than that, I am reminded of the woman I used to be," she proclaimed with tears filling her eyes.

She paused and swallowed hard, just as she'd watched her ex-husband, Dillon, do many times, whenever he wanted his members to sympathize with him. Raven had also seen the good Reverend Curtis Black breaking down and crying before his congregation. He'd go on to tell them about his awful childhood and his sinful past and then announce how God had delivered him from all of it.

So Raven had decided early on that there was no reason to change what worked. She also saw no reason to stop insisting that she was called by God to minister, even though, like her former husband, she hadn't been. Her position as founder and pastor of New Vision Christian Center had materialized by choice, and there was nothing wrong with that.

"Some of you know my story and some of you don't, but there was a time when I did some terrible things. And while I never try to use my childhood as an excuse for my actions,

I do know that being raised in multiple foster homes and being physically abused and raped at one of them wasn't good. It was unbearable. Although, I will say this, my childhood nightmare is what made me determined to get good grades and work my way through college so I could have anything I wanted. But before long, wanting material things became a huge obsession, and when my paycheck didn't cover my expensive tastes, I started to gamble. First I played the lottery. Not like normal people, mind you, but I played it heavily and regularly. There were times when I would buy a hundred dollars' worth of tickets in one day. And I would win, too...but how many of you know that I lost a lot more than I won?"

"Amen," the members said, some nodding in agreement.

"Then, when I realized the state lottery wasn't providing the kind of money I needed, I slowly but surely began heading over to the casino. I took that thirty-minute drive sometimes seven days a week, and the next thing I knew, I'd cleaned out my savings accounts, missed paying the rent on my condo for two months, and I'd refinanced my car. But worse than that, I'd begun working on the side for a dangerous loan shark, handling his finances."

Some members of the congregation showed expressions of shock, acting as though they'd never heard her story. Others actually hadn't heard it before and shook their heads in disbelief.

"Then, if that wasn't enough, I began stealing money from this loan shark, and ultimately, I even stole one... hundred...thousand...dollars from my former father-in-law. I stole from a pastor and his church, and I don't think there's anything else I'm more ashamed of. Pastor Black wasn't my father-in-law back then, but I worked as his church's chief financial officer. The worst thing about my gambling addiction, though, was that the stealing part of it is what sent me to prison. I did time, and to this day, I'm a known felon. The reason I say 'known' is because even though I'm not proud of it, I don't hide it. I openly share my story as a way to show just how much God can change any of us if we let Him. I tell my truth so that others who might be struggling with gambling addiction or any other kind of addiction—drugs, alcohol, sex, whatever it might be—can hear it and hopefully learn from it."

Now tears fell from Raven's eyes.

"But I also stand here, having to accept and admit that all my past sins and dirty deeds led to major destruction. I'm a true example that we all surely do reap what we sow. And for me, prison was just the beginning, because marrying my ex-husband proved to be my harshest punishment of all. You see, I fell deeply in love with a man who claimed to love me, yet he had an affair with not one, but two women."

Raven quickly glanced toward one of the front pews, where Porsha was sitting, but not long enough for anyone to notice it. She also thought about the fact that Porsha's decision to bring her that sex tape hadn't evolved simply because Porsha had wanted to do the right thing. She'd done it only after learning that she wasn't Dillon's only mistress, and she'd wanted revenge.

"I couldn't believe my husband had betrayed me in such

a cruel and humiliating way, yet he proudly stood in front of our members on Sunday mornings like it was nothing. Then, of course, once I decided to end our marriage, I suffered through a very humiliating, nasty, and highly public divorce. I even slipped into a deep state of depression, and for a while, I wasn't sure where I would live. Where my next meal would come from. My husband had withdrawn all the money from our joint accounts and left me with nothing, and I was destitute. But let me tell you about the awesome God we serve. *Our* God had a different plan for me. *My* God was true to His Word and forgave me for my transgressions. He brought me out of my depression and gave me all of *you*! He fixed everything. You hear me? He fixed absolutely everything in my life and showed me that His mercy really does endure forever."

There was loud applause and some folks stood up again.

Raven wiped her tears with both hands, smiling, and then raised her hands above her head, praising God with her congregation. She may not have been called by God to preach, but she loved each and every one of her parishioners. She loved the way they responded to her and how dedicated they were to the ministry. She cherished the kind of life she was able to live, all because of their generosity, and she didn't want to lose that.

This was also the reason Raven turned her attention to Porsha again. To this day, no one except Raven, Porsha, and Dillon knew about that sex tape or even about Dillon and Porsha's affair itself...but Raven still had her copies of it—both the DVD and one on a USB drive. She kept it safe, and no matter how much she'd forgiven Porsha and had become friends with her, Raven would do whatever she had to when it came to protecting her ministry and position as sole founder. This also meant that Raven would have to monitor every one of these new "inspirational messages" Porsha had decided to incorporate. All services were recorded, and Raven couldn't wait to hear the words Porsha had spoken earlier.

But the more she thought about it, the more she realized she would also have to protect her ministry from Dillon — when he crossed her again. Because if she knew Dillon the way she thought, he wasn't going to simply accept the idea that she now had as many members as he'd once had and that she'd already surpassed his level of success, thanks to her massive online following. A following of folks who gave consistent financial contributions. She knew Dillon was likely monitoring everything she was doing and was searching high and low for ways to ruin her. She knew this because that was just who he was. But what she also hoped was that Dillon still remembered who she was, too. She hoped he understood that she would stop anyone who tried to destroy all that she'd accomplished.

She would do so at all costs.

Chapter 3

Porsha snuggled closer to her boyfriend, Steven McKnight, trying to catch her breath. He did the same thing, and Porsha wondered why he wouldn't just pack up his belongings and leave his wife. More than that, she wanted to know how he could continue to experience such explosive levels of lovemaking with her, the way he had only moments ago, yet ultimately go home to a woman he no longer loved. It simply made no sense to her, and she was getting a little tired of being his secret mistress.

Porsha also wondered if his wife knew that on Sundays, like today, he went to church with her and their son, ate dinner with them, and then hightailed it over to Porsha's. Sometimes he came here to her home, and sometimes, just to spice things up, they went to a hotel outside of Chicago. But nonetheless, he showed up every Sunday without fail. He came to spend time with Porsha and to make love to her, and he rarely canceled for any reason. Their regular Sunday-afternoon trysts were as common as the sun shining in Jamaica, and as far as Porsha was concerned, he might as well leave Denene and marry her.

But so much for logical thinking.

Porsha took another deep breath. "That was good...I mean *really, really* good."

Steve lay on his back, stroking her hair. "Is that right?"

"Very much so."

"All I want is to make you happy."

What a loaded statement, was all Porsha could think—the kind that was screaming for a direct response. "Well, if that's the case then why don't you leave her? Why won't you divorce Denene and marry me?"

"Baby, please. Not today, okay? Let's just enjoy each other. I mean, why ruin our precious time together?"

Porsha had heard similar words before when she'd been having an affair with Raven's ex-husband, Dillon, but that was a whole other story. "Fine. Whatever."

"So, how did things go this morning?" he asked, deliberately changing the subject. "You know, with that new inspirational message you told me you were doing today?"

"I think it went well. Everyone seemed to like it."

"I knew they would. Just like last year when you spoke at that conference we met at."

Steve was a deacon at his own church, and he was referring to the Christian leadership conference that they'd both attended.

"Hard to believe a whole six months have passed already," she said. "It's even harder to believe that we'd never seen each other before then."

"This is true. Had to go all the way to Charlotte, North Carolina, to find the one woman who drives me wild."

Porsha glanced up at him, smiling and shaking her head.

Steve laughed. "What? You do drive me wild. Then, on top of that, I discovered that you lived right here in Mitchell. I mean, what are the chances that we'd never met before? It's not like our city is all that big."

"I know, it was very strange, but I'm glad it happened."

"So am I," he said, leaning over and kissing her on the lips.

Porsha tried not to react, but whenever Steve kissed her, chills streamed through her body. He was everything she wanted in a husband. Everything she needed.

"So, are you still planning to give your message every Sunday?" he asked.

"I am. That is, until I start my own ministry. Or maybe even just join another church."

"Wow, when did you decide that?"

"I've been thinking about it for a while. I just hadn't said anything."

"Is there a problem? I mean, why do you want to leave? You've always been so committed to New Vision."

"That's all fine and well, but for the last few months I've noticed some changes with Raven. She's become a lot more full of herself, and she's acting as though she built the ministry all on her own."

"You're kidding. Have you spoken to her about it?"

"No, because it's not like Raven really listens to anything I say. She pretty much ignores all of my suggestions. Even when my suggestions make the most sense. That's why when I decided to add on my own segment, I didn't leave any room for her to object. I basically just told her, and I could tell it caught her off guard."

"Geez. Well, I'm really sorry things aren't going well between the two of you. Especially since you seem to work so well together. And you're great friends."

Yes, they were indeed *friends*...but they weren't nearly as close as Steve thought. Although Steve didn't know that Porsha had slept with Dillon behind Raven's back, either. And if Porsha could help it, he never would.

It was true that Porsha and Raven were cordial enough, though, and as Porsha lay there thinking about it, she couldn't deny that they were at least *fairly good* friends. But in all honesty, how close could a wife and mistress actually be? Porsha did believe that Raven had forgiven her, but she also knew that Raven only trusted her to a certain point, and rightfully so. Because, after all, Porsha hadn't thought twice about having an affair with her trifling husband.

And what a trifling man he was. It was bad enough that he'd been sleeping around on his wife, but it also hadn't been long before Porsha had discovered that he was seeing another woman, too. Taylor Thomas. Porsha hadn't spoken to Dillon in over two years, but rumor had it that he and this *Taylor* were engaged to be married. Porsha knew it shouldn't matter, but deep down, this bothered her and made her wonder about two things: Why was it taking him so long to marry Taylor, and why hadn't *she* been good enough to become his wife? Because being married to Dillon and living happily ever after was all Porsha had wanted—all she'd asked for from the man she'd loved with everything in her.

Needless to say, though, this was also the very reason she'd been trying hard not to become so emotionally attached to Steve—another married man. But she could tell that she was starting to slip into the same pattern she had with Dillon. At first, it had been all about the sex and how great it was between her and Steve, and then she'd found herself thinking about him more and more until more and more had become every single day. Then she'd found herself missing him and wishing she could see him a lot more than just once or twice a week. She wanted to be with him daily and not just when he could sneak away from his wife. The reason: She now had real feelings for him—deep feelings—the kind she couldn't ignore. She didn't want to care about him this way, but she could already tell that it was too late.

Porsha lay there thinking and then suddenly sat up. "Look, I'm sorry. I know you don't want to discuss this, but how long are you going to keep pretending? How long are you going to torture yourself like this?"

Steve rested one of his hands behind his head. "What're you talking about?"

"Your marriage. Your wife. When are you going to leave her? Because clearly you're not happy."

"Baby, I thought I asked you not to do this today."

"Like I said, I'm sorry. But this is really bothering me."

Steve just stared at her.

"Why do you stay married to her? That's all I need to know."

"Because I don't want to hurt my son. And, to be honest, even though I no longer love Denene, I don't want to hurt her, either."

"But you don't mind hurting me, though, right?"

"That's not true, but you knew I was married. I told you the very first night we were together at that conference. The first day we met. So don't make it sound like I ever lied to you."

"I'm not saying you did. But I also don't understand how you can stay with someone you don't love. But to each his own, I guess."

"The reason you don't understand is because you've never been married. Yes, I'm not happy with my wife, but I still don't want to abandon her. And I certainly don't want to abandon my son. Stevie is only fifteen years old, and if I left now it would ruin the rest of his high school years. He would be devastated, and I could never do that to him. I wouldn't *want* to do that to him."

Porsha raised both her hands toward him and stood up. "You know what? Just forget I mentioned any of this."

"But baby—"

Porsha never looked back at him. Instead, she slipped on a red silk robe, went downstairs to her family room, and turned on the television. She was angry, hurt, and disappointed. Nothing was going the way she wanted—not with her love life or with her position at the church. On the one hand, Steve didn't want to discuss leaving his wife, and on the other Raven was acting as though New Vision Ministries was all hers. Maybe as far as Raven, though, her new level of arrogance was a result of how huge her social media and general online following had become. Or maybe it was because of how quickly the local congregation had grown in only two years—which was the reason Porsha wondered why Raven always told that same lie to the congregation about how destitute she'd been when she'd left Dillon. Because truth was, Raven had gotten paid nicely the very first month that the church was founded. She'd taken part of the money from the investment capital Porsha had given her, which Porsha had been fine with, and part of it had come from the tithes and offerings that the initial two hundred members contributed weekly—and she'd even eventually won half of Dillon's savings in the divorce and half the equity from the house they'd owned. But regardless of what Raven's reasons were for becoming so vain and obnoxious, none of Raven's success could've happened without Porsha, and more important, her money. Yes, Porsha did collect 50 percent of everything minus expenses, but that wasn't enough for her. At least not anymore.

What she wanted now was the same kind of online following that Raven had, and more than that, she wanted to be loved by thousands and thousands of people—and to help those thousands and thousands of people. She also didn't normally envy anyone or anything on any occasion, but she couldn't deny that she sometimes envied all the love everyone constantly showed Raven—a lot more than they showed Porsha. This, of course, was creating a problem for her because being loved was the one thing Porsha longed for and needed, and now that her mother and father were gone—the only two people who had ever loved her unconditionally—she was desperate to find that kind of love again. She'd sort of shared this very thing when she'd spoken to the congregation this morning. And this was also the reason she wouldn't lose hope that Steve would eventually divorce his wife and commit to her.

But until he did, she would secure love and appreciation through her ministry. What she would do is work toward figuring out her purpose—her reason for being born. She also believed that this *purpose* of hers—whatever it was— had to do with helping women who had a specific problem. She had no idea what this problem might be, but she looked forward to discovering it.

But even with her own set of plans for the future, for some reason, she still couldn't shake Raven's growing ego. When they'd first started the ministry, the idea that Raven had quickly become much more well-known than Porsha hadn't mattered to Porsha in the least, but now it sort of did. This whole snobby, superior attitude of Raven's wasn't right, and if Porsha was completely truthful, she would also have to admit that she just didn't like having a woman like Raven—a thief who'd done time in prison—talking down to her. Porsha wasn't sure why she felt this way, because before meeting Raven, she'd never tried to compare herself to anyone, mainly because she'd lived a very wealthy life since childhood. Not to mention, even though she'd graduated from college with a business degree, she'd never had to work to earn a living. Her parents had given her everything and then some, but now she wanted something more. She wanted to accomplish great things that had nothing to do with her father's money. She wanted her own gifts and talents to bring her the kind of happiness she deserved. As it was, she was already good at organizing programs and preaching the word, so all she had to do was continue on that same path. The only difference now was that she would be much more focused and diligent about it. She would sit down and create a real plan and then execute it with great passion. She would make her greatest desires her highest priority. She would rise to the occasion in no time.

Chapter 4

Raven reached across her shiny, dark mahogany dining room table, gently holding Kane's hands. Miss Ethel, her part-time cook, had prepared dinner for them but had just left to go home. Miss Ethel would have been more than willing to stay and serve them, except Raven preferred spending her Sunday afternoons alone with the man she loved. To be honest, she couldn't wait to find a full-time cook now that she could afford it, but when she did she would still give her new cook Saturday and Sunday afternoons off. She, of course, wished she could simply keep Miss Ethel, but Miss Ethel had recently turned seventy-five and just wasn't interested in all-day work.

Raven and Kane bowed their heads and she said grace. "Dear Heavenly Father, thank you for this wonderful opportunity of fellowship with my dear Kane, and for the food that has been prepared for us. I ask that you please let it serve as great nourishment for our bodies and good health. In Your Son Jesus's name, Amen."

"Amen," Kane said.

"So," Raven began, lifting a baked chicken thigh from the glass dish and setting it on her plate, "did you enjoy service today?"

Kane spooned out some green beans from a ceramic bowl. "I did. It was a blessing, and your sermon was great."

"I'm glad to hear that."

Raven picked up a dinner roll with metal tongs and then scooped out some red potatoes from another container. She knew it should be the furthest thing from her mind, but for some reason, she thought about the kind of life she'd lived with Dillon. Not her married life, but her material life. They'd purchased a five-bedroom, six-bathroom home, and she missed that. She even missed the twelve-seat dining room table that they'd sat at daily for dinner. The house she owned now was fine, and it certainly wasn't anything to frown at, but it wasn't the same as her former residence. She knew there was nothing wrong with having a four-bedroom home, what with her living alone, but she wanted something bigger, something more luxurious, something people took a second look at when they drove by it. She wanted something even grander than the house Porsha owned.

Raven had decorated her current home with lots of expensive furniture and accessories, but it still didn't compare to the house she'd shared with Dillon. That was okay, though, because, with the way things were going with the ministry, it wouldn't be long before she was able to build herself a small mansion. If it was the last thing she did, she would construct something spectacular and memorable—something she could be proud of.

Raven ate some of her chicken and gazed at Kane, who was the kind of man most women dreamed about. He was tall, dark, and handsome and had just the right amount of muscle.

"So what are you looking at, my dear?" he teased.

"You, of course."

"Why? You like what you see?"

"No, I *love* what I see. I love everything about you."

Kane ate a forkful of his food. "Is that a fact?"

"It is."

"Then why won't you marry me?"

Raven wasn't sure how to respond and was sorry she'd set herself up this way.

"You're not going to answer?" he asked.

"Baby, you know I can't do that right now."

"Yeah, that's what you keep saying, but I have to tell you, that line is getting pretty old."

Raven showed no facial expression, but she was a little thrown by his response. He was never happy when they had this conversation, but he'd also never sounded so irritated.

"I just need you to be patient with me," she said.

Kane leaned back in his chair. "I know I've told you this many times before, but I'm not your ex-husband. I'm not a cheater, and I would never hurt you the way he did. Why can't you see that?"

"I do see that. I know you're a much better man than he was. A much better man than he'll ever be. But I don't want to marry you and then not be a good wife. I don't want you to feel like I'm not devoting the kind of time to you that I should."

"Well, I guess I need you to explain what that means,

because I don't see how that would be a problem. We spend lots of time together now, and we're not even married."

"I know, and I'm glad you feel that way, but I've been doing a lot of thinking. I've thought long and hard about it, and it's now time for me to elevate the ministry. Take it to a whole new level."

"I still don't see what that has to do with our relationship."

"Baby, it has everything to do with it. Taking the ministry to a different place will require a lot more of my attention. And I will likely be doing it on my own."

"What does that mean?"

"I don't know how long Porsha and I will be able to work together."

"Why? What's wrong?"

"We don't see eye to eye on certain things, and I can tell she wants more control. Just like today, when she spoke before I gave my sermon, that was all her idea. She never even told me until a few minutes beforehand. She did what she wanted whether I liked it or not."

"Maybe you just need to talk to her. Let her know how you're feeling."

"I think we're already beyond that. Porsha thinks her investment gives her the right to do whatever she pleases. I can just tell."

"When did you start noticing that there might be a problem?" Kane asked.

"I've noticed here and there for a while. But incorporating this new message of hers makes me wonder what else she's up to."

"I still say you should talk to her. Because the worst thing anyone can do is assume they know what another person is thinking."

Raven heard Kane, but she wasn't planning to discuss anything with Porsha. Not when she basically wanted Porsha out—something she'd decided on this afternoon, while driving home from church. She wasn't sure how she would sever their business relationship, but somehow she would.

"Maybe I will," she said, lying. "We'll see."

"Enough of that, though. What about us?"

"I just told you. I really need you to be patient."

Now Kane folded his arms. "Is it that you don't love me? Because if that's what this is really about, just tell me. Just be honest."

"What? That's not it at all. I do love you. With all my heart. You know that."

"I'm not sure what I know anymore. Not with you insisting that we have to wait to get married. I understand your desire to spend more time with the ministry, but if I'm not worried about being neglected then you shouldn't, either."

Raven shook her head, wiped both sides of her mouth with a black linen napkin, and scooted her chair back. Then she went around the table and hugged Kane from behind. "Baby, please. Let's not fight, okay?" she said, kissing him on the side of his face.

"I hate when you do this," he told her.

She knew full well what he meant but said, "Do what, baby?"

"You know what. Ignore my concerns and then try to use your little seductive ways to silence me."

"That's not true," she said, kissing his neck.

She could tell he was succumbing to her advances, so she caressed his chest with both her hands.

"What we're doing is wrong, anyway. Having sex outside of marriage goes against everything God stands for, not to mention everything you preach about."

Raven tuned out his words, steadily kissing him and undoing his tie. Then she unbuttoned his shirt. Kane still tried to act as though he wasn't giving in all the way, until suddenly he moved her hands away from him and scooted backward.

Then he stood up, drew her close to him, and kissed her forcefully on her lips. She loved when he showed aggression. It was clear that he could no longer resist her and wanted her badly—just like always. They were good together. They had been for a whole year, and not even Kane could deny that. Raven knew he wanted to be married, but she simply couldn't make that kind of commitment and still become the most powerful female pastor in history. It wasn't possible, and all she could hope was that Kane would eventually become satisfied with their current arrangement. Because she certainly didn't want to lose him. But if he continued pressing her, she would be forced to choose between him and New Vision Ministries, and sadly, her choice wouldn't be him. She did love Kane, but she loved her ministry so much more—much more than anything or anyone else she could think of.

Chapter 5

"There's a huge difference between true Christians who love and honor God and those who I refer to as 'lukewarm church people,'" Porsha heard Pastor Gwyn Shepherd say.

Porsha had been power walking on her treadmill for nearly an hour and could barely take her eyes off the television. Before becoming a minister, Porsha had rarely watched any televangelist, but once she'd decided to take on that position, she'd watched as many of them as she could. She'd done so because she'd known she could learn a lot about ministry and how to deliver a Christian message.

But for the last few months, it was mainly Gwyn, a prominent local pastor, who held her attention, and Porsha admired her—partly because she was a woman and she had a noticeable way with words, and partly because unlike Porsha and Raven, she seemed to live the same kind of godly life she encouraged others to live. Porsha enjoyed Gwyn's sermons so much that she rarely missed a single morning broadcast. There were times when she did get up a little later than normal and needed to get to the church, but even when she missed the early airings, she watched the DVR recording in the evenings.

"The Bible says, 'Beware of false prophets who come disguised as harmless sheep but are really vicious wolves,'" Gwyn said matter-of-factly, and Porsha swallowed hard. Then, strangely, she realized she was fighting back tears. It wasn't that time of the month for her, so she wondered why she was so emotional. But the more Gwyn spoke, the more Porsha identified with the sermon—and the guiltier she started to feel. Her parents had taught her to love and honor God, but she knew her real reasons for becoming a minister had nothing to do with that. And deep down, she struggled with her deception. This was also the reason that Porsha sometimes wondered why she did some of the things she did, although she couldn't deny that much of her wrongdoing had seemed to escalate when her father had passed. As it was, she'd lost her mom when she was only a young teenager—she'd been thirteen, to be exact— and then she'd lost her dad just a few years ago. Worse, she was an only child, the same as her parents had been, so she felt all alone. She *was* alone, and she'd finally had to accept that she'd been left fending for herself in this cold, cruel world.

But it hadn't been long before all the money her father had willed to her had begun to fill part of the void. Not to mention, even when her dad had been alive, she hadn't wanted for anything. He'd made sure of it. But when she'd learned soon after his death that he'd left her his entire estate—a few million dollars, plus all his properties and personal possessions—she'd begun traveling to new countries and beautiful islands she'd never gone to before. And while visiting those places, she'd purchased high-end clothing, handbags, and other accessories without paying much attention to the cost, and well...she'd simply enjoyed herself in every way she knew how.

The only problem with that, though, was the fact that traveling and buying material luxuries had only been able to hold her attention for maybe the first full year after her father's passing. It had all soon become old and boring, and what she'd ultimately realized was that she needed someone to love—and someone to love her back. Someone to happily spend the rest of her life with. So, of course, it hadn't been long after she'd stopped traveling and had begun attending church regularly again that she'd found herself strongly attracted to Pastor Dillon Whitfield Black. More than she'd ever been attracted to any man.

At first, he'd acted as though he wasn't interested, but once she'd made her intentions known to him, one Sunday after another, he had eventually surrendered and had driven over to the northwest suburb that she'd moved to outside of Chicago. She'd since sold that home and moved to Mitchell because of her dedication to NVCC, but it was there that Porsha and Dillon had become close. They'd quickly recognized and fully embraced the intense chemistry they shared, and their relationship had blossomed into something she'd been sure would lead to marriage. It was true that at the time, Dillon had been married to Raven, but Porsha had seen Raven as nothing more than a mere technicality. Surely—at least she'd thought so, anyway—if Dillon had genuinely loved Raven, he wouldn't have been sleeping with Porsha every chance he got. She'd been positive that it would only be a matter of time before he asked Raven for a divorce, and she would agree to it. Then Porsha and Dillon would finally become husband and wife.

But, sadly, not only had things not turned out the way Porsha had hoped, Dillon had begun having *another* affair. He'd cheated on Porsha with another mistress, and Porsha's discovery of this disturbing news had sent her into a fury. She'd become so upset that her love for Dillon had slowly turned to hate, and she'd soon decided that she couldn't let him get away with what he was doing. Of course, Dillon hadn't known it, but Porsha had recorded a couple of their sexcapades and had stored away the DVD for safekeeping. So, needless to say, when she'd learned about this Taylor woman, she'd contacted Raven right away. She'd told her everything and had then driven over to Mitchell to Dillon and Raven's home to bring her a copy. Porsha could still see the hurt yet seething look in Raven's eyes, and Porsha had understood completely. It was the reason, too, that Porsha had apologized to Raven more than once for sleeping with her husband. And her apology had been sincere. Porsha had very much regretted what she'd done, and surprisingly, Raven had thanked her for bringing her the ammunition she needed in order to get what she wanted from Dillon: to be named co-founder and co-pastor of his ministry.

But as it had turned out, Dillon's church had burned to

the ground before that could happen, and Raven had divorced him and founded her own ministry. Porsha had fully supported her vision, and because of the guilt she'd felt about having an affair with Dillon, she'd quickly offered to invest 100 percent of the funding that Raven had needed. Still, if Porsha could do things over, she wouldn't have acted so irrationally. Especially since there were times when she wondered if Raven might ever try to use that video against her or Dillon. Porsha hoped not, but with the way Raven had been acting lately, Porsha worried that Raven might be capable of anything.

Porsha watched more of the sermon broadcast and sighed. What was wrong with her, and why did she continue making such awful choices? She'd slept with a married man two years ago, and she was sleeping with another one now. Her parents would be so disappointed. They wouldn't be happy about the sins she was committing, and in all honesty, she wasn't sure why she couldn't just stop what she was doing. Why couldn't she simply be the good girl her parents had raised her to be and leave well enough alone? She also didn't understand this new desire she had to reach more people. Although, maybe she needed something that connected her to others because she didn't have much to be proud of on her own. She had money—lots of it—but money didn't validate a person. It couldn't provide unconditional love or guarantee happiness. It couldn't comfort or protect you. It couldn't shield you from loneliness and heartbreak.

Porsha swallowed more tears and revved up the pace

on her treadmill. She watched more of Gwyn and couldn't stop crying. Then she wept harder and worked her legs even faster, trying to push the woe-is-me thinking from her mind. But soon, she finally regained her composure, picked up the remote from one of the machine's cup holders, and turned the channel. She flipped through a few programs until she spotted a rerun of *Scandal*. As usual, Olivia Pope was taking total control of some wicked situation and fixing things in a powerful, no-nonsense fashion. Olivia was the person everyone turned to when they needed something handled, or worse, they needed some crime or sin they'd committed to go away. Porsha didn't want to be a fixer per se, but she did want to be a go-to person. She wanted folks from every walk of life to know her as a woman who could help them. She wasn't sure how she would go about accomplishing this, but she knew anything was possible if a person had the right kind of resources and connected with the right people. So just as Porsha had been thinking yesterday, all she had to do was figure out her true calling. Because if there was one thing she knew for sure, every human being on this earth had one.

Chapter 6

Raven signed on to the ministry's YouTube channel, preparing to watch yesterday's service from her home office. This, of course, was something she did every single Monday anyway, so she could critique her sermons, but today, she was more interested in hearing Porsha's little message. Actually, Raven had planned on viewing the recording last night. But by the time she and Kane had finished making love and watching a couple of movies, she'd been too exhausted. He also hadn't left until sometime after eleven, and as soon as he had, she'd gone straight to bed.

Raven pressed Play on the video and then clicked it to full-screen on her twenty-seven-inch computer monitor. She relaxed in her chair, the one situated behind her shiny wooden desk, and watched the opening of praise and worship—but it wasn't long before she pursed her lips in disgust. For the most part, she loved her praise and worship leaders, all of whom she'd personally selected through individual auditioning, but she didn't like some of their song selections. Although, it wasn't so much their choice of songs as it was the fact that they sometimes sang the same ones two Sundays in a row. The congregation didn't seem to mind, likely because it didn't happen regularly, but Raven preferred variety. She wanted to keep things interesting and different, and they knew that. So it was obviously time to have another meeting with them.

Raven fast-forwarded to Porsha's segment, but when she realized she'd advanced the video too far, she rewound it. Now she saw Porsha walking into the pulpit and taking her place behind the glass podium.

"Good morning," Porsha said, smiling.

"Good morning," the congregation responded.

"Today, I would like to offer you a few words of encouragement, and I'd like to begin by quoting one of my favorite scriptures. First John four and seven, which says, 'Beloved, let us love one another, for love is from God, and whoever loves has been born of God and knows God.'"

Many of the parishioners said, "Amen."

"For some reason I have always loved that scripture. Maybe because when my parents were alive, they showered me with the best kind of love any child could hope for, and I miss that so very much. And please don't get me wrong. I am truly grateful for the wonderful love I receive from all of *you* here at New Vision and from other friends. But ever since my parents died, things haven't been quite the same for me. There's a certain void I feel. And while I know what I'm getting ready to say is likely going to be one of the most transparent moments I've ever shared publicly, I just need to be honest. I want to tell you my greatest desire...which is to meet the right man, fall in love with him, and get married. More than anything, I want a man who loves me as much as I love him. Someone who loves and cherishes me as his wife. There was a time when I used to be ashamed to admit that truth, even to my closest friends, but now I know that sharing my struggles, wants, desires, and even my pain can really help someone. And in this case, I know that there are likely many single women here today who feel the same as I do."

The video camera was zoomed directly in on Porsha, so Raven couldn't see the congregation. But she still heard *Amen*s and people talking among themselves. She could tell that they earnestly felt for Porsha, and that many of them could relate to her. They loved what she was saying.

And Raven didn't like this at all.

"But I'm here to tell you that I'm not giving up, and neither should any of you," Porsha said, smiling again. "God can do all things and He will...if we just believe in Him. If we just depend on Him. If we can simply trust Him with every...fiber...of...our...being. And we have to do it without wavering. We have to have faith minus all the doubt that the enemy tries to confuse us with. We have to see the enemy for who he is—an evil force who cares nothing about us. Then we have to stand on God's eternal Word."

There were more *Amen*s all around, and Raven squinted her eyes at her computer monitor. This mini message of Porsha's was sounding more like a mini sermon, and it was obvious that she was trying to outdo Raven. She was baring her soul to the congregation, hoping to gain sympathy. Worse, she was trying to ease her way further up the ministry ladder, just as Raven had thought, and Raven wasn't having it. New Vision Christian Center, New Vision Ministries, Inc., and more important, New Vision's members belonged to *Raven*. They'd all joined because of *Raven*. They'd told others to visit the church because of *Raven*, and she wouldn't let Porsha or anyone else steal them away from her. She simply wouldn't and couldn't allow that to happen.

Raven watched the remainder of the video, which lasted another couple of minutes, and then replayed it. She was becoming angrier by the second, so she quickly clicked out of YouTube, closed her eyes, and took a deep breath. In about a half hour, it would be time for her to speak to her online followers via Facebook Live, so she needed to calm her nerves. She needed to settle her thinking and forget about Porsha for the time being.

So she took more deep breaths and finally opened her eyes. She felt better, and as she clicked on a folder containing some of her personal financial documents, her spirits lifted even further.

She scanned a few of them and felt a strong sense of accomplishment. Things were certainly going well, and who would've guessed that she would ever have this kind of cash? It was one thing to be able to save for a rainy day, but having a money market balance of just over a hundred thousand and then right at eighty thousand in one of her checking accounts, Raven couldn't complain. It still wasn't nearly the kind of money that would categorize her as wealthy, but she was clearly on her way. Especially since she'd saved this $180,000 all in the last twelve months. There was so much potential for the ministry—so many possibilities for her as a pastor—and she was thrilled about the awesome way her local members and worldwide followers were contributing. They were being so generous that it wouldn't be long before she finally hired a financial planner to begin investing in a diversified portfolio. As a matter of fact, the only reason she hadn't done so already was because she hadn't wanted the stock market to trigger her gambling addiction. She hadn't attended any local Gamblers Anonymous meetings, but while in prison, she'd read as much literature on the subject as she could. She'd also worked through all twelve steps of the program on her own, and she lived by the GA philosophy.

Not everyone saw the stock market as a form of gambling, though, and for normal people it wasn't. But for recovering addicts like her who'd once believed that taking a risk on any amount of money and trying to make much more of it, well, it could become a problem. So, because of that, she'd shied away from stockbrokers and the like. But now she wanted to begin investing and planning for her retirement years.

Raven closed the folder and then scanned some of the church's financial statements. Their local giving was increasing every week, as was their membership, so eventually they would need to find or build a larger church. But for now, Raven thought it was best to focus on growing her online ministry and to begin strategizing another way to reach people on a national level. Doing online broadcasts and live-streaming their Sunday-morning services was working great, but in the future Raven wanted to host her own syndicated TV talk show. She wanted to have a weekly or even daily hour-long segment that aired nation-wide. This was something she'd been dreaming about doing for a while, and although she'd not shared that dream with another living soul, she couldn't wait to become a house-hold name. The kind of celebrity she deserved to be.

Raven left her office and went into her bedroom. She strolled past her king-size sleigh bed, which was covered with four plush, deep tan pillow shams, five throw pillows, and a matching silk comforter. Frances, her housekeeper, came every morning at seven a.m. sharp, except on Sun-days, to clean. She washed any dishes that Raven left in the sink the evening before, which was rare, and she made up her bed and dusted every room in the house. She also washed Raven's sheets and towels twice a week, on Mon-days and Fridays. Frances was usually finished and out the door by eleven, though, and Raven loved how meticulous and fast she was.

Raven went over to her boudoir area, sat in front of the table, and gazed into the lighted mirror—the same kind that top celebrities housed in their own dressing rooms. Brooke, her makeup artist, had done a perfect job already, so all Raven had to do was powder her nose a bit. When she finished, she did another once-over for each aspect of her makeup and turned her head to the side to check her

chignon. She was good to go and ready to deliver her online message.

In just a few minutes she would access Facebook Live,
so she went back into her office and sat in front of her computer again. She scrolled onto her public-figure page and
saw the last three status updates that Michelle had posted.
They were reminders about today's noon broadcast. Raven
loved that she was able to speak to everyone live, but she
also loved that broadcasts could be replayed later for those
living in other time zones, both in the US and worldwide.

She read a few other Facebook posts that Michelle had
posted for her and some that she'd posted herself over the
last few days, but when she saw that it was only two minutes to show time, she set her smartphone into its cradle.
Then she opened the video feature for Facebook Live on
her app and immediately saw viewers joining the session.
One after another, she saw more and more names pop up,
and she was grateful to have this real-time platform. Earlier this morning, she'd thought about a number of topics
to speak on, but then it had dawned on her. She needed
to tell her story—the one about her pitiful childhood and
dreadful marriage. She'd done this very thing at church
yesterday, but it had been at least four weeks since she'd
shared it on Facebook. And since new people tuned in regularly, she wanted to make sure they all knew about her
journey; both the truthful parts of it as well as those various details she sometimes fabricated. She wanted them to
remember everything she said today and feel sorrier for her
than anyone had in the past, even if she had to embellish

things a bit...or a lot. But more important, she wouldn't let Porsha outdo her with that little transparency stunt she'd pulled yesterday. In a few moments, Raven would prove to be more transparent than she *or* Porsha had ever been.

Raven now looked straight at her phone camera, first smiling and then not. "Good afternoon, everyone, and thank you so much for joining me. I really appreciate it, and it is my prayer that you walk away from this message feeling inspired and filled with much hope. It is my greater prayer that none of you will ever have to live the kind of awful childhood I lived or marry the kind of man I loved and believed in. I've shared these two stories many times before, but the reason I do is so I can remind everyone that any obstacle can be overcome. Which is why this afternoon, I'm going to share with you something I've not shared with anyone before. And that is...before I went to prison, I was raped by a very prominent pastor. Someone who just about everyone knows. He raped me, got away with it, and continued on with his life, business as usual. He went on to become one of the most successful pastors today, but as you can see...I'm...still...standing, too. God brought me through every bit of the pain and humiliation I endured, and now I have a testimony."

Raven paused for full effect with tears streaming down both sides of her face. She would certainly never go as far as saying Reverend Curtis Black's name, but with her having worked for him in the past, she knew many people would decide on their own that it was him she was talking about. Of course, Pastor Black hadn't done a thing to her—except send her to prison—but this kind of rumor would get folks talking the way she needed them to. Especially since many people already knew that she'd been raped as a child and felt sorry for her. This new tragedy would elevate the circulation of her name and position, and before long, more and more members would join locally. She would also secure more social media followers and rise just a little closer to the top.

She did what she had to do to get ahead. She did what powerful men had been doing for centuries.

She did what was required, and she wasn't ashamed of it.

Chapter 7

O h … my … goodness," Porsha said out loud, covering her mouth with both hands and falling back in her chair. She'd just watched Raven's Facebook Live broadcast, and she was stunned, to say the least. Porsha was the absolute last person to question any woman who said she'd been raped, but in this case, she already believed Raven was flat-out lying. And there was a reason for that, too: Porsha had worked side by side with Raven for two whole years, and she usually knew when Raven wasn't being honest. Today, though, she was being downright deceptive, something Porsha could tell just from watching her.

It was true that Porsha wasn't a saint herself, not even remotely, but there were simply some lines she wasn't willing to cross. In the beginning, there had been certain sins Raven wouldn't have committed, either. But the more powerful she became, the more invincible she thought she was. Then, of course, there was all the money she was now earning—income that was increasing every month. To put it plainly: The success of the ministry had gone straight to her head, and Porsha had a bad feeling about it.

But now Porsha thought about something else and shook her head. The only pastor who Raven had worked for prior to going to prison was Pastor Black. Surely she wasn't referring to him. Would she actually go that far, trying to create the kind of rumor that would get more folks feeling sorry for her? Something that would get more people following her?

Porsha tried to weigh every possibility, but then decided that she should at least give Raven the benefit of the doubt. She didn't believe her accusation at all; however, she would also be less than a woman and friend to ignore it.

Porsha dialed Raven's cell phone.

She answered on the first ring. "Hey, Porsha."

"Hey. So...did I hear you right? I just saw you on Facebook."

"What? About being raped?"

"Yes."

"You did."

"Wow. I had no idea," Porsha said, trying to sound empathetic.

"That's because I've never told anyone. Only God, me, and the person who raped me know about it."

"This is awful."

"Yeah, but it happens. To more women than most people realize."

"Do you mind my asking who it was?"

"At this point, I just think it's best to leave it all in the past. And the only reason I shared what I shared today was because I felt led to help others who were watching. Those who have been raped and are silently trying to cover up their pain."

Porsha couldn't believe Raven was stooping to such a cruel level. Because what if people thought she was telling the truth? And that it was Pastor Black who'd actually raped her?

"So, I watched your message," Raven said, effortlessly changing the subject.

"Really?" Porsha said.

"I did. Saw it on YouTube this morning."

"What did you think?"

"I thought it was okay."

"Just okay?"

"It was fine, but down the road I think it could be great. You know, once you do it a few more times."

Porsha wanted to laugh out loud. Raven was a real piece of work, and of course, there was no way she was going to say anything nice about what Porsha was doing. She never had, and Porsha knew it was because she wanted her to stay in her place. Collect her 50 percent of income and go about her business.

"Advice noted," Porsha said.

Raven didn't say anything else.

"Well, I guess I'll see you tomorrow at our staff meeting."

"Yes. See you then."

"Talk to you later."

"Bye."

Porsha set her phone down, but for as long as she and

Raven had been friends she couldn't remember Raven speaking so dryly to her. They'd said "bye" to each other many times, but today, it was the *way* Raven had said it that was different.

Porsha took a deep breath and returned her attention to next Sunday's inspirational message. This was what she'd been working on right before tuning in to Raven's ridiculous Facebook broadcast, anyway.

But as soon as she wrote a couple more sentences, her phone rang. Given Raven's nasty attitude, she doubted that it was her—and it wasn't. Surely, though, Porsha must have been seeing things, because displaying across her screen was the name *Dillon*. For some reason, Porsha had never removed him from her contact list, and now she was glad she hadn't. Otherwise, she might've answered it by reflex, since she did tend to answer all calls, including those she didn't recognize.

The phone stopped ringing, and Porsha wondered if Dillon was leaving a message. But as soon as she'd finished her last thought, her phone rang again. This time, her stomach felt as though it were turning flips, and she debated answering. She couldn't deny, too, that a part of her wanted to know why he was calling.

She lifted her phone from her desk. "Hello?"

"Hey, how are you?"

"I'm good. You?"

"Couldn't be better."

Porsha didn't respond, and now Dillon was quiet, which meant the conversation had already turned awkward.

But then he continued, "So, I'm not even going to beat around the bush. What's going on with that witch, Raven? Why is she doing this?"

Porsha pretended to be clueless. "I don't know. What do you mean?"

"I just saw her Facebook video. And from the sounds of it, she's trying to say my dad raped her."

"I don't know," Porsha said again.

"She conveniently didn't say the name of this so-called prominent pastor, but everyone knows her history with my family. She worked for my dad, robbed his church and went to prison for it, and of course, she badmouths *me* every chance she gets."

Raven was always saying how she was sure that Dillon was monitoring her every move, and now Porsha knew she was right.

"I don't know what to tell you," she said.

"The truth. Is she purposely lying on my dad to make herself look good? To gain sympathy from people? To make money? What?"

"I think you need to talk to Raven."

"Yeah, well, I certainly plan to. Tripping out on me is one thing, but telling the kind of lies that could damage my father's ministry, or worse, get him arrested, is something else."

Porsha listened but wasn't sure what he wanted her to say.

"And you know what else?" he said.

"What?"

"For the life of me, I still can't believe you became friends with that tramp."

"Well, I did."

"Why?"

"Because I was wrong for sleeping with you. Having an affair with her husband."

"Yeah, but it wasn't like you really even knew her."

"No, and it wasn't like I was your only mistress, either," Porsha spat back.

"True, and I know I deserve that. But you and Raven friends? Please."

"Why do you even care, Dillon? Why does it matter to you?"

"Because if you think you can trust Raven, you're being naïve. If you think she's going to stay all partnered up with you, you're sadly mistaken."

"Why do you say that?"

"Because Raven only cares about Raven, and she's the kind of heartless woman who wants to run things—all by herself. She's drunk with power, and she wants to be rich."

Porsha knew he was right, but she wasn't about to give him the satisfaction of knowing she agreed with him. "I would really rather not talk about this."

"Fine, then let's talk about you," he said matter-of-factly.

"Meaning?"

"How have you been doing? You know, since the last time we talked."

Porsha chuckled. "You're really something else. So just like that, you're going to call here, acting as though nothing happened between us. Like you didn't start dating someone else behind my back."

"I'm not saying any of that. I know I was wrong. Way wrong, and I admit that. But I'm sorry, and I certainly never meant to hurt you."

"Yeah, I'm sure you didn't, Dillon."

"I'm serious. I had no business treating you the way I did. I should've divorced Raven just like you kept suggesting."

"Well, you didn't, so that's that."

"I still don't get it, though."

"What?"

"You and Raven? Running a ministry together? Who would've guessed?"

"Stranger things have happened, right?"

"True, but wives and mistresses don't become friends."

"First time for everything," she said. "And who's to say we're the only ones?"

"If you say so."

"I do. And since we're catching up on everything, how's your fiancée doing?"

"She's doing well."

"Good for her."

"Do I detect a little saltiness? Maybe a little jealousy?"

"Dillon, please. You and your fiancée are the least of my worries."

"Doesn't sound like that to me."

"Well, you are."

"So how much money did you have to give Raven?" he said out of nowhere.

"Excuse me?"

"How much money did you have to invest so she could start her church?"

"Why?"

"Because there's no way Raven would allow you to hold a position there otherwise. Not without money being involved. Raven might pretend to be your friend, but she'll never get over the fact that you were my mistress. She'll never fully forgive you for that."

"I have to go."

"Okay, wait," he hurried to say. "I'm sorry. I didn't mean to upset you, but for whatever it's worth, you need to be careful. You need to watch your back."

"Really? You mean just like I should've done with you?"

Dillon laughed. "Touché. I guess I deserve that."

"I guess you do."

"Still, just be careful. Because believe me, Raven can't be trusted."

"Good-bye, Dillon."

"Bye, baby."

Porsha hung up the phone and frowned. *Baby?* Was he serious? After all that had happened between them? Surely he didn't think she wanted him. Because she certainly didn't. And she never would again. That's what she'd been telling herself, anyway, for two whole years. She'd told herself that because it was true. She was completely done with Dillon for good.

Chapter 8

*E*veryone gathered into the conference room for the
Tuesday-morning staff meeting. In attendance were
Raven, Porsha, Michelle, and also John Green,
NVCC's chief financial officer; Trudy Dennison, NVCC's
marketing and promotions director; Melvin Lane,
NVCC's media broadcasting director; and Kathy Bowman,
NVCC's online director. The church also employed a
board of elders who led individual ministries, but for the
most part, Raven, Porsha, and Michelle met with them sep-
arately. They only did so twice per month, and because
Raven was happy with all of them, she allowed each elder
to operate his or her respective ministry as he or she saw
fit. Although, to tell the truth, the reason she gave them
such free rein was because they ran things exactly the way
she'd instructed them.

As the meeting attendees assembled in the room and began taking their seats, Raven, who sat at the head of the
long wooden table, glanced to her left at Porsha. Porsha was
chatting with Kathy, and Raven wished Porsha had decided

to stay home today. She didn't want to see her, and she still couldn't believe Porsha had mustered enough audacity to call her yesterday. She'd acted as though she was genuinely concerned, but Raven wasn't stupid. No, what Porsha had actually been trying to do was question the validity of Raven's allegations, and Raven wasn't happy about it.

"So," Raven said when everyone seemed situated and ready to begin. "By now, I'm sure you've all seen my Facebook video. If you didn't see it live, then you've likely viewed the recorded version."

Everyone nodded, but Porsha just stared at her.

"Good. Well, I first want to apologize for not preparing all of you, but I didn't even know I was going to share anything new about my past until minutes beforehand. I've never told anyone what happened to me, but yesterday, I felt led to discuss it. I believe God wanted me to share my story as a way to help many others, so I did."

"I'm really sorry," Michelle said. "I know I've already told you that, but I truly am."

Raven smiled. "Thank you."

"We're all sorry," John added, and Raven smiled at him, too. The only difference now, though, was that she forced tears into her eyes just for him. She didn't allow them to fall down her cheeks, but she could see how hurt John was about her being raped, and she liked that. John was an extraordinary number cruncher, even better with finances than she was, but he was also ridiculously attracted to her. The only problem with that, however, was that he was far too straightlaced and wasn't her type—he wore

nerdy-looking glasses, multicolored socks, and loud bow
ties with his suits—but she always treated him well. She
even gave him bonuses for all his hard work...and she'd
slept with him a couple of times, too. Of course, John knew,
though, that she was dating Kane, and Raven believed that
was the reason he never pressured her. But she also knew
she could sleep with John again anytime she wanted. And
she would if that's what it would take for him to doctor
a few financial statements and bank account details. She
hadn't quite figured out what she needed him to do just yet
or if she would need him to do anything at all, but she kept
him right where she wanted him just in case. Since hiring
him, she'd known that having a CFO who was shamelessly
attracted to her would eventually benefit her in some way,
so she'd always subtly but regularly flirted with him for
good measure. It didn't hurt, too, that he was only thirty
and didn't prefer younger women. He had conveniently
mentioned that fact on more than one occasion, knowing
that Raven was nine years older than he was.

"We're here for you," Trudy said. "Anything you need."

"For sure," Melvin agreed.

"Thank you all so much. I love and appreciate you for
your concern, but I'm fine. Really."

Raven waited for someone else to speak, but when no
one did, she pulled a tissue from a box of Kleenex sitting near her and dabbed the corners of her eyes. She was
mostly hoping that Porsha would offer at least some sort
of support or kind word—not because she cared one way
or the other, but just so they could keep up appearances

among their staff. But Porsha still stared at Raven in silence.

Until finally she said, "A person like that should be reported. Arrested and locked up before they hurt someone else. I mean, just think of how many other women this lunatic may have victimized."

Raven tried to keep her composure, because it was clear that Porsha was only trying to get her to say who'd raped her.

"I just want to leave well enough alone," Raven said. "I don't mind sharing my story as a way to help other women, but that's where it ends. I don't want to identify the person, have to deal with the media, or have to testify in court. It's just not worth it."

"Why would the media want to get involved?" Porsha asked.

"Because people know me on a national level."

Porsha locked her hands together and rested them on the table. "That's even better. You just said you want to help other women, right? And if you identified your attacker, that might encourage others to do the same. It would also prevent innocent people from being accused."

Raven wasn't sure how to respond, but she was getting pretty sick of Porsha. None of this was even her business. Yes, Raven had gone on record saying that her rapist was a prominent pastor, but that jarring piece of information alone was all most people cared about—that he was a pastor and well . . . that it might be world-renowned Reverend Curtis Black. This was the only thing that mattered to Raven, too, as this kind of widespread gossip and raging curiosity could keep people talking for months. The whole scenario could do wonders for Raven's publicity, and if the good reverend, his pathetic son Dillon, his crazy daughter Alicia, or anyone else in the Black family suffered consequences, then so be it. As far as Raven was concerned, they would only be getting what they had coming to them.

Raven didn't bother responding to Porsha, though, and instead turned to her online director. "So, Kathy, while I handle my own social media pages, how are things shaping up with the church's?"

"Everything's going well. And as you can probably imagine, once I shared your video on the church's public page yesterday, it became our most shared video ever. As of this morning, people were still sharing it on their personal pages, commenting, and in some cases admitting that they'd been sexually assaulted themselves."

Raven feigned a look of surprise because the first thing she'd done this morning was check the ministry's Facebook page. "Really? I expected people to maybe comment, but not make this our most shared video."

"Yes," Kathy said, "people can relate and it always helps when someone learns that they're not alone. That someone such as yourself has experienced the same things they have."

"It might not hurt for you to do some sort of an internal video announcement," Trudy said. "Not for the overall public, but specifically for our church membership. I know you've shared your story online, but instead of sharing it with our local members this coming Sunday from the pulpit, maybe you could go into the studio with Melvin to record it. That way we could play the video before you actually speak to the congregation."

Raven liked this whole idea but masked her enthusiasm. "Well, if you all think it might help, then I'm more than happy to do it. I didn't disclose my rape just so I could get a lot of public attention, though," she said, lying. "But again, if even one person can be helped, I'll do whatever I have to."

"Good," Trudy said. "And is that okay with you, Melvin?"

"Absolutely. We can do it any day this week, Pastor."

"Sounds good," Raven told him. "Tomorrow or Thursday should work fine, and I'll confirm with you later."

Michelle read aloud the final four topics on the agenda, and when all had been discussed, Raven said, "Okay, then. Unless someone has something else, I think we can adjourn."

"Actually, I have something," Porsha said.

It took everything in Raven not to groan, cringe, and scream at the top of her lungs. But she didn't. Instead, she pretended to be highly interested in what *Minister Harrington* had to say. "Please, go ahead."

"I've thought about this before, but now I believe it's the perfect time to start a singles ministry."

Raven half frowned. "But we already have a singles ministry. Elder Carter holds meetings for it every month."

"I know, but that one is open to men and women. I want to create something for women only."

"I really like that," Trudy said. "And if you do this, I'll be one of the first members to sign up."

Kathy agreed. "Well, I'm not single, but my sister is, and I know she would love being able to fellowship with other single women."

"What about you, Michelle?" Porsha asked.

"I think it's a great idea, too. I look forward to it!"

Raven hated this. It was bad enough that Porsha had created a new message segment for Sunday mornings, and now she wanted to start her own singles ministry? What would she want to do next? Deliver all Sunday-morning sermons? Change her title from minister to senior pastor? Decide that she was head boss in charge of the whole NVM operation?

Only over Raven's dead body.

"So what is it that you think would be different?" Raven asked. "I mean, in comparison to the singles ministry we already have?"

Porsha relaxed further in her chair. "For one, each woman could share a lot more freely about women's issues. They could share their innermost concerns and fears about being single and also about men as a whole," she said, and then looked at John and Melvin. "No offense."

Both men laughed, and Melvin said, "None taken."

"None at all," John added.

Then Porsha continued. "They could talk about anything they wanted in more of a girlfriend sort of setting. They wouldn't have to feel guarded or worry about saying the wrong thing in front of male participants. This would be something created strictly for them."

"Actually, us single men could stand to have a ministry

like that as well," John said, laughing a little, but he seemed very serious. "It would be great to have one for women, one for men, and a combined one."

"I agree," Porsha said. "Because let's face it, men and women are very different. Women have different needs than men."

Trudy folded her arms. "Yes. So this will be perfect."

Raven was speechless. For the first time since she'd started her ministry and hired everyone sitting in this room, they'd all sided with Porsha. Worse, she knew Porsha was going to do whatever she wanted, regardless of what Raven had to say about it.

"I'm glad you all like the idea," Porsha said, "and if no one opposes, I'd like to begin writing the mission statement right away and then figure out which day and time of the week will work best. After that, I'll start brainstorming some fun things the ladies can do together as well."

Raven hoped and prayed that someone—anyone—would realize that this singles ministry for women was a total waste of time. But no one did. Instead, they were excited about it, and at this very moment, they were still raving over it and offering Porsha their blessings.

But nonetheless, Raven wanted to shut it all down. She wanted to object to any- and everything Porsha was proposing, except sadly, she knew it wouldn't look good to the others. Which was the reason Porsha had to go. There was just no getting around it.

Chapter 9

*N*ow Porsha knew for sure that Raven was lying about being raped. She'd actually known this since yesterday, but watching her interact with some of the staff members during the meeting two hours ago had confirmed Porsha's suspicions even further. Raven was pretending to be a victim and doing it well enough to deceive lots of people, and Porsha wondered how long she was going to get away with it. As it was, Dillon was already onto her, which meant his father was, too, so no good could come of this for Raven. Porsha didn't actually know Reverend Curtis Black personally, but she knew enough about his past to predict that things wouldn't go well for Raven if she didn't stop what she was doing. She was playing games with the wrong man, and if Raven's theory was right about Dillon burning down his own church, then he wasn't someone Raven should be messing with, either.

But that wasn't Porsha's biggest worry at the moment. Not when she'd felt a bit uneasy ever since speaking to Dillon yesterday afternoon. She'd tried to forget about his calling her, but she couldn't. In fact, she'd thought about him all evening and again this morning, and she didn't like how some of her old feelings had resurfaced. She didn't like it at all, especially with his being engaged to someone else—even though when she'd asked him about Taylor, he'd immediately asked if she was jealous. Then, there was the way he'd ended their call by referring to her as "baby." Porsha wasn't sure why he'd spoken to her in that respect if he was in love with and was planning to marry his fiancée. Although with Dillon's history of cheating, she knew she shouldn't be surprised. Which was even more reason she didn't want to feel the way she did, and she hoped he didn't contact her again.

Porsha pulled a legal-size writing pad closer and picked up her black Montblanc pen. She smiled when she thought about the fact that Steve had given it to her for her birthday earlier this year. He'd also bought her a gorgeous set of diamond studs, and a part of her did wonder what his wife would think if she knew the kind of money Steve had spent on Porsha. He owned a successful home health care company and could likely afford it with no problem, but there was no denying that these were the kinds of gifts a husband should be buying for his wife. This was something Porsha tried her best not to think about, though, because she knew having an affair with Steve was wrong. Sleeping with any married man was wrong, and strangely, when she'd woken up this morning a wave of guilt had nearly paralyzed her. It had overwhelmed her so much that she'd thought she was going crazy.

Then, when her mind and body had seemed to relax, she'd thought about her singles ministry for women. For so long she'd been lying and telling people that God had called her to preach, but this morning she'd felt as though God truly was speaking to her. It wasn't that she'd heard His actual voice, but He'd seemed to speak to her soul. He'd made it very clear that all the sins she was committing were wrong, and that He had something good He wanted her to do. Something that would help someone other than herself.

It had also been then that she'd decided to call her new singles ministry for women Daughters of Ruth. She hadn't shared this information during the staff meeting because she hadn't wanted anyone thinking she'd jumped ahead of the game, that is, before asking for their blessings. But again, she'd known since waking up this morning that this was the perfect name for what she wanted to accomplish. She felt so much passion for her new ministry, more than she had for anything else she'd worked on, and this meant everything. Because to her, the best ministries were started by people who could relate to the folks they were planning to help. Needless to say, as a thirty-four-year-old single woman hoping to find her own Boaz, she knew what it was like to feel alone and to want to be married. This was also the reason she would think that Raven would've been more supportive and would've seen how important this ministry was for the church as a whole. Especially since Raven was single and five years older than Porsha. But, of course, Raven didn't want to see Porsha creating anything that wasn't Raven's idea, and she would never say anything good about it.

Porsha Googled a few articles that offered statistics about single women. She shook her head when she saw one that stated that the reason some women were single was because there just weren't enough men to go around. Then it mentioned how, on top of that, the ratio of women to men turned bleaker when you considered the fact that some women had pretty high standards—the kind that didn't make a lot of sense but were also the kind that likely meant they wouldn't find a husband. For example, there were some women who wouldn't date a man who didn't have a college degree, even if he earned a better living than some men who did. There were also women who refused to date a man who didn't fall into the *exceptionally handsome* category, even if they weren't the most beautiful specimens themselves. Porsha didn't understand any of the above, because as wealthy as she'd always been, she'd never cared about a man's educational background or the amount of money he made as long as he worked somewhere full-time. Even being the finest man of the century didn't matter to her, as long as he took care of himself in all other areas. She did, however, want a man who treated her well, and most of all, she wanted to be loved at the highest level. Second only to God, she wanted her man—her husband—to love her more than anything or anyone else until death.

Porsha jotted down a few agenda items for the first ministry meeting, but then her phone rang. She glanced over at the screen and saw that it was Steve. He'd tried calling her twice yesterday and again first thing this morning, but she hadn't answered. She was still upset about his saying he wasn't going to leave his wife, and she hadn't wanted to talk to him.

She reached for her phone, barely catching his call before it went to voice mail. "Hello?"

"Well, it's about time," he said.

"Time for what?"

"Oh, so I guess you think that's funny."

"I don't think it's funny at all. But I'm also not going to pretend like you don't have a wife."

He sighed loud enough for her to hear him. "Why are you still talking about that? Why are you acting this way?"

Porsha leaned back in her chair and turned toward her window, but she didn't respond.

"Hello?" he said, sounding annoyed.

"I'm here."

"Look, we need to talk."

"Then talk."

"Not now, this evening."

She scrunched her eyebrows. "Since when do you visit me on weeknights? I mean, maybe you do every now and then, but that's rare."

"I really want to see you. Is that a crime?"

"You tell me."

"Look, I know you don't like our situation, but there's nothing I can do about it right now. It won't always be this way, though."

"You could do something about it if you wanted to."

"I can't help that my son is still in high school."

"This isn't just about your son. Have you forgotten what you said on Sunday?"

"What?"

"That you didn't want to abandon your wife?"

"Look, baby, let's just talk about it tonight, okay?"

"Fine."

"I love you, and I'll see you then."

Porsha didn't bother saying good-bye, because she doubted he was planning to actually show up anyway. She was pretty sure his church had Bible study on Tuesday nights, and he never usually missed going. Maybe it was time to end things with Steve. She did love him, but what if he strung her along until his son graduated high school and then still refused to divorce his wife? She'd seen this exact scenario many times before with other women. The same thing had sort of happened to her with Dillon. Maybe in a different way, but nonetheless, he'd ended up engaged to someone else. Porsha still resented him for that, too. So once again, she told herself that she didn't want to think about Dillon. That she didn't have feelings for the man who had betrayed her—feelings that had been buried for two years straight. Feelings that were slowly returning whether she wanted them to or not.

So, what she had to do was stop this madness from re-curring. She had to end it before it ever got started.

Chapter 10

Raven was still livid. Ever since returning to her office from the meeting this morning, she'd been trying to calm her anger and settle her nerves, but nothing was working. Porsha was going too far with all this I'll-do-whatever-I-please mentality, and she had to be stopped.

Raven picked up her desk phone and dialed Michelle's extension. "Can you come in here?"

"Of course. I'll be right there."

Raven sat up straight and took a deep breath.

Michelle knocked on the door, walked in, and then closed it behind her.

"I hope you weren't in the middle of anything," Raven said.

Michelle sat down. "No. Well, I was working on a small project, but it wasn't something urgent."

"Good."

"Is everything okay?"

"Not really."

"Is there something I can do to help?"

"I'm glad you asked that, because for the last hour I've done a lot of thinking. I've tried to weigh my options and figure out who I can really trust, and it's you who keeps rising to the top of that list."

"I'm glad you feel that way."

"I first want to say this up front, though. From this moment on, everything I discuss with you, business or personal, has to remain between us."

"Of course. Absolutely."

"I know that you work for Porsha, too, but if I had to guess, the things you do for her only take up maybe twenty percent of your time?"

"That's about right. Some weeks, she doesn't have anything for me to do at all. Mostly because she likes to handle a lot of her own scheduling and communication."

"I can tell. This is actually a good thing now, though, because I'm planning to make some major changes within the ministry. These changes won't happen overnight, but they'll be gradual and might become a bit uncomfortable for everyone here."

Michelle looked confused. "Okay."

"I know you're a little curious about why I'm getting ready to do this, but before I explain further I need to know that you'll be loyal to me and only me. Because even though I believe I can trust you, I still need for you to look me in my eyes and tell me that yourself."

"Pastor Raven, you can trust me with anything. I promise you that."

"I also need to know that regardless of what happens, you will support me and have my back. That you will defend me and remain in my corner."

"That's not a problem, either. I give you my word. I'll do anything you need me to do."

"What if it means helping me to get rid of Porsha?"

Michelle stared at her in silence, and Raven wondered if she'd told her too much too soon. But then Michelle said, "I'm actually not surprised."

Raven raised her eyebrows. "Really? Why?"

"I don't know. Just a feeling I had. I mean, don't get me wrong, I like Porsha. But I've also noticed that you and her don't seem to be as good of friends as you were when I first started attending here. And it seems like you've become even more distant over the last couple of months."

"Well, I was sort of hoping that no one had noticed. But I guess you can't hide obvious tension between friends. Or foes, even."

Raven now wondered if any of the other staff members had discovered the same thing.

Michelle crossed her legs. "It's not that you seem upset with each other or anything. Just different. You know, like you're each doing your own thing."

"That's because we are. I'm the pastor and founder of NVCC, and Porsha is only a minister—or so she says. But whatever. Anyway, I'm the face of New Vision Ministries and NVCC, and Porsha just works here."

"But if you don't mind my saying this, that's not how

everyone on staff sees it. Porsha has made it clear to all of us that she invested the initial start-up money, and that you and her are equal partners."

"On paper we are, but that's about to change," Raven said. "That's why I want her out."

Michelle looked at her, waiting for more details, but didn't say anything.

"I know that sounds harsh," Raven offered, "but it's also the truth. I don't want her here, because she's trying to control too much. You saw the way she added on this new Sunday message of hers, and now she's getting ready to start a new singles ministry. And she never talked to me once about either."

"That's too bad, and why do you think she's acting this way all of a sudden?"

"Because she doesn't like playing second fiddle. She wants to be in charge of the ministry. She never says she does, but her actions prove everything."

"I really wish things hadn't turned out like this," Michelle said. "Especially with how well the ministry is doing. It's growing weekly, and I just hope these problems with Porsha don't turn people off."

"I agree, and that's why we'll have to handle this whole situation as carefully as possible. I don't want this thing to turn ugly, but I won't lie . . . I'm willing to do whatever I have to when it comes to getting Porsha out of here."

"Do you already have something in mind?"

"No, not exactly, but I will. And soon. In the meantime, though, there's something else. I debated telling you this, but I think you should know who your friends are. And who they aren't."

Michelle looked astonished. "I don't understand."

Raven hated lying to her. Michelle was so innocent in all of this, but she also had a huge heart, and Raven needed to toughen her up. She also needed to turn her as much against Porsha as she could.

"Porsha has never liked you. She never even wanted you to work here."

"Really? I guess I don't even know what to say. Except that she must be a really good actor."

"She is. Just look at how she claims to be called by God to preach when she knows she was never called by Him to do anything. Porsha is a phony, and it's time you know the truth about everything."

Michelle shook her head. "This is too much."

"I can imagine, and I'm sorry she had you so fooled. And that I allowed it to happen."

"It's really wrong for her to deceive people this way. Some of the members in our congregation are really vulnerable. They've been through a lot or they're currently going through a lot, and they trust her."

"I know, and it's time for all that to stop. It's the reason we—you and I together—have to put an end to this. You're the only person who can help me."

"Just tell me what you want me to do."

"I'll take the next week or two to think things through, and then you and I'll talk again."

"Sounds good."

"Thank you for understanding, Michelle. Thank you for being here for me."

"Anytime."

Raven almost told Michelle her whole history with Porsha, specifically how Porsha had slept with Dillon behind her back. But she decided to save that damaging information for another day. As it was, she could already tell how shocked and hurt Michelle was, so it was better to feed her more details a little at a time. That way, Michelle's dislike for Porsha would evolve gradually and solidly.

Soon she would begin to hate Porsha just as much as Raven did, and this would make all the difference.

Chapter 11

Steve was out of breath and sounded as satisfied as always. He and Porsha had just made love—at least that's what he likely had thought it was, but to her, they'd merely had sex. Actually, Porsha hadn't been in the mood to do anything with him, but being intimate was the norm for them so she'd gone along with it. Now, though, she was glad it was over. She was puzzled by her feelings because for the first time since they'd met and had slept together, she hadn't enjoyed herself. She'd even felt an unusual amount of guilt, almost the same as when she'd woken up this morning. And, as much as she hated to admit it, she'd also spent part of the last few minutes thinking about Dillon. She so didn't want to keep doing this, but no matter how much she tried to push Dillon from her mind, she couldn't. If anything, she was thinking about him more and more, and she didn't know what to do about it.

Porsha turned her back to Steve.

And he obviously knew something wasn't right. "Baby, what's wrong?"

"Nothing."

"Then why are you acting this way?"

"I'm fine."

Steve sighed. "Look, I'm sorry about my situation. I'm sorry I can't leave my wife the way you want me to."

Porsha didn't even bother responding.

Steve caressed her arm. "But tell me what I *can* do to make things better."

"Maybe you should just get dressed. Go home to your family."

"Why?"

"Because it's not like you can spend the night, anyway."

"No, but what if I start visiting you more? Maybe seeing you no less than three times a week? And I can take you on some of my business trips? We can start with the one I'm traveling to at the end of this month. You know, the health care conference I told you about."

Porsha still didn't comment, but she did like that he was trying to make her happy. She knew most women wouldn't see Steve's offer as anything spectacular, since traveling to a work conference still didn't compare to his divorcing his wife. But for some reason, it made her feel better about their relationship, because maybe if she could spend more time with him, she'd then be able to make him see that it was her who he truly loved and wanted to be with—it was her who he wanted to be married to.

Still, she responded less positively. "I'm not sure any of that will make a difference."

Steve moved his hand away from her. "Then I'm not

sure what else I can do. I mean, what is it that you want
from me?"

Porsha sat up and squinted at him. "I've already told you
what I want. The whole package. I want to be your wife and
not your mistress."

"But we've already discussed that. And it just can't happen. Not right now."

"Well, I'm tired of living this way."

"Then why did you start seeing me? Huh? Because you
knew I was married. You knew I couldn't see you whenever
I wanted to."

"That's beside the point. What matters now is that I
don't want to be your nasty little secret anymore. I don't
want to be some petty side chick. I want more than that."

Steve shook his head. "You're impossible."

"Why? Because I know my worth? Because I've changed
my mind about what I need?"

"You should've thought about that when you first laid
down with me."

"And you should've thought about the fact that not every
mistress is crazy enough to wait years for a man to leave his
wife."

"So what does that mean exactly? You don't love me anymore? You want us to end things?"

Porsha hated herself for not being able to say "yes," but
she couldn't. And it was mostly because she didn't have
anyone else. She didn't want to believe that something was
better than nothing, but she sort of did. "Look, I know this
isn't what you were expecting, but the last thing I want

is to be hurt. I also don't want to be alone for the rest of my life. Can you understand that? I mean, here I'll be thirty-five next year, and I've never been married. And I want to have children, too."

Steve pulled her closer to him and wrapped his arms around her. "Sweetheart, I would never hurt you, and things won't always be this way. At some point, I will leave Denene. I just have to wait until Stevie finishes high school and leaves for college."

"I know you keep saying that, but isn't he only going to be a sophomore this fall?"

"He is."

Porsha sat up straight again and looked at him. "And you think it's fair for me to wait another three whole years? Not to mention how long it will probably take for your divorce to be final."

"I know it seems like forever, but if we start spending more time together three years will pass quickly."

"I don't think so."

"You just have to be patient. And if you really love me the way you say you do, you will."

"And if you love me, you'll do whatever you have to to make me happy."

"Where is all this coming from?" he asked, dropping his feet onto the floor and sitting with his back to her.

"I told you. I want more. Life is short. And I don't want to spend the next three years hiding out here at home with you."

"I understand that, and that's why I suggested you go on some of my business trips."

"Why? So I can hide out in your hotel room?"

"This is crazy."

"I'm sorry you feel that way," she said, "but if you want to know the truth, I also don't want to keep sleeping with someone else's husband."

Steve laughed. "Oh, so now I guess you've turned into some sort of saint."

"You know as well as I do that what we're doing is wrong. You're an ordained deacon, and I'm a minister."

"Yeah, well, we didn't just become them. You were a minister when I met you, and I've been a deacon for years. So, as much as I hate to say it, we're not perfect. But who is? The Bible says that we all fall short of the glory of God."

"Yeah, but it also says that you will know the truth and the truth shall set you free."

"Did you read that scripture *before* you slept with me the first time or just this week?"

Porsha didn't respond, but that same feeling of guilt she'd struggled with this morning was consuming her again. It was so intense, she felt dirty.

So she finally got up, grabbed her maxi-length robe, and slipped it on. But then her phone rang. She couldn't imagine who might be calling her this late in the evening. Interestingly enough, though, when she went over and pulled it from her handbag, she saw that it was Dillon again. She wondered what he wanted, but she hit Ignore and dropped her phone back inside her purse.

"Who was that?" Steve asked.

"Nobody important."

"Yeah, right. Maybe that's why you're all of a sudden trying to act so holier-than-thou."

"Meaning?"

"You're seeing someone else."

"Steve, please. Don't turn this on me. You're the one who's married, and the only reason you're upset is because I'm not okay with that anymore."

Steve stood up. "Whatever you say. And you know what? Maybe I *should* just leave."

"Do whatever you think you need to."

Steve rolled his eyes at her and went into the bathroom.

But at the moment, Porsha couldn't have cared less. Not when she was still trying to figure out why Dillon was calling her. Regardless of what his reason was, she knew it was best to leave her past exactly where it was, because she didn't want any trouble. She didn't want to create more problems for herself than she already had.

Chapter 12

Porsha could kick herself for doing this. About an hour after Steve had left, Dillon had phoned her back, and unfortunately, she'd answered him.

"So I'm sure you're wondering why I keep calling you, huh?" he said.

"Hmmph, you must be a mind reader."

"No, but the thing is...I miss you more than you can imagine. I realized that a while ago, but as soon as I heard your voice yesterday it brought back a lot of good memories."

"Really? So you call what we had good memories? Us sleeping with each other behind Raven's back and then me giving her a video of us having sex?"

"You know what I mean. When things were good between us, they were good. Very good, and you know it."

Porsha couldn't argue with that, but she kept quiet.

"I'll tell you something else, too," he said. "If I had it to do over again, I wouldn't have started seeing Taylor at all. I would've divorced Raven and married you like you wanted."

"Yeah, but you did start seeing Taylor and you got engaged to her. And for the record, even when things ended between you and Raven, it wasn't you who filed for a divorce. Raven did. You would've stayed married and messed around for as long as you had to."

"That's true, but I was a different person back then. I had a lot of personal issues going on with my dad, I started drinking again, and I was confused about life, period."

Porsha made herself more comfortable in her bed and leaned back against three pillows. She crossed her legs, and even though her television was on mute, she saw that the news was coming on. She hadn't realized it was already ten o'clock.

"Are you there?" he asked.

"Yep."

"You don't have anything to say?"

"About what?"

"What I just told you?"

"You mean about you being different back then? Well, even if that's true, I was the one who ended up hurt. The one left looking stupid." Porsha thought about how she was allowing Steve an opportunity to do the same thing to her. It was the reason she'd let him know tonight that she wouldn't keep seeing a married man or wait for him to get divorced three years from now.

Porsha wondered why any woman, including her, got involved with married men in the first place—why they fell in love with them. But she didn't want to think about that anymore and changed the subject. "So when you called me yesterday, you still didn't say a whole lot about what you've been up to."

"Well, if you're talking about my relationship with my dad, things couldn't be better. We finally have the kind of father-and-son connection we should have, and even Matthew has somewhat warmed up to me," he said, referring to his younger brother.

"That's really good to hear. I know you wanted that, so I'm happy for you."

"Thank you. It was a tough road, but I can't complain."

"What about a church, though?" she asked. "Are you planning to start a new one?"

"No, I'm not."

"Is there a reason?"

"I just don't have any desire to preach sermons anytime soon. I'm content working behind the scenes at my dad's church. Right now, I'm his VP of broadcasting."

"I didn't even know you had an interest in that."

"Neither did I, but I really enjoy it. And I only have one more year to go before I finish my degree in that area."

"Wow, you've been busy."

"I have."

Porsha was still a bit surprised that Dillon had given up on having his own church, because once upon a time, he'd wanted nothing more than to be a megachurch pastor. But maybe working things out with his dad had truly changed his thinking.

"So what else is going on?" she asked.

"Can I come see you?" he said.

"What? Maybe you didn't hear me. I asked you what else is going on?"

"I heard you. But I don't want to talk about that. I don't want to talk at all. I just want to come see you."

Porsha didn't like this. Their whole conversation was starting to make her nervous, and she worried about where it was headed. So she quickly told him, "No, definitely not."

"Why?"

"For one, you're engaged to be married, and two, I'm a minister at your ex-wife's church—a church we run together, remember?"

Dillon chuckled.

"So I guess you think that's funny?"

"I didn't say that."

"Well, I doubt you're laughing for no reason. So what is it?"

"You really want to know?"

"I do."

"Okay, you asked me so I'm going to tell you. I'm laughing about you being a minister. I mean, what's that all about?"

"Oh, so you don't believe that God calls women to preach?"

"I never said that. I just can't believe *you're* a minister."

Porsha didn't like the way Dillon was ridiculing her, but sadly, she understood his skepticism. She would never admit to him that the reason she'd settled on giving herself the title of minister was because she hadn't known what other position in the church would give her regular interaction with the whole congregation. And as it had turned out, her choice had been a good one, because everyone seemed to like having her in that role. Except now, of course, Porsha was regretting her decision to become a minister more and more and didn't want to play with God any longer. She didn't want to keep lying to people about what God's purpose was for her. The only problem, however, was that she didn't know how to stop being a minister without being humiliated. Public shame and condemnation wasn't something she wanted to deal with, which meant she would have to continue her façade a little while longer. Maybe if she stopped delivering sermons, though, it wouldn't be so bad.

"Baby, come on," Dillon said. "Because I know you haven't forgotten all those Mondays we used to spend together. Remember, that was my day off from the church, and I would drive over to your suburb. We would make love on and off all day long. We never got tired of each other."

Porsha knew he was telling the truth, and she couldn't help thinking about the way they would in fact make love multiple times.

Of course, Dillon was thinking the same thing. "Don't you remember how it used to be? Multiple times, all the way into the evening. Plus, we just liked being together. Remember?"

Porsha felt herself becoming weak, but then she thought about Steve and how she'd just had sex with him earlier.

"No. It's not happening."

"Why are you trying to be so hard about this? Because I know you want me. I can hear it in your voice."

"I have to go, Dillon. I'll talk to you later."

She hung up before he could say anything else. Now, though, she breathed in and out. Why was he doing this to her? Contacting her and trying to be with her again after all this time? This just couldn't happen, and she had to end whatever scheme he was plotting. She had to put things to rest between them once and for all. She would try to forget that he'd called her tonight, and that he'd been right about what he'd said. Because, God help her, she did want him—more than ever. She knew she shouldn't, but she couldn't help the way she felt. She couldn't help wanting to commit the very same sin with Dillon she was committing with Steve. The only difference was that Steve had a wife, and Dillon had a fiancée. Still, sleeping with either of them was wrong, and there was no changing that. Facts were facts, and she couldn't pretend otherwise.

Chapter 13

Kane was vice president of human resources for a logistics company, and since he and some of his colleagues were entertaining out-of-town clients for dinner, Raven was home alone this evening. To be honest, she wasn't all that sad about it. Because had Kane not been so busy with work, he would've already seen her Facebook video. He rarely viewed them live, but he almost always watched them the same evening she recorded them and definitely by the next day. The reason she knew he still hadn't seen it was because if he had, he would've immediately called to let her know how upset he was. He would've gone on and on about how wrong it had been for her to go public with something so personal when she hadn't even had the courtesy to share it with him first. But it wasn't like she'd had time to call him. She'd decided on a whim that she needed to shake things up a bit with her online viewers. Still, she knew it wouldn't be long before she would have to explain herself to Kane, but she wouldn't worry about that until she had to.

Now, she sat watching one YouTube video after another. Instead of looking at her own, though, she watched those of Reverend Curtis Black. She did this regularly, seeing what she could learn from him. It was true that she had zero respect for Pastor Black, but she couldn't deny his natural-born charisma, his complete knowledge of the Bible, his great gift for delivering sermons, or his exceptionally good looks. The man had children in their thirties—at least his two eldest were, anyway—but he was still as handsome as always. He was the kind of successful pastor Raven aspired to be, and she was well on her way. The only difference was that she was a woman, and as it was with any other career or calling, a woman had to work five times as hard and be ten times as good in order to receive even similar respect as a man.

This made Raven angry, but there wasn't a whole lot she could do to change the backward, sexist way some men thought. And interestingly enough, some women didn't believe women should vie for positions that were mostly dominated by men, either. But Raven wasn't going to let that kind of foolish thinking stop her from becoming who she wanted to be.

She watched another video and then came across one that she hadn't listened to in a while. Because of yet another very public scandal that Pastor Black had gotten himself involved in, he'd decided to step down from his position as senior pastor. But this sermon had been delivered years ago, on the first Sunday he'd returned to his post. Raven clicked Play and turned up the volume.

"My, my, my. Well, today is the day the Lord hath made, so let us rejoice and be glad in it. And I guess it goes without saying that today I am a very happy man, and I am also a very humbled and grateful man of God. As my wife mentioned earlier, this has been one of the toughest years of our lives, but thank God it has also been a wonderful learning period for all of us. It has been a learning process that we truly needed to experience. A little over a year ago, I stood here, letting you know that because I'd made a ton of mistakes it was time for me to step down as your pastor. And that's exactly what I did. I attended service each week the same as you, I participated in Bible study on Wednesday evenings as a member, and I read and studied my Word daily. Sometimes I studied from my home office for hours on end, and I'm here to tell you, it was very much worth it. Then, there were days when I turned out all the lights and closed the shutters in my office and got down on my knees so I could meditate. I did this so I could listen and hear from God without any distractions. I spoke to Him regularly, because I still had a lot of repenting to do. And it is because of all of this that I am totally recommitted to God's work and this entire ministry. I now see things completely different than I did before. I've learned so much and improved so many things in my life, I really wish more pastors would step down and take a backseat when they know they're not walking in God's purpose. When they know they're not doing all that God wants them to do and what He expects from them. I finally feel as though I'm not just on the right path this time around, but instead, I'm now on an eternal path when it comes to my relationship with God. And believe me when I tell you that there's definitely a difference."

Raven pursed her lips. He'd sounded sincere enough, she gave him that much, but who was to say whether he'd kept his word and hadn't done any more dirt? In all fairness, she had to admit that since that particular year, she hadn't heard any rumors about him, not even while she was in prison, but she still didn't trust a man who'd slept around on three different wives and who'd had two of his children with mistresses. The whole family was crazy if you asked Raven. Because for the life of her, she couldn't believe Curtis's current wife, Charlotte, had accepted that child and was raising Curtina as her own daughter. It was true that Curtis's former mistress had died, but there was no way that Raven would have even considered raising a child that her husband had conceived with another woman—while he was married to her. Every time she looked at that child, it would've reminded her of her husband's affair, but maybe Charlotte was different. Either that or she was willing to accept any- and everything if it meant she could keep her position as first lady of the largest church in Mitchell. Or more important, she could continue being married to one of the most well-known pastors worldwide, a man who made sure she wanted for nothing. Charlotte and Pastor Black were so wealthy, Charlotte would likely never want for anything *ever*.

So the more Raven thought about it, the more she realized that Charlotte had done what she needed to do. It was exactly what Raven would've done, too, if it had meant living the kind of lifestyle she longed for. Although there was something else that Raven had forgotten as well. Charlotte's son, Matthew, had been conceived with Pastor Black while he'd still been married to his first wife, Tanya. So maybe this was the real reason she'd been able to accept Pastor Black's outside daughter and move on. Maybe she felt guilty about what she'd done to Tanya. And now that Raven kept thinking about it, Charlotte had also gotten pregnant by a man she'd had an affair with on Pastor Black. She'd had a daughter who Pastor Black had raised as his own child, but that little girl had passed away when she'd been very young. So maybe *this* was the primary reason Charlotte had no problem with Curtina. But with the Black family, there was just no telling.

Raven watched the rest of the sermon, paying attention to the way Pastor Black read scriptures and the way he worded his sentences. But then she snickered. She wasn't sure why she suddenly thought about those two times she'd tried to seduce Pastor Black: once when the two of them had stayed behind in one of the church conference rooms after a meeting to discuss more financial business, and once when she'd pretended her car was in the shop so he would give her a ride to work. She'd known he would eventually be on his way to the church, so she'd called him bright and early. But after all these years, what she still didn't understand was why he'd turned her down on both occasions. It didn't make sense, not when he'd always loved smart, beautiful women—not to mention, he had certainly been unquestionably attracted to her. But rejecting her was exactly what he'd done. Then he'd also had the nerve to have her arrested and sent to prison.

Raven still hated him for that, too, and although no one knew this except God and her, getting back at Pastor Black had been the reason she'd married his son, Dillon. Dillon had known that Raven couldn't stand his father, but to this day, he didn't know that Raven had ever tried to come on to his dad. Maybe because even though Raven's initial connection to Dillon had only been revenge related, eventually she had genuinely fallen in love with him. She wished with everything in her that she hadn't, but it had happened before she'd realized it.

Raven watched sermon videos from five other nationally known pastors. The difference between them and Pastor Black, however, was that while they were each dynamic speakers, too, Raven honestly believed they were *true* men of God. She could tell just by listening to them, and she also had never heard anything bad about any of the men character-wise. She knew no one was perfect, but these men walked with great integrity. There was no doubt that Raven had different motives than they did for becoming a pastor, something she never lied to herself about, but she still had the utmost respect for pastors who seemed to care about doing the right thing. She loved that these particular men stayed clear of scandal.

Raven slid back from her desk, preparing to head up to her bedroom, but when her phone rang she stopped in her tracks. Her eyes must be playing tricks on her, was all she could think. Because she just knew Dillon hadn't found the audacity to call her. Although, there was no doubt that he was calling about that video she'd broadcast yesterday, and she didn't want to hear anything he had to say.

So she waited to see if he was bold enough to leave her a voice message. It took a little longer than she thought, which meant that he either hadn't left one or he was leaving a pretty lengthy rant.

She looked at her phone a few seconds more but then went upstairs. Not long after, her voice message signal beeped, and she swiped her screen to check it.

"I don't know whether you're ignoring my call or if you're legitimately not available. But either way, I need you to hear me and hear me good. Don't start something you won't be able to finish. We all watched that video of yours, and people are already posting comments and saying that they wonder if my dad is the pastor you're talking about. So if you know what's good for you, you'll retract that accusation of yours. My father would never do anything like that to you or any woman, and what a dirty trick you are for trying to insinuate that he would. And you call yourself a pastor. Please! More like some fake harlot standing in a pulpit. You might have those members at your church fooled, but we all know who you really are. We know everything about you, and if you keep playing games, you're going to regret the day you ever met my father. You'll regret you ever met me, too, or even heard of the Black family. So I'm telling you now. Either you make a public statement clearing my dad or else. And just so we're on the same page, these are the kinds of words we expect you to say: 'While it has come to my attention that some people believe that when I said I was raped, I was referring to Pastor Curtis Black, I just want to say that it was not. Pastor Black never touched me or violated me in any kind of way.' And I expect you to do it before noon tomorrow. And if you don't, then consider this your first of very few warnings. Because I'm not playing with you, Raven. It's bad enough that you dragged *my* name and reputation through the gutter during that divorce, so I owe you, anyway. But trying to ruin my dad is something different. So I advise you to do what you need to do. And do it quickly."

Raven clicked the button on her phone and laughed. Was he kidding? Did Dillon actually think she was afraid of him? Did he believe she was going to do anything he told her? Well, if he did, he was crazy, because she wasn't going to retract anything—unless she would get something out of it. Maybe if Pastor Black wanted to verbally endorse her ministry in some beneficial way, or even better, drop a seven-figure contribution into one of NVCC's collection plates, she would be happy to tell her viewers whatever the Black family wanted her to. But if not, she was leaving the allegations as is. She would allow all the suspicion and accusatory rhetoric to continue running rampant, because every bit of it was working nicely for her. Since yesterday, she'd gained ten thousand new followers on her Facebook page and nearly the same on her Twitter and Instagram accounts. Plus, there were all those candid and very touching comments that women nationwide were posting about their own sexual assaults. Some were sharing their stories for the first time, and they loved Raven for giving them the courage to do so. They were thanking her across the board, and she wasn't about to give up such visible attention. Not when she needed this kind of publicity to grow her ministry. Not when the online donations from new viewers were steadily flowing in. But at the same time, it was like she'd just been thinking before: If Pastor Black paid the right price, she would retract whatever he wanted.

For seven figures, she'd do just about anything.

Chapter 14

Hi, Michelle, do you have some time to come chat with me?" Porsha asked.

"Uh, do you know how long it'll take? I have a report that I need to finish by this afternoon."

"Not more than twenty minutes or so."

"Sure, I'll be right in."

Porsha set her phone on its base, wondering why Michelle sounded a little strange. But maybe Raven had her working on something important.

Michelle knocked, walked inside, and sat down.

Porsha smiled. "I really appreciate your taking the time to sit with me."

"No problem," she said with no feeling in her voice.

"Are you okay?" Porsha asked.

"I'm fine."

"Are you sure? Because you seem a little preoccupied."

"Just busy is all. But what can I do for you?"

"Well, as you heard at our staff meeting yesterday morning, I'm starting a new women's ministry."

Michelle nodded.

"And what that also means is that I'll be giving you a few more assignments than usual. I'll need you to research a number of items, too, and as we move along over the next couple of months, I'll want to plan outings for the women. I'll, of course, need you to assist me with that as well."

Michelle barely blinked and acted as though she didn't want to be there. "Okay."

"I've already decided on the name of the ministry, too, which is Daughters of Ruth. But over these next few days, I'm going to begin working on multiple documents. For each monthly meeting, I'll need you to create a formal hand-out that will include helpful information for single women. For the second meeting, I want to give them something that lists the top reasons women who want to be married are still single. I'll also want to give them something that talks about the best places to meet really decent guys. But for the first meeting, the handouts will be more intro related."

Michelle looked at her but still didn't say anything. This was so unlike her, and even though she claimed nothing was wrong, Porsha knew something was.

"Okay, look, Michelle. If this isn't a good time, please tell me. If you're having a bad day, you know I'll understand."

"No, I'm good."

Porsha wondered why she was lying but didn't call her out on it. "That's pretty much all I have, anyway, so unless you have questions I guess that's it."

"When are you planning to have your first meeting and on what day of the week?" she finally asked.

"Every fourth Thursday," Porsha said, flipping through the calendar on her desk. "So I'd really like to start two weeks from now."

"You don't think that's too soon?"

"No. Today is only Wednesday, and I plan to work on this every single day through Saturday. Then, this coming Sunday, I'll be personally announcing it to the congregation. A few days later, you can send it out to our membership mailing list, and I'll talk about it again the next Sunday. After that, you can send out another mass e-blast two days before the meeting."

"I'll do my best," Michelle said. "Raven has a few things she needs me to work on as well, but I'll be fine."

Raven always had projects for Michelle to work on, and even when Porsha did sometimes add a few responsibilities to Michelle's workload, she never complained or made excuses. Today, however, she sounded as though she was hoping Porsha would say, *Oh, well, that's okay. I'll handle my own research and administrative needs, and you just focus on Raven's.*

"Again, I really appreciate you taking the time to sit down with me and for all your help."

Michelle stood up. "No problem. Just send me what you need me to do, and I'll get it done."

"Sounds good, and thank you."

When Michelle left and closed the door, Porsha lowered her eyebrows. Something was very wrong, and Porsha knew she wasn't just imagining things. Michelle was distant, and the more Porsha thought about it, she seemed cold, even. Maybe she was dealing with something personal and simply didn't feel comfortable sharing it with Porsha. If so, Porsha hoped this was only temporary, and that tomorrow would be a much better day for her.

Porsha researched more information online regarding single women until her cell phone rang. It was Steve.

"Hey," she said.

"Hey yourself. Are you busy?"

"Sort of, but what's up?"

"Not a lot. Just wanted to hear your voice...and ask if you enjoyed our time together last night. You know, before things turned a little ugly."

"It was okay."

"Oh, so I see you're still upset."

"Nope."

"Look, baby," he said. "You know I don't like it when we argue like this. It really bothers me. And I barely slept two hours."

"I don't know what to tell you."

"Let's let bygones be bygones. At least for now."

Porsha flipped through a couple of documents on her desk and didn't respond.

"So have you thought more about my suggestion?"

"Which is?"

"Going to my conference with me next month."

"I'll have to let you know."

"Why? Do you have other plans?"

"Not that I'm aware of, but I'm starting a new singles ministry for women. And I'm going to be very busy with it."

"Really? When did you decide this?"

"Just recently, but now it's official."

"Well, it's not like you're really single."

"Excuse me?"

"You're not."

"Yeah...I am. I'm not married to anyone."

"But you and I have a commitment to each other."

"No, *you* have a commitment to your wife. A broken one maybe, but it's still a commitment. I'm not committed to anyone, though."

"But eventually you'll be my wife, and you know that."

Porsha felt herself becoming irritated. "Can we talk about something else?"

"I'd rather talk about this singles ministry you're starting up. Because the next thing I know, you'll be hanging out with some of these women, looking for men."

"First of all, I don't *hang out* anywhere. But if I do meet a nice single man, why shouldn't I be able to date him?"

"I'm going to pretend you didn't say that."

"Pretend all you want."

"What is going on with you? Why are you suddenly acting like you don't care about us anymore?"

"I explained all of that to you last night. I just want more, Steve."

"Hmmph, maybe. Or maybe it has more to do with whoever called you last night."

"What are you talking about?" she said.

"Porsha, don't do that."

"I told you it was nobody important."

"Then why can't you tell me the name of this *nobody*?"

"Because it's not necessary."

"Whatever you say, baby. Look, I have to get going, but I'll call you tomorrow before I come by."

"Yeah, right. I won't hold my breath."

"I'm serious. You'll see."

"I'll talk to you later, Steve."

"I love you."

"See ya."

"You're not going to say it back? I noticed you didn't say it back yesterday, either, before we hung up."

"Love you, too."

"I really do love you, Porsha."

"So do I. Talk to you later."

Porsha laid her phone down and swiveled her chair around so that she faced her office window. She was so confused. As wrong as it was, she did love Steve. She'd loved him for months, but she was no longer comfortable with their situation. She knew that this was partly because God was dealing with her conscience—something she now realized for sure, just at this very moment—and partly because of Dillon. She had no idea why all of this was happening to her, not to mention all at one time. She'd been positive that she was over Dillon, and that the only man she loved was Steve, but she could no longer deny that she still had strong, passionate feelings for him. She cared about both of them.

Still, she was baffled by all of it, and even more so when it came to Dillon because he'd already proven that he couldn't be trusted. Actually, Steve couldn't be trusted, either, what with the way he was cheating on his wife with her, but at least Steve wasn't seeing anyone else—as far as she knew, anyway.

Porsha closed her eyes, attempting to relax her mind. Her life was so not what she wanted it to be, and she wondered how she was going to fix it. But maybe the passion she had for her women's ministry was the answer. She knew it was going to help lots of other women, and she hoped and prayed that it would help her just as much.

She needed all the help she could get—before things got worse.

Chapter 15

Kane walked into Raven's office without knocking and shut the door behind him, fuming. "So when exactly were you going to tell me?"

Raven hurried out of her seat and then stepped around her desk, trying to embrace him. "Baby, I knew you were going to be upset, but please let me explain."

Kane pushed her arms away from him. "Explain how? I mean, here we've been seeing each other for all this time and you never told me you were raped? Yet you told the entire world about it?"

"I didn't mean for it to happen that way. Honestly, I didn't."

"I don't believe you. It's bad enough that you won't marry me, but now you're keeping secrets? The kind of secrets people in love don't hide from each other?"

This was turning out worse than Raven had thought it would be, and since Bible study would be starting in thirty minutes, it was such bad timing. "I didn't want to, but I was so ashamed. Sometimes just thinking about it is way too painful, and that's why I never talk about it. I've never told anyone."

"Until two days ago. On Monday you told everyone except me."

"I know, baby, and I'm sorry. If I could do things over I would, but I can't."

"No, you're right. What's done is done, but at least now I know where we stand."

Raven walked closer to him again.

"Don't touch me," he said. "That's not going to work this time."

"Please let me make this up to you. I have to get ready for Bible study, but I promise I'll answer any questions you have right after. I'll explain everything when you come to my house."

"No, I think I'll pass on both."

"You're not staying for Bible study?"

"No."

"Baby, I get that you don't understand any of this, but you also don't know what it's like to be a rape victim," she said, searching for anything she could that might make him forgive her. "You don't know what it's like to be traumatized the way I was and then have to walk around all this time as though nothing happened. But for some reason when I got ready to do my broadcast on Monday, I felt led to tell the truth. I felt obligated to share my story so that I could help other women."

Kane stared at her, and Raven had never seen him so furious. She'd never seen him so hurt.

"So who did this to you?" he asked matter-of-factly.

This was the one question that Raven had already thought up a lie for. "That's not something I can tell even you. I know it might sound strange, but if I did, it would stir up too many awful memories. It's just better to forget about it and move on."

"You're too much. You know that? And to think I thought you loved me."

"I do love you. But I can't allow my past to take over my life. I won't do that."

"So you're going to let a rapist go free? Let him ruin some other woman's life? And who's to say he hasn't raped lots of other women already?"

"I can't worry about that. I have to worry about me."

Kane shook his head. "Please tell me you're not serious. You're a pastor, trying to save souls, yet you can't worry about other victims?"

"I'm sorry."

"Well, then which is it, Raven? You just said that the reason you shared your story was to help other women, but now you're saying you're only worried about yourself?"

Kane was trying to use her words against her, the same as Porsha had done during yesterday's meeting, but it wouldn't change Raven's mind about anything. How could it? Because it wasn't as though she had a real name to give. It wasn't like she'd been raped—at least not as an adult.

"Baby, please. I'm begging you to understand. I know it's hard, but let's just get through Bible study and then we'll continue this later."

"I already told you. I'm not staying for Bible study, and I'm not coming to your house."

Raven wasn't sure what else to say.

Kane shook his head again. "I'm out of here."

Raven grabbed his arm, but he jerked it away from her and left her office. She would have to work hard to ease back into his good graces, but right now, she couldn't worry about that. Instead, she skimmed through tonight's lesson and the list of scriptures she would be teaching from. She closed her eyes, breathed in and out, and sat there in silence. In a matter of minutes, she felt a great sense of calm. It was as though Kane hadn't burst into her office and confronted her about anything.

Raven greeted everyone and then closed her eyes. "Dear Heavenly Father, we come to You this evening just to say thank You. Thank You for watching over us, for protecting us, and for providing for us. Thank You for blessing our entire church family and for allowing us this great opportunity to study Your Word. We ask that You would open our minds and hearts in the best way possible, so that we can learn and receive the message You have for us. But most of all, Lord, we sincerely thank You for Your mercy, grace, and favor on each and every one of our lives. In Jesus's name. Amen."

"Amen," the members said.

Raven moved her typed lesson to the side, picked up her Samsung tablet, and walked down from the pulpit. She locked eyes with Porsha but only for a second. Raven looked forward to the day when she wouldn't have to see her. Not on Wednesday nights, Sunday mornings, or any other day—but those thoughts had to be saved for a different time.

For now, Raven acted as though Porsha were invisible. Then, she swiped through her Bible app until she found the line she wanted to begin with. "Tonight, I want to talk about David and Goliath, so if you would, please turn your Bibles to First Samuel, chapter seventeen, verses thirty-two through forty-nine."

Raven glanced across the sanctuary, slowly walking back and forth, waiting for everyone to either turn to the correct page of their Bibles or pull the scripture up on their electronic devices.

Finally, she began reciting the first six verses. "And it reads as follows: "'Don't worry about this Philistine," David told Saul. "I'll go fight him!" "Don't be ridiculous!" Saul replied. "There's no way you can fight this Philistine and possibly win! You're only a boy, and he's been a man of war since his youth." But David persisted. "I have been taking care of my father's sheep and goats," he said. "When a lion or a bear comes to steal a lamb from the flock, I go after it with a club and rescue the lamb from its mouth. If the animal turns on me, I catch it by the jaw and club it to death. I have done this to both lions and bears, and I'll do it to this pagan Philistine, too, for he has defied the armies of the living God! The Lord who rescued me from the claws of the lion and the bear will rescue me from this Philistine!" Saul finally consented. "All right, go ahead," he said. "And may the Lord be with you!"'

"I don't know about you, but I smile every time I read about David," Raven said. "And I think it's because even though David was only a small boy, he trusted and believed that God would see him through no matter what. Everyone, including King Saul, was afraid of Goliath, but not David. No, David had the kind of faith we all should have, the kind that never wavers."

"Amen," seemingly every member said. They loved this lesson already, and Raven was glad she'd one-upped Porsha again. Porsha had talked about faith while giving that petty message of hers on Sunday, but Raven was going to take the topic of faith to a whole other level this evening.

"And I have to tell you," Raven continued, "as a female pastor I sometimes feel like David. But then there are times when my faith really does weaken. There are times when I meet various men of God at ministry conferences or even when I visit churches right here in town, and they don't accept me. They look at me as though I don't belong, and as if I don't know my place."

Many members shook their heads with sadness, and Raven wanted to high-five herself. Last night and again this morning, she'd tried to figure out a good way to draw in more sympathy. Telling everyone about her "rape" had certainly caused thousands of people to feel sorry for her, but here, locally, she wanted to add just a little something more to sweeten the pot. She wanted her local members to support her and defend her to anyone, and she knew teaching this sort of lesson would get their attention.

Raven held her tablet against her chest and broke into

tears. "You all just don't know what these last couple of years have been like for me. These last nine years. I won't go into what I talked about during my Facebook broadcast on Monday, but for years, I have been fighting to have peace in my life. And I went from that tragedy to getting married and divorced and then to becoming a pastor—a pastor who isn't accepted by everyone," she said, sniffling, and one of the older ladies of the church got up and gave her a cotton handkerchief. Raven could tell just from wiping her cheeks that it wasn't the same quality as her own, but she acted as though she couldn't be more grateful to the woman.

"Thank you for being so kind. For being so thoughtful."

When Raven finished drying her eyes, a fortysomething woman raised her hand.

"Yes," Raven said, still sniffling.

"Thank you so much, Pastor Raven. For being such an awesome minister and for being so transparent about your life. As you mentioned, most of us watched your video, and I am so sorry about what happened to you. I replayed that part three different times, and I cried my eyes out."

"Thank you, my sister. Thank you for caring about me in such a wonderful way."

"Of course. Then, as far as tonight's lesson, my question to you is, how do you stop your faith from wavering? What happens if you're not as steadfast with your faith as David was, and how do you get back on track?"

"That's a good question," Raven said. "And my best answer is to never get off track. Wake up every single morning believing that God will do exceedingly, abundantly, above all that you could ever ask or think. Focus specifically on keeping your faith strong throughout your day and even when you pray before going to bed. The Bible says to pray without ceasing, and I believe we have to have faith without ceasing as well. Because if we become lax, we can begin to doubt God. We can start to feel as though nothing is going to work out right for us."

The woman nodded and smiled. "Thank you, Pastor Raven."

"Let's continue reading chapters thirty-eight through forty. 'Then Saul gave David his own armor—a bronze helmet and a coat of mail. David put it on, strapped the sword over it, and took a step or two to see what it was like, for he had never worn such things before.

"'"I can't go in these," he protested to Saul. "I'm not used to them." So David took them off again. He picked up five smooth stones from a stream and put them into his shepherd's bag. Then, armed only with his shepherd's staff and sling, he started across the valley to fight the Philistine.'

"So as you can see, David's faith was solid. Concrete. Unshaken. And what that also teaches us is that even if we have no one to help us through our trials and tribulations; even if our own family members and friends forsake us; even if we feel totally and completely alone in this world, we can still fight for ourselves. We can still win any battle, no matter how massive it is, but the only way we can accomplish this is through God. As long as we keep God first in our lives, obey His Commandments, and believe, believe,

believe in Him with our entire beings, we will never be defeated. In other words, if we have God, we have everything."

Raven read the next few chapters and answered questions from a young man and also from his mother. Then she ended with the last two verses. "And finally, 'As Goliath moved closer to attack, David quickly ran out to meet him. Reaching into his shepherd's bag and taking out a stone, he hurled it with his sling and hit the Philistine in the forehead. The stone sank in, and Goliath stumbled and fell face down on the ground.'

"It was as simple as that," Raven said, smiling. "David slew Goliath, the giant, the pagan Philistine who everyone in the land was afraid of. He did it by way of faith and through his belief that God was with him."

"Knocked him clean out," Brother Pascal, an eighty-something gentleman, said.

Everyone laughed out loud, and so did Raven.

"You are so right, Brother Pascal," she said. "He knocked him out big time."

When everyone settled down, Raven looked across the sanctuary, checking to see if there were more questions. But when she spied the man standing with his arms folded, her heart sank. He stood there, bold and intimidating, dressed in a black shirt and black jeans. It was D. C. Robinson, the loan shark she'd stolen money from years ago.

He never even gave her a chance to ignore him. "Good evening, Pastor Raven."

Her nerves twirled in an uproar. "Good evening."

"I know your lesson tonight is about David and Goliath,

but since I'm strugglin' with somethin' a little different, I wondered if I could ask you about it."

"Yes, go ahead."

"Well, in my line of work, I deal with a lot of people who don't keep their word. They don't do what they promise, and then I end up takin' a major loss. So I just want to know how I should handle somethin' like that. Especially someone like me who hasn't been the best Christian in the world. But I do know one scripture in Matthew that talks about a person usin' a sword, and how he will die by the sword."

Raven wondered how D.C. equated that scripture to someone owing him money and not paying it back, because she knew unpaid debts were what he was actually talking about.

"Well, I don't think that's necessarily the right scripture to meditate on. Not in this case, anyway. I would suggest that you focus more on the many scriptures that speak about forgiveness. I would also suggest that you maybe not do business with certain people anymore. That might be your best solution."

"Then I guess my real struggle is more with me wantin' to get revenge on people who have lied to me. Folks who have deceived me. I've even had some so-called *Christians* betray me, and that's when I think about this other scripture I used to hear my grandfather quote. It had something to do with wolves in sheep's clothing. So my other question is, how does revenge work for these kind of people? Do they end up reapin' what they sow just like nonbelievers?"

Raven hurried to answer him as best she could, and

thankfully, D.C. finally took his seat. Why on earth was this man attending her Bible study lesson? She knew she'd never paid him back the money she'd stolen from him, but he'd also never bothered her about it. She hadn't heard from him while she was in prison, while she was married to Dillon, or even since her divorce. So she'd just assumed that D.C. had moved on and forgotten about her—or that maybe once she'd been released from prison and had become Pastor Black's daughter-in-law, he'd decided to cancel her debt. Because in the past, D. C. Robinson had never waited as much as nine days beyond a due date, let alone nine years.

But then it dawned on her. What if Dillon or Pastor Black had sent him because of her rape accusation? Especially since Pastor Black had known D.C. for years and considered him a friend, even. But would Pastor Black and Dillon actually go this far? Using a criminal to try to scare her? Raven wasn't sure one way or the other, but what she did know was that she didn't need this kind of drama. What she wanted was for D.C. to leave and never come back there.

Yet he still sat staring at her—like he hated her. He never took his eyes off her, and she knew he wanted his money back. All thirty thousand dollars of it. This, of course, wouldn't have been so bad, except if she knew D.C. the way she thought she did, he would also want interest. But to get rid of him, it would be well worth paying him and moving on. It was best to take care of this and be done with it.

Chapter 16

R aven was still a nervous wreck. She'd just left the church, heading over to Kane's, but she couldn't stop thinking about D.C. He'd ended up staying until right after Bible study had been dismissed, and thankfully, that had been only ten minutes after she'd answered his questions. He'd sat patiently, acting as though he was daring her to even look at him the wrong way, and it was then that she'd known she would have to pay him his money as soon as possible. Either that or Raven would end up beaten to a pulp—or sent to a hospital with broken bones. She knew this because while working for D.C., she'd seen his "people" do all of the above. And D.C. didn't care if the person who owed him money was a man or a woman. He treated everyone the same, no matter what.

Raven drove her black BMW 750 through a four-way intersection, barely beating a red light, and for the first time in years, she wanted to gamble. She knew it wasn't an option for her, but she just needed something to clear her mind. Something to make her forget about this disaster of a situation she now faced.

Raven sighed with frustration but jumped when her phone rang. She glanced at the media screen on her dashboard, and although she didn't recognize the information displaying, she had a feeling D.C. was calling her. There was no reason in the world why he should have her cell number, but her gut told her it was him and that she'd better answer.

She pressed the speaker button on her upper console. "Hello?"

"Ruthless Raven."

"Hello?" she said again, mostly because she wasn't sure what else to say.

"Long time no hear from."

"What is it that you want, D.C.?"

"Trick, please. You know exactly what I want."

"After all this time? All these years?"

"Yep."

"Why now?"

"Because you owe it to me. Plain and simple."

Raven could hear the not-so-cordial tone in her voice and decided to speak a bit more gently. "Look, I'm sorry things turned out the way they did. I was wrong for taking your money, and I apologize. I had a real problem back then, but I'm not like that anymore."

"To be honest, I don't care about any of that. You can be whoever you wanna be. I just want my money."

"I'll need a couple of days, but I'll have it for you by next Monday."

"Why not tomorrow?"

"Because I'm guessing you don't want me to write you a check."

"You know how I operate."

"Well, then it's not like I can just walk into my bank and pull out thirty thousand cash. At least not without sending the wrong message."

"Wait a minute," D.C. said, laughing. "Did you say thirty thousand?"

"Yes, isn't that how much I owe you?"

"Now, boo, you and I both know how I do when it comes to late payments. *You* of all people know exactly how I roll."

Raven did know. But she couldn't help trying to get away with mentioning only the principal amount. She'd known it was a long shot, but she'd just been hoping that maybe he would have mercy on her and would let her slide without paying anything more than that.

"Then how much do I owe you?" she asked.

"Two hundred and seventy Gs."

Raven bugged her eyes and nearly lost control of her vehicle. "What?"

"You heard me."

"D.C., what are you talking about? I only took thirty thousand dollars from you."

"I know exactly how much you stole. But for every year you went without paying me, I multiplied that by the principal."

"You can't be serious. Why are you doing this?"

"I'm no great mathematician, but last I checked, nine

years times thirty thousand dollars equals two hundred and seventy Gs. But you're the smart one, so you tell me how much all that adds up to."

Raven wanted to cry. She knew D.C. was no joke, and that he rarely showed leniency to anyone who crossed him. But $270,000? He wanted her to pay him that kind of money all at once? And why was his interest rate so astronomical? Or again, why was he just now contacting her about any of this? She sat in silence, trying to steady her shaking hands on the steering wheel. But then she thought about Dillon and Pastor Black again. She'd wondered earlier if they'd had something to do with this, and now she knew that D.C.'s showing up at the church tonight, only two days after her video broadcast, was no coincidence. D.C. would never admit it, but she knew her suspicions were correct. She was also willing to bet that Dillon was the lowlife who had given D.C. her cell number.

Raven shook her head. "Where am I supposed to get that kind of money?"

"That's not my worry. All I know is that you'd better get it to me or else. You'd better pay me every single dime, or things won't end well for you."

"I don't have it. I mean, I can maybe pay you half by next week, but I'd have to take care of the rest with monthly installments."

"No, I already told you. I want *all* my money *all* at once. And I don't care what you have to do to get it. Actually, you're pretty good when it comes to stealing, anyway, so I'm sure you'll do what you need to."

Raven hated begging anyone for anything, but she didn't see where she had any other choice. "D.C., you have to help me out here. I know what I did was wrong, and you have no idea how sorry I am...how much I regret doing what I did to you. Which is why I will definitely pay you what I owe you, but I need more time."

"You should've thought about that when you stole from me. When you took me for a complete fool and thought you could get away with it. I've been waiting on this day for a very long time. Now, you either pay up or deal with the consequences."

"If you could just try to understand—" she pleaded, but all she heard was a deafening silence. D.C. had hung up on her, and she felt as though she were fighting to wake up from a nightmare.

What was she going to do? Although, what if this was in fact related to her rape accusation, and Dillon was merely trying to force her to retract it? If so, all she had to do was go on Facebook Live again and clear Pastor Black's name. When she did, D.C. would leave her alone. There was no doubt that he would still want her to pay him his money back, but it wouldn't be nearly the amount he was asking for.

Raven drove for another ten minutes, pulled into Kane's driveway, and parked only a few feet from his three-car garage. She could see a light shining through the front window of his two-story brick home, so she knew he wasn't in bed yet. Plus, it was only nine thirty, and Kane rarely went to bed before eleven.

She turned off her ignition and took multiple deep breaths. This thing with D.C. had stirred her emotions to a level she hadn't experienced in years, and the last thing she wanted was for Kane to see how upset she was. She certainly didn't want him finding out about the money she owed D.C., and that he was calling in her debt to him. Kane, like everyone else who knew her, was well aware of her former gambling problem and that she'd once worked for and stolen from a loan shark, but he didn't know D.C.'s name or that Raven had never paid him back. Now, she realized how careless she'd been to continually include this part of her criminal history in her testimony. It had been downright stupid, but she just hadn't counted on D.C. reentering her life and then demanding nine times the amount she'd taken.

Raven picked up her leather tote and got out of the car. She proceeded down the winding brick sidewalk, which was lined on one side with tracking lights that shone toward Kane's house. After walking up the three steps to his front door, she rang the doorbell.

It took nearly a minute, but he finally opened the door. When he saw her standing there, he turned and walked away.

Raven came in, shut the door, and followed him into his family room.

She sat down next to him on the dark green leather sofa. "Baby, I know you're not happy with me right now, and I don't blame you. But I really am sorry for not telling you what happened to me. I'm sorry for everything."

Kane tossed her a look of fury. "Why are you even here, Raven?"

"Because I love you, and I don't want to lose you. Not over something like this. Not because I made this one little mistake."

"Really? So you think telling people you don't even know before telling me is just a small mistake?"

"That's not what I meant. I know I should've told you, but I really didn't know how."

"Well, you sure knew how to tell the world, though, didn't you?"

"Like I said, I know I was wrong for doing that. But I also can't change it. So I'm just asking you to please forgive me."

"I'll forgive you. Eventually. But I've also been doing a lot of thinking. Not just today, either."

"About what?"

"Us. I mean, this thing you did this week really hurt me, but that was mostly just the icing on the cake."

"What are you saying?"

"That I've finally come to the realization that you don't love me, and that you never plan to marry me. To be honest, I've known that all along but was just hoping things would change."

"But I do love you. I know I haven't been up front with you about certain things, but I would never lie to you about the way I feel," she said, touching his arm. "Honey, I've never loved any man the way I love you."

"Then you certainly have a funny way of showing it. And

if you want to know the truth. I don't even think you know what real love is."

"That's not fair."

"Maybe not, but you do talk a lot about how you were never loved as a child."

"But I still know what love is."

"Maybe we should just take a break for a while," he said.

Raven rested her hand under his chin and turned it toward her. "Please tell me you don't really want that."

"No, but I think it's best. Maybe some time apart will give us both a chance to think and figure out what's what."

Raven thought about her conversation with D.C. and then about Kane wanting to break up with her. Everything in her life was falling apart all at once, and she could barely wrap her mind around it. Just three days ago, when she'd been preparing in her study for Sunday morning's service, she'd felt as though she were on top of the world. She'd thought about the future and how things were only going to get better for her. But now, Kane wanted to end things, and D.C. was making demands and threatening her with bodily harm.

Raven laid her head against the sofa and burst into tears. She sometimes faked her emotions when it was convenient, but this time they were real. She was troubled, afraid, and overwhelmed with uncertainty.

At first Kane didn't move or as much as look at her. But soon, he pulled her into his arms and she pressed her face against his chest, wailing.

"Baby, I'm sorry," Kane said. "I'm sorry that things aren't working out for us, but please don't cry."

"Please don't leave me," she said between sniffles, and then looked up at him. "All I'm asking for is another chance. Baby, please."

"I don't know. I love you, but I just don't want to keep going through this. And playing this waiting game with you."

"Can we at least try to work this out?"

"I would love nothing more than that, but this feels too one-sided. I feel like I'm all in, and you're just basically going through the motions."

"I know, but I'll do better. And I will never hide anything from you again," she said, wishing she could tell him about D.C. and the six figures she owed him.

"I know I'm going to regret this, but fine. We'll see how things go, but if they don't get better, I'm out."

Raven gazed into his eyes while still lying in his arms. "I really do love you, Kane."

"I love you, too. I always have," he said, kissing her.

Then Raven stretched all the way out on the sofa, and Kane lay on top of her, kissing her again. He did so with the kind of passion she never wanted to live without.

And she wouldn't.

Not if she could help it.

Chapter 17

"So how was Bible study?" Steve asked.

He was on his way home from the deacons' board meeting at his church but had called Porsha a few seconds ago.

"It was fine."

"I was hoping to call you before now. But since our chairman had a prior engagement, our meeting didn't start until eight. And we're just getting out."

"Oh, okay," she said.

"If it wasn't so late, I would try to come by."

"Yeah, I'm sure you would."

"I'm serious. Especially with you talking all this craziness about some singles ministry for women. What about the men?" he said, laughing.

"I'm glad you find this funny."

"If you want to know the truth, I don't think it's funny at all. I'm sort of irritated by it."

"I don't know why."

"Because you've never talked about attending a singles ministry before, let alone starting one."

"We've always had a singles ministry. For men and women. I just realized it was time our women had one just for them."

"Maybe I'm not giving it to you good enough. Not taking care of my job as well as I thought I was."

Porsha frowned. "So you think sex is all I'm interested in? That I don't need a whole lot more than that?"

"No, I'm just saying that if I was taking care of business the way I should be, we wouldn't be having this conversation."

"Well, unless you're planning to get divorced, you'll never be able to give me what I want. It's just not possible anymore."

"Now I *know* you're seeing someone else," he said. "Because nobody just up and changes like this for no reason. It was just this past Sunday when you were all over me in bed and wanting us to get married. Now, three days later, you're acting like I'm no big deal. Like you could take me or leave me."

"That's not true. I do love you, but I also don't want to keep foolishly hoping for something to happen. Wishing you would leave your wife. For a long time, I didn't think about that very much. I guess because I only cared about what *I* wanted. But now I find myself thinking more about how your wife must be feeling. And how if I was married to you, I wouldn't want you to sleep around on me."

"Look, I know you're not happy with things right now. And that's why I want us to take this trip together."

"I don't see how spending a week out of town is going to change anything. You'll be busy with the conference during the day, so where does that leave me? Waiting for you in some room?"

"It wouldn't be like that. We'll be able to go out to restaurants for dinner or do anything you want."

"Really? So you're not worried about your colleagues seeing you with another woman?"

"How would they know who you are? If anything, everyone will probably just think you're there for the conference. That you own your own health care business."

Porsha wished he'd stop pressing her about this trip that she didn't want to go on. At first, she'd sort of considered it, thinking that it might help their relationship—make Steve realize what he was missing by not marrying her. But now she didn't feel as comfortable with the idea as she had. She dreaded having to travel somewhere in secret.

"I'll let you know," she finally said.

"When?"

"Soon?"

"Well, I'm leaving in two and a half weeks, so it would be great if I could get your plane ticket booked as soon as possible."

Porsha rolled her eyes toward the sky and moved her phone to her other ear. No matter what she said, he didn't seem to want to give up. "I'll let you know tomorrow."

"Good, and I hope you don't disappoint me because I really want you to go."

"I'll call you tomorrow for sure."

"That's fine, and don't forget I'm coming by when I get off work."

Porsha was a little shocked that he was still planning to. That would make three times this week. But instead of being excited about it, she wondered what lie he would be telling his wife.

"I'll see you then," she said.

"I love you, baby."

"I love you, too."

"Rest well."

"I will."

Porsha hung up, but for some reason, Raven fell on her mind again. Toward the end of Bible study, she'd seemed beyond out of sorts. Nervous even. And her demeanor and body language had only seemed to change just after that mysterious guy had stood up and asked questions. Porsha had never seen him before, not on Sunday mornings or at Bible study, so she wondered who he was. He'd asked some very strange questions, too. But regardless, all Porsha knew was that Raven had seemed uncomfortable and almost as if she was afraid of the man. Which meant Raven must have known him personally.

Porsha removed the jeans and sleeveless white dress top she'd worn to church this evening and slipped on a knee-length black silk spaghetti-strap nightgown. She went into her bathroom and washed off her makeup and wrapped her hair with a satin scarf. It had been a long day, and for some reason, she was a little more tired than usual. So she got in bed and flipped through the onscreen guide to see which guests were going to be on the night-time talk shows.

But before she could decide which she wanted to watch, Dillon called her. This now made three consecutive days that he'd done so, and she'd be lying if she said she wasn't happy about it. Because truth was, when she'd been on her way home this evening, she'd found herself hoping he might contact her again.

"Hello?" she answered.

"Hey, you."

"Hey yourself. What's going on?"

"Not much. Just thinking about you."

"Really? And why is that?"

"Because I want to see you, and you won't let me."

"You're not going to start that up again, are you?"

"I don't see why not."

"So did you do anything special today?" she asked.

"Oh, I see. You're just going to change the subject, I guess."

Porsha laughed. "I don't know what you're talking about."

"Yeah, okay."

"But hey, can I ask you something?" she said. "And I'm being serious now."

"What is it?"

"When you and Raven were married, did she have any run-ins with people from her past?"

"Not that I know of. Why?"

"Because some guy showed up at Bible study tonight, and something wasn't right with it. He looked a little scary, and he made Raven pretty nervous."

"Who knows. That witch could've crossed anybody. You know how she is. Or at least *I* know how she is, anyway."

"I just hope he's not going to be trouble."

"Well, I'm sure I don't have to tell you this, but I really don't care one way or the other. Raven deserves whatever she gets, and all I want is for her to retract that statement she made on Facebook. We were all checking more web sites today, and we saw a lot of new comments. People wondering if maybe my dad is in fact the pastor Raven was talking about. No one is specifically saying he did it, but his name definitely keeps popping up. That's why I called her behind yesterday."

Porsha was a little stunned. "You talked to her?"

"No, she wouldn't answer. I left her a message, though."

"Interesting."

"So I guess she didn't tell you about it, huh?"

"Nope."

"I'll bet she didn't. She's the same sneaky witch she's always been, and she's not your friend, either."

"Why do you keep saying that?"

"Because it's true. But enough about Raven. I want to talk about us."

"No, I have a better idea. Let's talk about your fiancée," Porsha said.

"What about her?"

"Does she know you're calling me?"

"No, why would she?"

"You're being sarcastic, but I want an answer."

"We broke up. Our engagement is off."

Porsha laughed. "Dillon, I know we haven't seen each other in a while, but what do you take me for? Some kind of teenager?"

"No, we really broke up. We decided to go our separate ways."

"When? Today?"

"Three weeks ago."

"Why? What happened?"

"She went back to her ex-fiancé. The same man that cheated on her for a whole year before she found out about it."

"Well, I wish I could say I feel sorry for you, but I don't."

"I don't expect you to, and I've already told you how I never should've started seeing Taylor. I'm not saying I didn't love her, because I did. But we also didn't get together under the best circumstances. I should've divorced Raven before I started seeing you or Taylor. I know that now."

"Well, I guess this explains why you all of a sudden started calling me."

"I won't lie. Had Taylor and I not broken up, I wouldn't have. But I still never stopped thinking about you. Then, when Raven made that video, it gave me a reason to call you the other day."

"So what you're saying is that you lost the woman you love and then thought you could just start back seeing me? That we could simply pick up where we left off?"

"No, it's not like that. I know you don't believe me, but I don't just want to see you. I want us to have everything you wanted us to have in the first place."

"Uh-huh. And what's that, Dillon?"

"An exclusive relationship."

"Do you want to have that with me or with the money you know I have?"

"I won't lie to you about that, either. When you and I were messing around before, I did want you to keep giving money to my church. But now I just want to be with you. I want to do things the right way this time."

"That could never happen."

"Why?"

"Because I don't trust you."

"Even with me pouring my heart out and being completely honest about everything?"

"I still don't trust you."

"I'm sorry for all the pain I caused you, but my life was really messed up back then. I was selfish, and I hurt a lot of people. But I'm telling you, I'm not that person anymore."

Porsha heard him and hated that she was allowing him to get inside her head this way. Dillon had proven who he was a long time ago, but she couldn't help that she still had feelings for him. She didn't want to, but how did anyone simply stop loving someone just because they knew they shouldn't? People judged women like her all the time, trying to figure out how they could still care for a man who had betrayed them. But it was only because they'd never been in that kind of situation. They hadn't been in love with someone the way she'd fallen in love with Dillon. Then, there was Steve, who Porsha still loved, too.

But at this very moment, she knew she didn't love Steve

nearly as much as she'd once loved Dillon. Over the last couple of years, she'd forced herself to block Dillon from her mind as much as she could, but just hearing his voice for the last three days had done wonders for her. She wouldn't tell Dillon this directly, but when she spoke to him, she felt a certain sense of gladness and contentment she hadn't felt in a while. Yes, she'd started seeing him when he was married, too, and he'd betrayed her with Taylor—something she'd reminded herself of on Monday, yesterday, and again today. But she still felt a connection with him, and she wasn't sure how much longer she'd be able to pretend she didn't. Even now, she wanted to tell him to jump in his car so he could come over and make love to her.

She wasn't proud of any of what she was feeling, but this was her truth and she couldn't deny it. At the same time, though, she also couldn't deny Dillon's history. She couldn't ignore everything she knew about him—or forget that some people never changed for the better. So what was a girl to do? Take a chance on love or leave well enough alone? She just didn't know and wondered if she ever would—that is, without getting hurt again.

Chapter 18

Raven hadn't slept a wink. Maybe she had for ten minutes here and there, but that was about it. Now she was up, pacing back and forth in her bedroom, trying to figure a way out of this mess. For one, she was definitely planning to record another Facebook Live message, clearing up any questions about who might have raped her. She wouldn't take back the part about *being* raped, but she would clarify that Pastor Black wasn't the man she was talking about. She would even state that while she and his son were divorced, Pastor Black had never been anything but a gentleman to her. She would then go on to say that he'd been a joy to work for, and that she was very sorry if her words had led anyone to believe anything else.

But before doing any of that, she wanted to call D.C. again. That way she could try to reason with him one more time about installment payments. He'd already told her that he wanted the entire sum, but maybe she could convince him otherwise. That way, when she clarified the rape story and he lowered the amount she owed, she could still spread it out over several months.

Raven picked up her cell phone and dialed his number before she lost her nerve.

He answered on the first ring. "Banks open up this early now?"

Raven hated how arrogant he was. "No, I just needed to talk to you about something."

"Unless you're callin' to say you have my money, we don't have a single thing *to* talk about."

"D.C., please just listen. This won't take very long."

"What is it?"

"I know you said you want all the money, but I just don't have it."

"Then what you *do* have is a problem. A really *big* problem."

Raven had planned on offering to pay half of it now, but with the way he was sounding, she decided to up the ante a bit. "Can you at least accept a hundred and fifty thousand, and then twenty thousand over the next six months?"

"What part of 'I want all my money' don't you understand?"

"It's not that I don't understand. But I can't give you what I don't have."

"I don't believe that. I think you have two-seventy and a whole lot more. You're just tryin' to get out of payin' me."

"I would never do that."

"A trick like you who used to lie and steal like it was nothing? Of course you would."

"D.C., I don't have it. But as I said, I can pay you part of it and then give you the rest over the next six months."

"I'm gonna say this again. I want all of my money or nothin' at all. But let me warn you about somethin'. If I end up with nothin', I'm gonna handle things the way I see fit."

Raven knew he was threatening her with bodily harm again, and before she could stop herself she said, "Did Pastor Black or my ex-husband put you up to this? Is that why you waited nine years to contact me?"

D.C. laughed at her. "Why would my money have anything to do with them?"

"I don't know, but it just doesn't make sense that you would wait all this time."

"Heifer, I think you need your head examined. Because right now, you're soundin' real stupid. Paranoid even."

Raven didn't know if he was telling the truth or if he was only pretending that this wasn't revenge for Pastor Black and Dillon. She just didn't, and that worried her.

"I don't know what else to say," she finally admitted.

"So does that mean you won't even have the money by next week the way you claimed?"

"D.C., how many people do you know could go to the bank and bring you almost three hundred thousand dollars?"

"I know exactly who could do it. Big-time pastors like you. Those with large congregations and huge online followings. Plus, from what I saw, you're easily livin' in a four- or five-bedroom home. A big, beautiful one at that."

Raven's heart skipped several beats. "Excuse me?"

"What? Are you shocked that I know where you live? With all my many contacts and as small as Mitchell is? Sweetheart, not only do I know where you live, I know what kind of car you drive, where you work, and as you know, I have your phone number. So if you're thinkin' about trying to dodge me, you can forget it."

"D.C., I'm asking you again. I'm begging you. Please let me pay you what I can. Let me get you the hundred and fifty now and the rest later. Please."

"No, you're now makin' way more money than some people make in a lifetime, and that's why I want my two seventy. You're out here using God's Word to fool people out of their money—innocent people, at that—so it's like I told you last night, pay me or deal with the consequences."

Raven tried to figure out what else she could say, but before she could, D.C. said, "The clock starts tickin' now. You hear me, heifer? Tick-tock, tick-tock, tick-tock. You had better get me my money."

When D.C. hung up, Raven dropped down on the chair in the corner of her bedroom. What if he was telling the truth? What if his wanting all this money from her had nothing to do with Pastor Black or Dillon? What if she was dealing with two different scenarios, and all three men were out to get her?

But something told her that her instincts were right, and that this had everything to do with that video she'd broadcast. It was true that Raven despised Dillon and Pastor Black, but now she sort of regretted the way she'd led people to believe that Pastor Black might've raped her. Until this morning, she hadn't noticed just how many comments had been left about her ex-father-in-law, those from folks speculating about whether he was her predator. She had certainly hoped that at least a few people would think it was him, because it was getting her a lot of new attention, but now the rumor mill was turning a lot quicker than she'd planned for.

Which meant she had to figure out both a way to change her statement and a way to get every dime of the money D.C. was asking for. He was adamant about receiving it all at once, and now she knew there was no changing his mind about it. She wasn't sure how she would find so much money so quickly, but she knew she had to. Because when it came to D.C. and his vicious rules, her life depended on it.

Chapter 19

Raven had just finished recording her internal video announcement with Melvin for Sunday, and now she was heading back to her office. She'd considered letting her members know that her ex-father-in-law was not the man who'd raped her, but she'd decided to wait. She also had planned on updating her online following with the same information, but she was putting that on hold as well. The reason: She needed proof that D.C.'s financial demands were in fact connected to Dillon and his father. D.C. had claimed that they weren't, but Raven just couldn't be sure. She'd even decided this morning that D.C. was definitely in cahoots with them. But again, what if he wasn't and she went ahead and exonerated Pastor Black, anyway? D.C. would still end up wanting $270,000 from her, and she would lose all leverage with Pastor Black for no reason. In the beginning, she'd only wanted people to think he'd done something to her for publicity purposes, but she'd also known that her accusation might create a chance for her to blackmail him in some way.

Raven continued down the carpeted hallway, smiled at a couple of her staff members, and walked inside her office. She closed her door, sat behind her desk, and opened her laptop. Then she leaned back in her chair, weighing her options again. Maybe she should call Dillon to see if she could feel him out. Maybe he would slip up and say something he shouldn't. Although, with Dillon that was highly unlikely. He was too clever for that kind of thing, and whether he was the mastermind behind this D. C. Robinson drama or not, he would never let on. He would much rather see Raven squirm and suffer with curiosity. He was dirty that way, and he had no mercy on anyone he couldn't stand. And with her it was worse, because he outright hated her.

But maybe it wasn't Dillon who she should be calling, anyway. Maybe Pastor Black was the person she needed to talk to. Especially since he was the person all the rumors were circulating about.

Raven debated what she should do and then picked up her smartphone. She Googled the phone number for Deliverance Outreach and dialed it.

"Pastor Curtis Black's office. This is Lana speaking."

"Uh, hi. Is Pastor Black available?"

"May I tell him who's calling?"

"Raven."

"Is there a last name?"

"It's me, Miss Lana. Pastor Black's ex-daughter-in-law."

"Oh, how are you, Raven?"

"I'm doing well, and you?"

"I'm good. Please hold for a moment."

"Thank you," Raven said.

Miss Lana had been cordial enough. And although Raven hadn't spoken to her since she'd embezzled the money from the church, she knew she probably wasn't one of Miss Lana's favorite people. Not when Miss Lana saw Pastor Black as her surrogate son and was very protective of him and his family. It also didn't help that because Dillon had been estranged from his dad the whole time he and Raven had been married, Raven hadn't seen Miss Lana in nine years. She'd never even had a chance to apologize to her, but it wasn't as if Raven felt she needed to, either.

Lana came back on the line. "I'll transfer you now. And you have a good day."

"Thank you."

Raven waited a few seconds for her ex-father-in-law to answer.

"Pastor Black speaking."

"Hi, Pastor."

"Raven," he said with no feeling in his voice.

"I'm sure you're wondering why I'm calling you, but if you have time I'd like to speak to you about something."

"Go ahead."

"I'm not sure how this happened," she began lying, "but for some reason when I shared online that I'd been raped by a pastor, some people took it the wrong way. They assumed I was talking about you."

"Uh-huh, and why do you think that is?"

She could already tell he wasn't happy. "I don't know. Maybe because I worked for you."

"Well, for one thing, you and I both know that I never touched you in any way, let alone raped you. I also understand that my son already contacted you about this."

"He did, but I just wanted to call to say how sorry I am. Because not once when I bared my soul to the public did I think they would start mentioning your name."

"Well, they did, and it's already causing people to think the worst of me. It's damaging my reputation."

"I never meant for that to happen, so I hope you can forgive me."

"Have you corrected your statement? Made it clear to everyone that you specifically weren't referring to me?"

"No, but I'm going to...but I did want to ask you about something else, too."

"Which is?"

"D.C."

"Robinson?"

"Yes."

"What about him?"

"Did you ask him to contact me?"

"No, why would I?"

Raven closed her eyes with disappointment. "I don't know. I just wondered if maybe you'd done it to get back at me about the video."

"Look," Pastor Black said. "First of all, I know I'm not guilty of raping anyone, and second, Dillon already told you what you needed to do. Retract your statement...correct it or do whatever you need to do to clear my name. That's all I want. Nothing else."

"Well, it just seemed strange that I broadcasted live on Monday, and two days later D.C. showed up at my church. He literally came to Bible study last night."

"Why?"

"To scare me, I guess. But that's not the worst part. He wants his thirty thousand dollars back."

"Well, Raven, it's not like you don't owe the man. So I suggest you pay him."

"Well, I would, except he wants one hundred percent for every year I was late. So instead of the original thirty thousand, he wants two hundred and seventy."

"I guess I don't know what to tell you, because I don't get involved in D.C.'s business."

"But you did before I went to prison."

"Did he tell you that?"

"No, but I just had a feeling that you did, because D.C. doesn't let anyone get away with not paying him. Even after I was arrested and was going back and forth to court, he never bothered me. For years, I never heard from him."

"I'm sorry about your situation with D.C., but you'll have to work that out with him."

"I already tried, but he wants his money. And I don't have it."

"Well, it's like I just told you, Raven, I don't get involved in D.C.'s business."

Raven wanted to plead with him to help her, just like she'd pleaded with D.C. earlier, but she didn't.

"I need to get going," Pastor Black said, "but I trust you'll be clearing my name as soon as possible."

"I will," she said.

"I appreciate it. You take care."

Raven ended the call and set her phone on her desk. She wasn't sure what to think or what the truth was. Would Pastor Black lie about hiring D.C. to do his dirty work? He didn't sound as though he was, but what if he were? What if he'd only told her what she'd wanted to hear, and once she cleared his reputation, D.C. would still be waiting to collect six figures from her? Because it wasn't like she could ignore her gut feeling about this. Or what if Dillon had hooked up with D.C. on his own as a way to finally get back at her? He'd lost his church, his power as a pastor in the community, and his popularity with women, and he blamed her for all of it. Not to mention, she'd divorced him, and she also had that sex tape of him and Porsha.

This last thought sort of lifted Raven's spirits a little. She'd always told herself that there might come a time when that lurid sex video might become her saving grace. She hadn't known how or when, but she'd always thought that she would use it if she had to. So maybe it was time she stopped being a scared little wimp—maybe it was time she stood up for herself. At least when it came to Dillon. She still had to figure out how to handle this D.C. state of affairs, but if Dillon contacted her again, she would remind him about his and Porsha's sex tape. If he threatened her, she would threaten him right back with no fear in her heart.

This was also the reason she wasn't retracting anything about her rape story. She was leaving everything as is, and if Dillon or his dad wanted her to fix her statement, they would have to pay. They would need to compensate her dearly—by way of $270,000.

Chapter 20

Four days in a row. That's how often Dillon had called Porsha, and once again, she was happy to hear from him.

"So you do realize we just talked last night, don't you?" she asked, leaning back in her office chair at the church.

"Yeah, but what does that have to do with me calling you today?"

"I guess I don't understand *why* you're calling. Not after all the drama we've been through."

"That's all in the past."

"Maybe, but I still remember every single thing that happened."

"I'm sure you do, but I'm not giving up on us. I'm going to keep calling until you agree to see me."

"I don't think that's a good idea."

"Why?"

"I just don't."

"Okay, wait a minute," he said, as though he'd had some

huge lightbulb moment. "Are you seeing someone? Is that why you keep turning me down?"

Porsha scooted slightly away from her desk and crossed her legs. "As a matter of fact, I am."

"Is it serious?"

"Why do you want to know?"

"Because if it is—or even if it's not—I want you to end it."

Porsha chuckled. "Wow, you have some real issues."

"No, I just know what I want, and I'm not afraid to go after it."

Porsha didn't comment.

"Are you there?" he asked. "Because I don't hear anything."

"What do you want me to say?"

"That you're willing to give me another chance. That you never stopped loving me. Because I certainly still love you."

Porsha closed her eyes, trying not to let his words affect her. But they did. She didn't need this kind of thing happening in her life right now. Not when she was already struggling with her conscience and the fact that she knew she wasn't honoring God the way she should. What she wanted was to focus on her singles ministry for women, figure out a way to end things with Steve, and also tell Dillon that they could never be a couple again. That a relationship between them would never work. But she couldn't bring herself to do it. She couldn't convey any of what she was thinking, because in all honesty, she *did* want to see him. More than ever.

"You only *think* you still love me," she finally said. "Or

who knows? Maybe you never loved me at all. Maybe what we had was only about sex."

"The sex was out of this world. You and I both know that. But I also cared about you and loved you."

"Right. You loved me so much that you started seeing that woman, Taylor, and then you asked her to marry you."

"I know, and I realize now how much I hurt you. I mean, I always knew that I had, but talking to you this week has let me know how much it really affected you. And I'm sorry."

"Sorry won't change what happened. It also won't guarantee that you won't hurt me again."

"No, but if you love me you have to at least try to trust me again. I know I don't deserve anything from you, but it's like I just told you. I'm not giving up."

Porsha wanted to tell him how much she did want to give him a chance but also that she was terrified of what the outcome would be. Especially since she had so many scenarios playing out in her head. What if Dillon was only using her to eventually find out all he could about Raven? That way, he'd be able to possibly get back at her. Or what if he simply just wanted to start sleeping with her again? What if he was merely looking for yet another woman to mess around with? For all Porsha knew, Taylor could've ended things with him because he hadn't been faithful to her. It was certainly possible.

"So can I come over?" Dillon asked.

"We've already discussed that."

"Well, like I said, I'm not giving up. So if it means calling you every day until you say yes, then that's exactly what I'll be doing. It's up to you."

"I really wish you wouldn't do that."

"Why, because you don't want me to or because you know you want the same thing I do?"

"I have to go," she said.

"I'll bet you do, because you know I'm telling the truth."

"Good-bye, Dillon."

"Talk to you tomorrow."

Porsha could barely contain herself, and she didn't like how she was feeling. She wasn't happy about the way she was steadily allowing Dillon to wear her down. At first it had been easy to tell him no, but now she struggled with it.

Porsha took a deep breath and pulled her laptop closer. Before Dillon had called, she'd been writing her inspirational message for Sunday morning's service, and she wanted to get it finished. This would only be her second time delivering one, but the entire process already felt natural to her. It was as if she didn't have to think hard about what to write or say, and the idea of hopefully helping one or more of their parishioners on a weekly basis made her feel even better about it. Then, what excited her more was her singles ministry, which she was planning to spend all of this afternoon working on.

She spent the next hour finalizing her message, but then her cell phone rang. She looked at the display and hesitated. It was Steve, and although she was tempted to let his call go to voice mail, she didn't.

"Hey," she said.

"Hey, baby, how are you?"

"Good. You?"

"I'm great. So have you made a decision about our trip?"

"I have, and I can't go."

"You can't or you just don't want to?"

"Steve, please try to understand my position. I love you, but what we're doing isn't right."

"Porsha, where in the world is all of this coming from?" he yelled. "I mean, why don't you tell me what this is really about."

He rarely called her by her first name, so she knew he was livid. "Steve, all I can say is that I'm sorry. I know this isn't what you were expecting to hear, but I don't feel good about our relationship any longer."

"Just like that? In a matter of days, you somehow fell completely out of love with me?"

"No, that's not what I'm saying. I do love you. That part hasn't changed, but there's something inside of me that's different. Something I've never felt before."

"Yeah, and what is that exactly?"

"I don't want to keep sleeping with another woman's husband."

"And you just woke up one day this week and decided that?"

"I know it sounds strange, but yes. I mean, I've always known that what we were doing was wrong, but now I feel really bad about it. Much worse than I used to."

"So I guess you don't want me to come over tonight, either."

Porsha didn't respond because a part of her did want to

see him, but a part of her didn't. Her whole way of thinking was so wishy-washy now. So baffling and worrisome.

"I don't think it's a good idea," she said.

"Baby, please don't do this."

"I'm sorry. I really am."

"And that's supposed to make me feel better? Because right now, the word 'sorry' isn't doing very much for me. It means nothing."

Porsha wasn't sure why, but tears filled her eyes. She was so torn over this.

"Baby, I know you're going through something," he said. "That part I believe. But please don't end things between us. Let me come see you. We don't even have to make love. Just let me come hold you and spend time with you."

Maybe it was best to see Steve at least one last time. Because it wasn't as though they'd just met a couple of weeks ago. They'd been seeing each other regularly for months.

"Okay, fine."

"I'll see you tonight then. And baby, please don't give up on me. Please give me a chance to make things right."

Porsha didn't respond, but she couldn't help thinking about the conversation she'd just had with Dillon. He'd spoken similar words, except he'd professed how he was the one who wasn't planning to give up on trying to be with her.

"I'll see you later," she said.

"I love you, baby," he told her.

Porsha saw the call ending and set the phone down. She'd agreed to let Steve come over, but she still knew it was wrong. It had always been wrong, and if she could do things over she would never have begun sleeping with him in the first place. She never would've begun sleeping with Dillon when he was married, either. But this was all wishful thinking, and it wasn't possible to change what had already been done. That was the unfortunate truth when it came to making terrible choices, committing awful sins, and hurting innocent people. A person couldn't erase any of it. But what she did know was that *different* choices could be made, and that even though everyone fell short sometimes—just as the Bible confirmed—there were still certain sins that could be eliminated for good. Because again, it had to do with choices.

She still didn't know why her conscience had chosen this particular week to overwhelm her, but then she remembered something her father used to say. "When God decides that it's time for you to make a change, a change you will surely make. He will get what He wants, and you won't be able to stop Him."

Porsha missed her father so much, and now tears streamed down both sides of her face. There was no doubt that she was going to have to make lots of changes, and she just hoped she was strong enough to do the right things. She wanted to become a better person, and she knew there was one thing in particular that she had to stop doing: pretending that God had called her to preach. She wasn't sure how or when she was going to make this known to everyone, but she knew it was inevitable. It was time she stopped playing with God before something bad happened.

Chapter 21

It was Friday morning, and while it had only been two days since that thug D.C. had shown up at Bible study, Raven felt like she'd been dealing with this nightmare for weeks. It was weighing on her mind in more ways than she could count, and she'd gone another night without sleeping. So much so that when she'd finally gotten up this morning, she'd noticed small bags under her eyes. She'd looked tired and not at all the way she normally did when she took a shower, applied her makeup, and got dressed. Even now, she didn't look awful, but she certainly didn't look her best, and something had to change. Something had to give, and she knew she had to fix this money ordeal sooner rather than later.

Raven scrolled through the church's financial documents on her computer, trying to figure out how she might be able to take a larger cut of income for the next few months, but her cell phone rang before she could. When she saw it was Dillon, she shook her head.

Then she lifted her phone from her desk. "Why do you keep calling me?"

"You know why."

"Well, I wish you would stop."

"Not until you do what I told you."

"So, you're my boss now?"

"No, but I know you got my message."

"You don't know anything."

"According to my dad, you admitted that you did."

"Look, I'm really busy."

"Do I sound like I care about that? I don't care what you're doing. I just want to know when you're going to clear my dad's name."

"And if I don't?"

"You heard my message the other day, right? When I said I wasn't playing with you, I meant it."

"Is that why you sent D.C. over here to threaten me?"

"Excuse me?"

"Excuse me, nothing, Dillon. I know you sent him, and I also know that this is all part of your little scheme to make me do what you want."

"I don't know what you're talking about."

"I think you do."

"Think what you want. That's on you, but if you don't record a new video, I'll be taking matters into my own hands."

"I'm not afraid of you, Dillon."

"You should be."

"Well, I'm not. I never was."

"You're really starting to piss me off."

"Too bad."

"You'd better clear my dad's name, or—"

"Or what, Dillon?" she yelled, cutting him off. "What exactly are you planning to do? What *can* you do?"

"Keep stalling with that retraction, and you'll find out the hard way. I told you, I'm not playing with you."

"Good-bye, Dillon."

"Bye, trick."

Raven set the phone down and felt her heart racing. Ever since the day Porsha had brought Raven that sex tape of her and Dillon, Raven had hated him. And those feelings hadn't changed. What bothered her, though, was that even after talking to Dillon, she still couldn't tell whether he was behind the D.C. crisis. He hadn't overtly denied it, but he also hadn't admitted that he had any connection to D.C.'s calling in his loan.

But either way, she'd already made up her mind first thing this morning that she would pay D.C. She was, of course, still hoping that she wouldn't have to give him the full amount he was demanding, but even if he reduced it, she knew that the one hundred eighty thousand she'd saved wouldn't cover it.

Raven wondered again why this was happening to her now. Why were things leaning toward ruin when her ministry was doing so well? The local congregation was steadily growing, her online ministry was through the roof, and if she could get rid of Porsha she would become even more successful. Although, maybe getting rid of Porsha was the last thing she should be considering. Maybe

Raven was going about this all wrong, because with the millions Porsha had, maybe she was the one who could help her. The two of them weren't as close as they'd once been — or at least as close as they'd tried to be — but maybe it was time Raven changed the way she dealt with Porsha. If she did, she could tell her about the problem she was having with D.C., and maybe Porsha would loan her the money.

But then, if Raven told her the truth and Porsha helped her, there was a chance Porsha might use it against her in the future. Plus, the more Raven thought about it, the more she truly did want Porsha gone. It would be a while before Raven could buy her completely out of the ministry, but physically she wanted Porsha to leave the building. She wanted her to pack her things and set up shop somewhere else. Take her mediocre preaching skills to a different church or even a different city. Raven didn't care what Porsha did, as long as she didn't show her face again at New Vision.

So, no, borrowing the money from Porsha wouldn't work. But plan B would.

It had been just three days ago when Raven had been sitting in their staff meeting, thinking how there might come a time when she would need John, her chief financial officer. Originally she'd thought she might need his assistance with ousting Porsha, but now she needed him because of D.C. It would certainly take some time to reel John in all the way and lock him under her spell, but she knew it could be done. It *had* to be done, because it was her only feasible option. D.C. had stated more than once that he wouldn't take payments, but he would still have to give her at least until the end of the month. By then, she'd be able to convince John to do anything she wanted. She could make him secretly pull the money she needed from various church accounts and deposit it into one of hers. To be safe, she was going to ask for two hundred thousand dollars, because then she'd only have to use seventy thousand of her own money. This, of course, was only if D.C. still refused to back down from the full amount.

Raven picked up her desk phone and called her CFO.

"This is John speaking."

"Hi, John. Did I catch you at a bad time?"

"No, not at all."

"Good. Could you come talk to me for a few minutes?"

"Sure, I'll be right there."

By the time Raven stood up and walked around her desk, John was knocking on her door.

"Come in."

He strolled in, dressed in his usual nerdy attire, and Raven pointed toward her plush sofa.

"Please have a seat."

"Thank you," he said.

Raven sat next to him and wasted no time disclosing her intentions. "I could easily strike up some petty conversation and pretend I called you in here for something church-related. But as you know, I don't really believe in sugarcoating the truth."

John looked at her and then quickly turned his head away. "Okay."

"I've tried to keep things very professional with you. But I can't do that anymore."

John gently pushed his glasses farther up on his nose. "I'm not sure I know what you mean."

"Then I'll tell you. Since the very first day you started working here, I've been extremely attracted to you. So those two times we were together weren't just about sex."

John didn't respond, but he also seemed embarrassed by what she was saying.

Raven moved closer so that their hips were touching. "It's true."

"How long have you felt this way?" he said, still barely looking at her.

Raven crossed her legs so that her calf rested against his knee. "I just told you. Since the very beginning. And I think you've always been attracted to me, too. Am I right?"

John swallowed and seemed stunned by what she was telling him.

"I know this is probably catching you by surprise, but I couldn't keep pretending," she said.

"Well, if you want to know the truth, I've wanted to tell you how I feel for a very long time. But I also knew you were in a relationship with Kane, and it seemed serious."

For a second, Raven thought about Kane, too, and a bit of guilt eased up her spine. But as much as she loved Kane, he wasn't more important than her ministry.

"I am," she said, "but I've always wanted to be with you."

"Well, I also didn't want to damage our working relationship," John admitted. "And you're also a pastor."

Raven removed his glasses. Then she held either side of his face and kissed him with total zeal. She moved quickly before he had time to think about it.

Still, John pulled away, and Raven smiled at him.

His chest heaved up and down, and she saw other physical signs confirming that he wanted her, too. So she got up and went over to her desk to call her assistant.

"Michelle, can you please hold all my calls? Actually, I don't want to be disturbed for any reason, because John and I are discussing some very important financial matters."

"Not a problem."

"Thank you."

Raven hung up the phone, went over to lock her door, and came back to the sofa. But she didn't sit down right away. Instead, she kicked off her pumps and then sat back down next to John.

Then she reached for his belt buckle.

Until he stopped her. "Pastor Raven, please don't. This isn't right."

"I'm just trying to please you. Prove to you how much I've been wanting to be with you."

Raven reached toward him again.

But he stopped her *again*.

"Why are you fighting me like this?" she asked.

"Because it's not right. You're with Kane, and you're a pastor."

"I also have feelings and needs, and I'm not perfect. And I really want you."

Now, John just looked at her...and then he relaxed his body against the sofa.

Raven reached toward his belt buckle again, and this time all he did was watch her.

This time, he let her do whatever she wanted.

Chapter 22

Porsha lay quietly, staring up at the ceiling, wondering how she'd allowed any of this to happen. Why hadn't she fought harder to say no to Dillon the way she'd been planning? Because if she had, she wouldn't be lying next to him in his bed. She also wouldn't have felt the need to lie to Steve last night, claiming that she had church business and couldn't see him. Steve had called her around six o'clock after he'd left work and had been on his way, so needless to say, he hadn't been happy. But she'd promised him that he could come by on Sunday the way he always did, and that had seemed to calm him down a bit.

But what Steve didn't know was that Dillon had called her a half hour before that, saying all the right words in all the right ways, and she hadn't been able to resist him any longer. He'd come on to her so strong that before she'd even been consciously aware of it, she'd invited him over. Then she'd slept with him only minutes after he'd arrived—and tonight she'd slept with him again at his place, and she was ashamed of herself. But, God forgive her, she also had enjoyed being with Dillon, and she couldn't help it.

Dillon turned toward her on his side, propping himself up on his elbow and caressing her face. He still looked as handsome as always.

"I have really, really missed you," he said. "You know that?"

"You missed *me* or what we just did?"

"Both. Being with you feels like old times. You and I were always so good together, but we couldn't share our love publicly. Now, though, we can be together anytime we want."

Porsha thought about Steve and the affair she was having with him behind his wife's back. Without question, that was a sin she no longer wanted to commit, but even though Dillon wasn't married, she was still sinning with him, too. She was fornicating, and no matter how "good together" they were, it was wrong. It had always been wrong, but for years, the idea of sleeping with a married man or even sleeping with a single man out of wedlock hadn't bothered her. She wished she could say she'd felt bad about it, except mostly she hadn't. But now she did, and at this very moment, she knew God was speaking to her heart about it whether she wanted Him to or not.

This was also the reason she was having a hard time reconciling the many thoughts that were spinning through her mind. She was struggling with the idea of wanting to do the right thing but still doing wrong.

"Can I ask you something?" Dillon said.

"What is it?"

"How long are you planning to keep dealing with Raven?"

Porsha knew that it was only a matter of time before she left New Vision, but she still didn't trust Dillon enough to confide that kind of information. So she said, "Is that what you came over here for? To talk about your ex-wife?"

"No, I just can't understand why you got mixed up with her. And did you know she called my dad yesterday, apologizing and saying she would change her statement? But then never did it?"

"Really?" Porsha said, realizing now that Raven was no longer sharing *any* news with her. Not about her personal life or church business. She'd been blowing off their friendship for a while, which was fine with Porsha, but now it was a lot more noticeable.

"Yep, and I'm not about to let her get away with what she's doing," he declared.

Porsha didn't comment.

"Not when my life is finally in a place that it's never been in before. This is the first time I've felt extremely close to my dad and the rest of our family, and my dad's ministry is doing better than ever. So we don't need to be involved in some new scandal."

Now Porsha rolled on her side, facing him. "I'm really sorry that this is happening."

"Actually, none of us should be surprised about anything Raven does, but all I know is that I won't let her ruin us or our church. I'll protect it any way I have to."

Porsha wondered what he meant by that, but once again,

she didn't say anything. She sort of wished she had, though. Because maybe if she'd kept talking, they wouldn't have heard her phone vibrating in her purse. Of course, Dillon couldn't wait to question her about it.

"Aren't you going to answer that?"

"No."

"Why? Is it your man calling?"

"No."

"Maybe I should answer it for you," he joked while raising his body up.

Porsha hurried to pull him back down. "No, don't."

Dillon laughed. "Now I *know* it's your man calling."

"It's not."

"How can you be so sure? Did you tell him you were coming to see your other man tonight?"

Porsha refused to acknowledge his accusations. "So, how is your sister? And her husband?"

"Yeah, change the subject, why don't you. But they're fine and couldn't be happier. They were made for each other. Just like you and me."

Porsha shook her head. "Whatever you say, Dillon."

"You think I'm joking?"

"How's everyone else doing?" Porsha asked, still refusing to acknowledge his questions.

"Everyone is good, and my baby sister, Curtina, and I are as thick as thieves."

"Really? How sweet is that, and how old is she now?"

"Eleven. I don't know if I ever told you this, but when she and I first met we didn't care much for each other.

Actually, none of my siblings cared for me, but then of course, Alicia and I eventually became as close as any brother and sister could be."

"I'm so happy for you, Dillon, because I know that's what you always wanted."

"I did, and although my stepmother and I mostly just tolerate each other, we get along."

"That's great, too."

"So all is good."

"That's really a blessing. But there's still something I don't understand."

"What?"

"Why you no longer want to be a pastor."

"I just don't."

"Do you still consider yourself a minister?"

"Nope."

"So just like that, you decided not to be one?"

"I was never a *called* minister in the first place."

Porsha couldn't believe what she was hearing, because the Dillon she had known would never have admitted something like this. But at the same time, she lay there thinking about her own choice to become a minister and how she hadn't been called by God, either. She seemed to think about this truth all the time now, and it wouldn't go away.

"Why are you so quiet?" he asked.

"No reason."

"I know you probably don't understand my decision, but I just didn't want to do that anymore."

"What, be a pastor?"

"No, keep pretending. I didn't want to end up like my dad, caught up in one scandal after another. I mean, even though my dad was really called by God to preach, he abused his calling. He talks about that all the time, and although it took him years to get things right, he finally did. I've watched him closely, and I've even tested him with a couple of situations, and he works hard not to do things that will go against God's Word."

Porsha got quiet again, but while Dillon had been speaking she'd been coming to her own decision. She would continue building her singles ministry for women, but she wouldn't accept any more invitations to preach at other churches. She was also going to cancel any that were confirmed on her calendar for the rest of the year. Even if Raven was planning to be out of town on any upcoming Sundays, Porsha would tell her to bring in a guest minister from somewhere else to fill in for her. Then, once Porsha got her singles ministry up and running, she would publicly announce that she was leaving pulpit ministry. She would make it known that her assigned ministry from God was something totally different, and that her purpose was to help women.

"Plus," Dillon said, "to me, our broadcasting division is a ministry in itself. So it's not like a person has to preach from a pulpit or be a senior pastor to have one. Ministry can be so many other things."

It was almost as if Dillon had read Porsha's mind. "I know, but you just seemed so determined to be a prominent pastor."

"Yeah, but only because I was angry at my dad and wanted to prove to him that I could be more successful than he was. That I could even take his members from him. But needless to say, I don't have to feel like that anymore, and I don't."

"It sounds like you've really made a lot of changes."

"I have," he said, moving closer to her and kissing her. "And the more we spend time together, you'll see just how much."

"I still don't trust you."

"Maybe not today. Maybe not even next week. But you will."

Porsha lay in his arms, wanting to believe him. She knew she shouldn't, but she couldn't help the way she felt. It was just the way things were, and all she could do now was hope for the best.

Chapter 23

Raven snuggled closer to Kane on her sofa, and he hugged her and kissed her forehead. It was shortly after ten a.m., and though Kane had dropped by last night around seven, he hadn't left. He'd come straight through the door like a wild man, and although Raven had never seen him this way, she'd loved every minute of it. He'd taken total control, and he'd acted as though they hadn't made love in years. He'd seemingly not been able to get enough of her, but she knew his actions were a response to the problems they'd been having. Raven had hurt him, and he'd wanted them to make love like never before. He'd wanted them to make up the way most couples do after a major argument, something she'd assumed they'd already done on Wednesday after Bible study. But now she knew that Kane hadn't officially made things right with her the way he'd wanted to until last night. Plus, as the saying went, there truly was a very thin line between love and hate, and Kane's emotional pain had heightened his ability to make deep, passionate love to her.

There was one thing Raven wasn't proud of, though: having sex with two men on the same day, only hours apart. She hadn't planned for things to happen this way, but she'd also had to do what she'd had to do. Still, Kane would kill her if he ever found out about John, so she had to be careful. There was at least one important difference, though. She'd only had sex with John, but she'd made love with Kane. Actually, she hadn't even meant to go all the way with John, at least not yesterday, but then she'd decided it was best to give him what he wanted. That way, he would soon become mesmerized and so obsessed with her that he could barely see straight. She'd wanted him to leave her office both lovesick and yearning for more, and he had. As a matter of fact, he'd already texted her this morning, asking if they could meet up today. She'd purposely not responded, however, because she'd known that ignoring him would make him that much more desperate. But she wouldn't force him to wait too long. She would keep him satisfied so he could get her that two hundred thousand dollars she needed. Thus far, she hadn't mentioned anything about money to John, but in due time, she would. Soon she would have him positioned just where she wanted him, and he would do exactly what he was told. He wouldn't ask questions or want lengthy explanations. He would merely do what was required to make her happy, or she'd never sleep with him again. And sadly, she'd also have to fire him.

"So did you enjoy yourself last night?" Kane asked.

"You know I did. You were like an animal."

Kane laughed. "Well, if I was, it's all your fault."

"Oh really? And why is that?"

"You do things that make me crazy, and then I have all this pent-up frustration I need to get out."

"Then maybe I need to make you crazy a lot more often."

"No, I don't think so."

"I'm just kidding, anyway. And, baby, I really am sorry about keeping secrets from you. I'm sorry for upsetting you the way I did."

"That's in the past, but I will say one thing. I'm now wondering what a lot of other people are wondering."

"What's that?"

"If Pastor Black is the person who did this to you."

Raven didn't want Kane thinking that, but she also didn't want him trying to pressure her into saying who had actually raped her. So she chose her words wisely. "It wasn't him, and all I want is to move on with my life."

"Well, you need to make that statement publicly. Have you seen all the rumors online? And yesterday, I overheard two of our employees talking about it. One woman said she's a member of his church, and that he would never do anything like that, and the other said she wouldn't put anything past any man."

"People are going to talk no matter what."

"But you know you worked for the man before you went to prison, and you were married to his son. So quite naturally, a lot of folks can't help but question who did this."

"That's not my fault."

"Look, baby, I know you don't have a great relationship with your ex-husband or his family, but a rumor like this is serious. Nobody deserves to be accused of something they didn't do."

"It's all in the past."

"I don't get that."

"Why does it bother you so much?" she asked him.

"Because it's not right. I mean, would you want people thinking I was a rapist?"

"No, but I never said that Pastor Black did anything. Not once did I mention his name."

"But you know the rumors are out there. You know people are talking, and you could end that."

"Yeah, and then everyone will start wanting to know who *did* rape me. Or they'll find other pastors here in town to start speculating about."

Kane raised his arm from around her shoulder. "You know what? You do whatever you think is best."

"So I guess you're mad at me again?"

He picked up the TV remote but never looked at her.

"I don't believe you," she said, sitting up straight and staring at him.

Kane flipped through a number of channels until he found a baseball game.

"So now you're just going to ignore me? All because I won't do what you want?"

Kane gazed straight at the television screen. "I don't want to talk to you right now."

Raven sighed and then got up. "Fine."

Kane drew his legs up onto the sofa and made himself more comfortable.

Raven went upstairs to her bedroom. It was amazing how a blissful Saturday morning could turn so disastrous. But she knew Kane had strong convictions about a number of different issues, and he didn't like what was happening to Pastor Black; not when he felt as though she could fix things anytime she wanted. What he didn't know, however, was that eventually she would clear Pastor Black's name. But not until John had embezzled the money she needed. Because if for some reason John couldn't get the full amount or something else went wrong, she would have to get it from Pastor Black. She would have to blackmail him, mainly because she wouldn't have any other choice. Not when she needed to pay D.C. his money.

Before he hurt her...or killed her, even.

Chapter 24

*P*orsha's thoughts were all over the place. One minute her mind was focused completely on the short message she would be delivering to the congregation this morning, and the next, it was fixated on Dillon. She'd tried to tell herself that it was best to take things slow with him, but not only had she seen him on Thursday and Friday, she'd also spent most of yesterday at his home. He did seem as though he'd changed for the better, but she also couldn't ignore her common sense. She couldn't pretend that he hadn't slept around on his wife, with both her and a second woman, not to mention, he'd done so while he'd been a pastor.

But then, who was she to judge anyone when it came to being a minister when she was knowingly deceiving innocent people? After leaving Dillon's home last night, she'd even considered confessing the truth today. Because in all honesty, she needed to clear her conscience. She knew this would prove to be her most humiliating moment, but she also knew she would be free. She wouldn't have to lie anymore about being called by God for pulpit ministry or walk around consumed with guilt. Her only worry, though, was the potential aftershock. Because what if publicly coming clean caused every person she knew to turn their backs on her? What if people questioned what else she'd lied about and then ended their relationships with her? As it was, she didn't have any immediate family members, but what if the few women at NVCC who she did see as friends distanced themselves from her?

Porsha clasped her hands together just under her chin, closed her eyes, and prayed for direction. "Lord, I come before You asking for full discernment and complete clarity. I know beyond a shadow of a doubt that I won't find peace until I boldly confess and repent of my sins. But even when I've done that, I'm asking that You would please give me the strength I need to do the right thing. I also ask that You would please guide me with proper timing. That I will have the courage to move forward when I should. I ask You for these and all other blessings in Your Son Jesus's name. Amen."

Porsha read through her message again and set the document back on her desk. She looked at her watch and saw that it was time she headed out to the sanctuary. But before she stood up, she thought about Steve and how he was coming to see her this afternoon. She didn't want him to, but she still felt it was better to end things in person.

When the praise and worship team took their seats, Porsha walked up to the podium. "Beloved, let us love one another, for love is from God, and whoever loves has been born of God and knows God," she said, quoting the same scripture she'd started with the previous Sunday. But over the last few days, she'd decided that she would begin with these particular words from now on, even with her women's ministry meetings. There were many wonderful passages in the Bible, but speaking about the importance of everyone loving each other was a priority for her. Especially since as far as she was concerned, most people didn't love each other enough. They either hurt or betrayed those whom they claimed they cared about, or they focused only on themselves.

"Before I share my inspirational thought with you this morning, I also want to announce the launch of NVCC's newest ministry. It will be called Daughters of Ruth, and it'll be designed to help our single women."

Many of the members nodded with approval, and some of the men made comments and chuckled a little.

Porsha smiled. "All right, gentlemen. I know you might feel a little left out, but please know that this was not my intent. I just feel that women and men have different concerns and problems, and sometimes it's a lot easier for us to discuss those issues privately. It's better to share openly amongst ourselves. Plus, I'm pretty sure that there are certain things men like to talk about that you wouldn't want us ladies to hear, either. Am I right?"

Everyone laughed, and it was at this moment that Porsha wished she could be honest about everything. Tell their members who she truly was. But no matter how hard she stood there trying, the words wouldn't come out. She just didn't have the courage.

"That's what I thought. Men and women are very different, and my hope is that one of our elders or one of our other members will start a ministry designed only for men."

There was more nodding of approval.

"So ladies, single ones that is, our first meeting will be held Thursday after next, and then we'll meet every fourth Thursday thereafter. But between now and then, Michelle, our executive assistant, will be sending out email reminders and also including that information on our automated phone calls. I think most of you are on the list for our weekly phone updates. But if you're not, you might want to register for it, because we make sure to keep you abreast of any news you might need to know before Sunday mornings. But either way, I really hope to see as many women as possible, and I look forward to everything we'll be doing together."

Porsha scanned the outline for her mini message. "Now, before I take my seat I just want to share a few words with you, which won't take long at all. Last week I talked about my desire to meet the right man. Someone who would love and cherish me. I still feel that way, of course, but what I also realized was that part of my true purpose in life is to help other women who are battling the same problem. Good women who have an amazing amount of love to offer but who can't seem to find a good man to love them back. Women who know that they have a soul mate out there, but they just haven't met him yet. Or in some cases, their true soul mate might be someone they already know, but they've somehow overlooked him. Or maybe the circumstances weren't lined up the way they needed to be when they first saw each other. As for me, I know I've struggled with relationships since college. I've been in and out of them, I've sometimes been misused and taken advantage of, and sometimes I've been hurt by men so badly that I curled up and cried like a child. But here's what I know to be true. And it's something that God only recently opened my eyes to. And that something is this: Until we truly begin living the way God wants us to live, nothing will work out the way it should. Until we fully begin trusting Him completely and praying to Him without ceasing, we will never truly be happy. So my final thought for you today is to trust in the Lord with all your heart. And as you know, in Proverbs, that passage finishes by saying, 'and lean not to your own understanding.' So, women, if you want to find the man of your dreams, then you must stop looking on your own. What you have to do is ask God to send you the man He wants you to be with. The same goes for single men. If you want to find that one special woman, then you have to ask God to bring that amazing woman into your life. But even if you're sitting here today and you don't have that sort of problem— maybe you're already happily married, but you're unhappy about something else—well, if so, the same message applies. Because if you're going to a job every single day that you hate, then you're not following your passion. You also aren't walking in your purpose. And if this is the case, then the only way you'll ever discover your true purpose is by asking God to tell you what that is. You have to ask and then spend lots of quiet time with Him, listening. You have to take Him and His Word a lot more seriously. You have to do what He expects you to do in all areas of your life. You have to stop *saying* you're a Christian who believes in God and start acting like one!"

The congregation applauded, and Porsha hadn't felt this good about herself—well, in a very long time. She still hadn't shared anything about her decision to leave pulpit ministry, but she knew she was on the right track. She wasn't so naïve that she thought she could fix all her wrongdoing at one time, but she was now looking forward to being a relentless work-in-progress. First, she would end her affair with Steve this afternoon, and then she would figure out how she was going to handle her situation with Dillon. From there, she would find the courage to resign from her position as associate minister and then figure out how to sever ties with Raven. She wasn't sure how the latter would work from a financial standpoint, but her hope was that Raven would be fair. Even if she wasn't, though, Porsha wouldn't fight over money—money that she knew she'd invested for all the wrong reasons. So if it came down to it, Porsha would walk away with nothing. She would find another church to attend, one that she could hopefully start her Daughters of Ruth ministry with. She would then work toward taking Daughters of Ruth online. She was so excited about all her new possibilities that she burst into tears. She had a lot to do, but at this very second, she felt more joy than she had in years—maybe even in her whole life.

Chapter 25

Raven heard a knock on her door, and smiled because of how efficient Michelle always was. As usual, she was right on time with bringing Raven a copy of her revised sermon notes.

"Come in."

The door eased open, and Raven smiled. But when she saw who it was, her happy demeanor vanished.

"Good morning," John said.

Raven wondered why he was dropping in on her unannounced. "Good morning."

He walked closer to her desk. "I know you're getting ready for your sermon, but I just needed to see you. I just wanted to tell you how much I appreciate your honesty."

"About what?" she said, forcing herself to smile again.

"Your feelings for me and how you've cared for me all this time."

"I'm glad we were finally able to tell the truth," she said.

"I also know that it will take you a little time to end things with Kane, but I'm fine with that."

Raven almost frowned, but stopped herself. Did he honestly think she was planning to break up with Kane for him? "I'm glad you understand, because we've dated for a while now. And it won't be easy."

"Of course, and that's why I'm willing to be as patient as you need me to be. But I won't lie, I hope it happens soon."

Raven leaned back in her chair. "Don't worry, it will. I promise."

"I'm sorry if I seem a little nervous, but I guess I just still can't believe this is happening."

Raven wondered how long he was planning to stay, because the last thing she wanted was for Kane to show up at her office. It also wouldn't be long before Michelle arrived with her sermon notes, so Raven had to get rid of him.

Finally, she stood up, walked around her desk, and wrapped her arms around his neck. "Well, it is happening. And I'm just glad we finally connected."

"I've always wanted you," he confessed. "Always."

Raven pecked him on the lips. "I've always wanted you, too."

John removed his glasses and kissed her like no one else was in the building, and she knew she had to end this little meeting of theirs.

"I don't mean to rush you, but Michelle will be coming back soon and I don't want her to suspect anything."

"It's not a problem, and I'll get going," he said, walking away and then looking back at her, smiling.

Raven waved good-bye to him and breathed a sigh of relief. She loved that he was clearly smitten with her, yet she also didn't want him showing up whenever he felt like it. She couldn't have people wondering what was going on between them, which meant she had to set some boundaries. She would have to make him understand that they needed to be more careful about their love affair—just until she broke up with Kane for good. She would need to tell that lie and many others to get what she wanted.

Raven looked across her congregation. "So by now, I'm sure all of you have seen my Facebook video. Which is why I first want to say how sorry I am for not sharing this part of my life with you first. Each and every one of you knows how much I love you and this church, so please know that it was never my intent for you to find out the way you did. But what I've had to learn, too, is that when God leads you to do something, you have to do it. You have to be obedient and not question Him, because He has a reason for everything. Even when I apologized to some of my staff members this past Tuesday for not telling them beforehand, either, I realized that my testimony isn't about me. It's about all the women and girls who God knew would be watching online that particular day."

Everyone gazed at her with much compassion.

"But with that said," she continued, "I've recorded a formal message just for all of you. My beloved members here at NVCC. Actually, Melvin and a couple of his media staff members were kind enough to come in at the last minute yesterday evening. I'd already recorded a quick message a couple of days ago, but the more I thought about it the more I realized that you deserved something different. Something that fully explains what I went through," she said, stepping back and turning to look at one of the large-screen televisions. "We're going to play it for you now, and it won't take very long."

Raven locked her hands together and held them low in front of her body. She waited for Melvin to cue up the message, and soon her face appeared on-screen.

"Good morning, NVCC. Today, I wanted to take some time to share a little more detail about what happened to me. As you know, nearly a decade ago, I was raped by a well-known pastor. It was before I was arrested and sentenced to prison, but until last Monday I'd never told another living soul. I'd walked around harboring this painful secret for years, pretending that it never occurred. I was devastated and traumatized in the worst possible way, but I still tried to forget about it. I tried to act as though it wasn't reality. And I was successful with doing that... until last week, when God seemed to will me to tell the truth. Then, He made me see that hiding my abuse wasn't helping anyone. So I did what I knew He wanted me to do, and I never thought twice about it. This was doubly hard for me to deal with because as some of you already know, I was also sexually abused while I was in foster care. I was raped twice and made to do other awful things to grown men, but I still went on with my life. I was strong and ambitious, and I did what I had to do to make it in this unkind and very vicious world. I did what women have been doing since the beginning of time. But then, when this happened to me again as an adult—and worse, I was violated by a prominent pastor—I was shaken to my core. I'd borrowed gambling money from him that I couldn't pay back, and he used that against me. He kept asking me for his money, and then one Sunday afternoon..." Raven said, tearing up. "One Sunday afternoon, he showed up at my condo and did what he wanted. Only hours after preaching a sermon at his church, he sexually assaulted me. He treated me as though I was some animal on the street, and then he left. So needless to say, I was left wondering if God really existed. I wondered what I had done to deserve such cruelty and why this was happening to me again. But thank God that while I was in prison, I regained my faith. Then, when I was released, I married my ex-husband, became first lady of his church, and well, you know the rest of the story. And today, I'm doing well, both mentally and emotionally, and I will be fine. But before I end, I do want to say that I have purposely decided not to identify my predator. There's a lot of talk online and also here locally about who it might be, but in order for me to move on from this, it's just better not to name anyone. I just don't want any old wounds ripping back open. Finally, though, I would like to ask that you would please keep me in your prayers and know that I appreciate your support. You all make my life complete, and I couldn't be more honored to be your pastor and servant. I love you with all my heart. Thank you so much for listening, and God bless you."

When the video ended, Raven turned back toward the congregation, and everyone applauded. They were proud of her for telling them more than what she'd shared with the general public, and this was the response she'd been shooting for. She wiped a few tears and thanked them again for supporting her, but when she glanced out at Kane he tossed her an angry look. John, on the other hand, seemed prouder than anyone, which she expected—but then her upbeat spirit vanished. And she tried to swallow the lump that was now lodged in her throat. She so wished her eyes had been playing tricks on her, but she knew they weren't. D.C. had just walked inside the sanctuary, staring at her.

As one of the female ushers escorted him to a seat toward the back, he never took his eyes off her. Raven could, of course, ask herself why D.C. was there, but she knew his presence served only as yet another warning about his money. He had shown up to taunt her and make her uncomfortable, and she knew he wouldn't stop until she paid him. She would've loved nothing more than to report D.C. to the police, but D.C. wasn't someone you called the law on. If you did, it wouldn't matter because one of his "people" would still be ordered to handle things accordingly. So again, she would have to pay D.C. his money as soon as she could, which meant John would need to be lured all the way in a lot sooner than planned.

Chapter 26

*P*orsha still couldn't believe it. Raven had secretly re-
done her internal video message, and this new
recording was much more damaging to Pastor Black
than the one on Facebook. It just didn't make sense for her
to continue down this path, so what was this all about? Was
Raven doing this to get back at Pastor Black for sending her
to prison years ago? Or was this some sick way of securing
revenge against Dillon? Porsha wasn't sure one way or the
other, but she had a feeling someone was going to get hurt.
She also hadn't forgotten about that mysterious guy who'd
shown up at Bible study.

Porsha slipped out of her black bolero blazer and matching sleeveless dress and pulled on a pair of heather-gray
workout shorts and a white NVCC T-shirt. As she stood in
front of her dresser mirror, looking at the church's logo dis-
played across her chest, she felt miserable. She'd helped
Raven start NVCC two years ago, and although she knew
she hadn't honestly represented herself to their parishioners, she was going to hate not being able to see them

anymore. That would be the hardest part about leaving, but nonetheless, she didn't have a choice.

Porsha grabbed her cell phone, left her bedroom, and went downstairs. But when she arrived in the kitchen, Dillon called her.

"Hey," she said.

"Hey, baby, how are you?"

"I'm good. You?"

"Couldn't be better. Just got home from church."

"Me too."

"So am I coming to your house or are you coming here?"

Porsha didn't want to lie to him, but she wasn't going to tell him about Steve either. "I can't."

"Why?"

"I have other plans. Something I need to take care of."

"I hope it's not with another man."

Porsha changed the subject. "We just saw each other yesterday, remember? Not to mention Thursday and Friday, too."

"I know, and I want to see you today."

"I wish I could, but I can't."

"You know you're enjoying our time together. We're both enjoying it."

"I never said I wasn't."

"Then why are you trying to make excuses about being busy?"

"I'm not. I really have something else I need to do."

"Well, you know that makes me wonder, right?"

"What?"

"*Who* you have these plans with."

"Look, Dillon, I would love to see you. I really would, but I can't."

"All right, all right, all right. I won't pressure you, but just so you know, I'm not happy about this."

"I'm sorry."

"So *now* what am I supposed to do on this beautiful Sunday afternoon? Especially since I already told my dad I wasn't coming by for dinner."

"It's not like you can't change your mind."

"I know, but that's not what I wanted to do today. I wanted to spend a few hours with you."

Porsha didn't say anything, and for a split second she thought about calling Steve and canceling their visit. But she knew she had to follow through on her decision to break up with him.

"We'll get together another day," she finally said.

"What about tomorrow?"

Porsha laughed. "You don't give up, do you?"

"No, and it's not like you want me to anyway."

Porsha thought she heard a car door and rushed toward her entryway and looked out. "I have to get going, okay?"

"Already?"

"I do, but I'll call you later."

"You promise?"

"Yes."

"If you don't I'll be calling you."

"I'll call you this evening. Really."

"Talk to you then. Bye, baby."

Porsha pressed the End button and switched her ringer to silent. Then she went back into the kitchen and set her phone on the island. Seconds later, her doorbell rang and she went and opened the door.

Steve smiled and walked inside, and as soon as he shut the door behind him, he pulled her into his arms.

Porsha pulled slightly away from him.

Steve let go of her. "Wow, so we've gone days without seeing each other, and this is the kind of welcome I get?"

"Let's go sit down," she said, turning away from him and heading toward her family room.

When they walked over to the sofa, Porsha took a seat and Steve sat next to her. Then he wrapped his arm around her, trying to kiss her.

But she leaned her head in the other direction. "I'm sorry, but we really need to talk."

"What's wrong now? What's going on?"

Porsha scooted over a couple inches and positioned her body so that she was facing him. "This is one of the hardest things I've ever had to do, and all I can hope is that you understand."

"What is it?"

"I can't see you anymore. This affair of ours is over."

"You have got to be kidding me. Why, Porsha?"

"It's not right. It never was."

Steve scooted to the edge of the sofa, fuming. "So let me get this straight. You just all of a sudden want out of the relationship?"

"It's not that simple."

"Well, being in love with someone and then cutting them off for no reason doesn't make sense. I mean, who does that?"

"I know you're upset, but I can't help the way I feel. I've had a huge change of heart, and I can't keep sleeping with another woman's husband."

Steve laughed like a crazy man, but Porsha knew this wasn't funny to him. It was actually just the opposite, because for as long as she'd known him she'd never seen him so outraged.

"I'm sorry, Steve. I really am, but every night this week I've gone to bed feeling guilty and I wake up the very same way. Each day this feeling has gotten worse, and I can't do this with you anymore."

Steve didn't respond for at least half a minute, seemingly trying to calm himself down or find the right words to say. "Okay, baby, I know you're going through whatever it is you're going through, but we can work this out. I love you with all my heart, and I don't want to lose you."

"I hear you, and I appreciate that, but I just don't have the desire to keep doing something I know is wrong. I don't want to spend the rest of my life claiming to love God and then sleeping with you. Hoping you'll leave your wife and child. Hoping you'll get a divorce and marry me. I just can't."

Steve shook his head. "I don't know what to say. I mean, tell me what to do and I'll do it."

As recently as last Sunday, Porsha would have quickly asked him again to file for divorce, but not today. "It's your wife who you need to work things out with."

Steve frowned. "And how am I supposed to do that?"

"Pray about it and go to counseling with her."

"But, baby, I don't love her. I haven't loved her in a very long time, and you know that."

"I'm sorry," she said.

"Why do you keep saying that? I mean, what is 'sorry' supposed to do about any of this?"

"Steve, I know you're upset, but I can't change the way God has been speaking to my heart."

"Yeah, go ahead why don't you. Blame this lie you're telling all on God."

Porsha stared at him. "Why would I lie about something like this?"

"So you can lay up with some other man. Because I know that's what this fake, holy-roller spiel of yours is all about. I'm not stupid, Porsha."

Porsha didn't even bother commenting. She couldn't deny that Dillon had helped make her breakup with Steve easier, but she was also telling the truth about the way God was dealing with her. Even she didn't know why He'd decided to shake her conscience as much as He had over the last few days, but none of that mattered. The reason: God didn't need a set hour or week to do anything. He worked in His own timing, and if He chose to, He did it quickly and without warning.

"So just like that?" he said, speaking louder than before. "You're breaking up with me and moving on? And you expect me to do the same?"

"I know this isn't what you wanted to hear, but I just needed to be honest."

"Honest, huh? Then why don't you be honest about Thursday night? You know, tell me the *real* reason you stopped me from coming over here."

"Let's not keep doing this," she said. "Let's not keep going back and forth with me trying to explain things and you calling me a liar. Because no matter what I say at this point, you won't believe me."

"Yeah, you're definitely right about that. And it's all because I know you better than this. I know you're seeing someone else. I'd be willing to bet every dime I have on it."

Porsha looked away from him, not knowing what else to say.

"This is what I get for sleeping with some so-called minister. Someone playing with God and then profiting from it."

Porsha squinted at him. "Really? So you're innocent in all of this, I guess?"

"I never said that, but you knew I was married, and if you weren't planning to stay in this for the long haul, you never should've started sleeping with me. You never should've become the reason that I cheated on my wife."

"Excuse me? So being an ordained deacon wasn't a good enough reason for you not to? It didn't make you think twice about having an affair?"

"You're impossible," he said, standing up. "Got me sneaking around on my wife and falling in love with you, and now you're done."

"You know what, Steve? I think it's time for you to leave."

Steve tossed her an evil look and left the room. He

never looked back at her, and soon she heard her front door shutting.

Porsha's nerves were shot, and she hated that their relationship was ending on such bad terms. She also couldn't deny that a part of her was hurt, because she did love Steve. But none of that mattered because she also knew she'd done the right thing. She would no longer be sleeping with someone else's husband, and that gave her peace. She was relieved and could breathe just a little easier.

Chapter 27

Raven turned on her side, watching John sleep like a baby. They were lying closely in his bed, and she'd just given him the best sex of his life. At least that's what he'd told her, and with the way he'd responded to her—before, during, and after—she believed him. He acted like some teenage boy who was infatuated with his first love, and Raven knew she was close to getting what she wanted. In due time, she would seize total control of his mind, and he would do as he was told. Actually, Raven hadn't known he was as gullible as he was or that he'd been *this* taken with her for as long as he had been. She'd certainly been aware of his attraction and strong admiration, but she hadn't realized how simple he was. Being a nerd didn't always mean a person was simple or gullible, but when it came to women, John easily identified with a sixteen-year-old.

Raven lay thinking a while longer, mostly about Kane and how he wasn't speaking to her again, and then she thought about D.C. Thankfully, he hadn't called her yesterday after service or today even, but she wasn't taking his latest visit

too lightly. She'd known then that it was a threat and a warning, and it was the reason she'd decided it was time to seduce
John to the *n*th degree. Raven still knew, however, that she
couldn't simply ask John to steal money from the church or
ask him to do it this quickly, so she'd added on a new part
to her plan. She'd decided that the only way to get John
fully behind her was to turn him against Porsha. Originally,
she'd thought it was Michelle who'd be able to help her oust
Porsha from the ministry, which was the reason Raven had
subtly begun carving a wedge between them. But for now,
she had to focus on getting D.C. his money. She had to tell
John whatever it took to make him feel sorry for her.

John moved around a bit, stretched his arms above his
head, and opened his eyes. He smiled and squinted at her,
and Raven knew he needed his glasses.

He, of course, wasted no time reaching for them and
sliding them on. "Where have you been all of my life?"

Raven smiled but then changed her expression to a
somber one. "Where have you been all of mine?"

"What's wrong?" he asked.

"Everything."

"Like what?"

"I don't want to burden you with my problems. I didn't
come over here for that. I just wanted to make love to you."

"It's fine. Tell me."

Raven waited for her eyes to fill with tears and then said,
"Are you sure?"

"Yes," he said, touching the side of her face. "Because it
might be something I can help you with."

This was way too easy, was all Raven could think. "Okay," she said, sighing and wiping the tears that now fell down her cheeks. "I learned yesterday from a very reliable source that Porsha is planning to take over the ministry. She's going to push me completely out of NVCC and the entire organization."

"Oh my goodness. Do you believe that?"

Raven sniffled. "I didn't want to. Not when I've been such a good friend to Porsha, but the person who told me would never lie about something like this."

"Can you say who that person is?"

"I wish I could, and it's not that I don't trust you, because I know I can. But I promised my source that I wouldn't betray their confidence."

"I understand, but this is crazy."

"I know, and I'm really sorry for unloading this kind of drama on you."

John pulled her close to him, and she laid her head on his chest.

"There's nothing for you to be sorry about," he said. "So please don't apologize."

"Well, then I might as well tell you the rest," she said looking up at him.

"What?"

"Porsha and Kane have been sleeping together behind my back."

"No way. Kane and Porsha?"

"Unfortunately, yes...and I'm sad to say that I haven't been completely honest with you about something else."

John looked at her in silence.

"Remember when I told you on Friday that I was tired of pretending that I didn't want you?"

"Uh-huh."

"Well, part of the reason I wanted to be with you that day, right there in my office, was because of how devastated I was. I'd just found out about Kane and Porsha the day before. But please know," she said, now resting her hand on his cheek, "that my attraction for you is real. And when I told you that I've always been attracted to you, I meant it. So can you forgive me?"

"There's nothing to forgive, so don't spend another thought on it. I can't believe Porsha and Kane."

"Well then, imagine how I'm feeling."

"Did you say anything to them?"

"No, and I'm not going to until I can figure out what to do. I'm definitely breaking up with Kane, though, and I'm eventually going to confront Porsha, too."

John shook his head and seemed puzzled about something.

"What is it?" she asked.

"I don't know. Porsha seems like such a nice person, and to be honest, so does Kane. That's why I never wanted to approach you in the wrong way. I didn't want to disrespect him."

Raven had known that John might somewhat question whether Porsha would sleep with Kane behind her back, so she'd come to his house very prepared.

"Porsha isn't the sweet, holy minister you think she is, and this isn't the first time she's done this to me. She betrayed me two years ago, but being the true woman of God I am, I forgave her and became friends with her. We became so close that she agreed to help me start the ministry, but then she became jealous of how success-fully I grew the following. Then she became jealous of my relationship with Kane. That's when I guess she started plotting behind my back to steal the ministry from me."

"This is awful, and so hard to believe."

Raven knew it was time to shatter any doubt he might have about Porsha being a whore. "If I show you something, can I trust you not to tell anyone about it?"

"Of course. What is it?"

"Can you give me something to throw on?"

John got up and went into his closet. When he came back, he passed her one of his white long-sleeved business shirts, and she slipped it on and buttoned it up. John wrapped a velour robe around himself and tied the belt hanging from it.

Raven then went over to her leather tote and pulled out a DVD. She'd also made a third copy on another USB drive, which she'd brought with her, too, just in case they needed to watch it on John's laptop. "Do you have a Blu-ray player?"

"Yeah, right under my television," he said, pointing to-ward his armoire.

Raven passed him the disc. "Here."

John reached for it and turned on the machine.

They both sat down at the foot of the bed and waited for the DVD to begin playing. There was moaning and groaning right from the start, and Raven saw how mortified John was. And rightfully so, because Dillon and Porsha were butt naked and having the time of their lives.

Raven watched more with him and then said, "So you see, I can't allow a woman like Porsha to take my ministry from me. She knows nothing about running it, and everything will be ruined. We'll have to close the doors of NVCC for good."

"Gosh," John said, holding his forehead with his hand. "This is too much."

"I know, but you have to promise me that you won't tell anyone about this."

John gazed at her with what seemed like total sincerity. "I would never do that to you. I would never betray your trust in me."

"Thank you for that, because you're the only person I've ever shown this to. Only Dillon, Porsha, and I even know about it."

"Well, something has to be done. I mean, you can't allow someone like that to become senior pastor. You can't allow this kind of woman to just push you out of the way. NVCC is yours," he said matter-of-factly, and Raven was shocked by how disgusted he was. In a matter of minutes, he'd lost all respect for Porsha, and Raven wanted to pat herself on the back.

"I know, but Porsha has a lot of money, John. A ton of it. And it would take thousands of dollars to stop her."

"Well, if there's anything I can do to help you, I hope you'll tell me."

"You really mean that?"

"I do."

"I first have to figure out the best way to handle this."

"Whatever you need, I'm here for you. And don't you forget that."

Raven gazed into his eyes. "You are such a sweetheart, but baby, this thing with Porsha might get ugly. And I don't want you to feel obligated to do anything that goes against your ethics. Or Christian values, for that matter. Because I'll be honest, I'm willing to do whatever it takes to stop Porsha. Even if it means doing something I shouldn't. To keep my ministry, I might have to sin and pray about it later."

"I don't blame you," he said, and Raven wanted to scream with joy. John was making it clear that he would help her at all costs, and from this point on, she would give him as much sex as he wanted. From here on out, she would satisfy him in ways he hadn't even heard about.

Chapter 28

After Raven had given John all the pleasure he could stand, she'd told him she had to get going. She'd then jumped in the shower, gotten dressed, and kissed him good-bye. Needless to say, he hadn't wanted her to leave and had found the gall to ask her to spend the night, but she'd let him down easy. She'd explained how they still needed to be careful until she broke up with Kane. The good news, though, was that he was completely on board with helping her get whatever amount of money she needed. He had agreed without much coaxing at all, and what she now realized was how good she was at tricking men and getting them to believe everything she said. Kane, of course, was starting to doubt some of what she claimed and did, but once she paid off D.C., got rid of Porsha, and cut off John, she would make things right with him. She would give him her undivided attention, and if he insisted, she would finally marry him.

Now, though, Raven was in her car heading home and plotting out her next move. First, she would tell John

that the simplest way to find her the two hundred thousand dollars would be to transfer it piecemeal from the
least-used church accounts. That way, the chance of their
getting caught would be next to none, and John could fun-
nel all of it into one new account—an account that would
be hers. To be safe, she'd also decided that she would tell
him that the funds she was taking were only a temporary
loan, and that she'd be paying it back over the next four
months. This wasn't true, but this particular story would
also lead him to believe that her "loan" was nothing more
than an advance she was taking against her normal income.

But even though she'd figured out that part of her plan,
she knew John would need time to make this happen.
Which meant she had to convince D.C. to give her a
month's extension. She knew he would still insist that she
pay him now, but she was hoping that she'd found the perfect solution. She wasn't sure he'd go for it, but she was
calling him now to make her case.

Raven dialed his number.

"Hey, Rev," he said. "Great sermon yesterday. You got my
money?"

"That's actually why I'm calling."

"I hope you're not still tryin' to talk me into some petty
payment plan, because for the kazillionth time, I'm not
havin' it."

"Not even if I'm willing to pay you a little more than the
two hundred and seventy?"

"Yeah, right. Heifer, you must think I'm a fool."

"No, this is real. If you can give me a month, I'll give you three hundred."

D.C. laughed the way he always did when he thought she was trying to get over on him. "If you don't have two seventy, how do you plan on gettin' me three hundred?"

"All I'm saying is that if you give me thirty days, I'll get you three hundred K."

"Make it three hundred K plus you go online and clear Pastor Black's name, and I might think about it."

A wave of anger and nervousness swept through Raven's body. She'd suspected all along that Pastor Black was the reason D.C. had decided to come after her. But when she'd asked him about it, he'd acted as though he didn't know what she was talking about. Dillon had lied, too, and now he was using D.C. to get the revenge he'd been trying to unleash on her since their divorce.

"Helloooo?" D.C. sang, trying to be funny. "Do we have a bad connection?"

"I can't believe you're doing this. All because of Pastor Black?"

"Well, believe it, sweetheart, and you should've thought about that when you stole money from him and me. You also had no business makin' that sick accusation. Pastor Black has done a lot of stuff over the years, but rapin' women ain't one of 'em."

"How do you know that, D.C.?" she asked, just to see what his response would be.

"Because I know he didn't. I also know you and what a lyin', manipulative trick you are. You showed who you were nine years ago, and pretendin' to be some holy pastor at a church hasn't changed that. You're just as sneaky and low down as you always were. You should be ashamed to step up in anyone's pulpit, let alone your own."

Raven wasn't sure why D.C.'s words sort of bothered her, but they did. That was only for maybe two seconds, though, because she was still livid about this Pastor Black turn of events.

"So who made you do this? Pastor Black or Dillon?"

"First of all, nobody makes D.C. do anything. *I* decide what goes on with my business. But if you must know, I contacted you on my own—at first. Because when that video of yours started circulating around, I realized how cocky and dirty you still were. And I decided right then and there that you were going to pay me."

"Well, if that's true, then why are you all of a sudden saying that you'll extend my deadline if I clear Pastor Black's name? Is part of that three hundred going to him?"

"Nope. This is just part of our deal, plain and simple. Now take it or leave it."

Raven wanted to slam her phone against her windshield, but she knew it wouldn't change anything. "Fine. Three hundred it is."

"And a new video. By tomorrow evening before midnight."

"What? I need more time than that. I have to figure out the best way to fix this."

"Then I suggest you get busy. I'm already bein' nice to

you as it is, because I could make you record that video tonight."

"I'll see what I can do," she said, trying to stand up to him.

"No, you'll either do it or our deal is off. And when you finish, that video had better leave Pastor Black lookin' like a saint."

"I'll take care of it."

"You'd better not be playin' games with me."

"I'll get it done."

"And my money?"

"I'll get you that, too. In thirty days."

"For your sake, I hope you do. Because if I have to contact you again...well, let's just say you know how I do. And I don't make promises without keeping them. I softened up a little before you went to prison, but not this time."

Raven tried to toughen up her tone, acting as though she wasn't afraid of him. "Like I said, you'll have your money in thirty days."

"And it better not be a day later."

D.C. hung up, and Raven wanted to cry. Not because she was hurt, but because she was outraged. The reason: Pastor Black was no longer a blackmail option for her. She'd been thinking that if she continued making accusations about him, he would eventually become so worried about his reputation that he would pay her whatever money she asked for. Worse, if she told enough lies, he might think he was facing prison time and he would pay her an even larger sum. But now, Pastor Black and D.C.

had beaten her at her own game, and she had to switch her plot to plan B.

She was now going to blackmail Porsha. Actually, this scenario would work out better for Raven, because with Porsha there wouldn't be any repercussions. When it came to Pastor Black and Dillon, however, if she'd tried to blackmail them, they would play a tit-for-tat war with her for years. She would end up doing something awful to them, they would do something worse to her, and the saga would continue. But with Porsha, Raven would only have to make her demands and wait for payment. And there wouldn't be any negotiating, either. Porsha would simply pay Raven three hundred thousand dollars, plus sign over all her rights to anything relating to New Vision Ministries, Inc.— including her ongoing 50 percent profit—or Raven would leak that sex tape. She would send that raunchy video of her and Dillon to every local and national media outlet she could find, and she knew Little Miss Goody Two-Shoes wouldn't want that. She would never allow something like this to happen, not when it seemed as though she was trying to become some new devout Christian. When Raven had viewed that mini message of hers last week, she'd seen something different about Porsha, and she'd also noticed the same thing when she'd watched her message from yesterday. Raven didn't know where this sudden change in Porsha's personality was coming from, but it wouldn't stop her from kicking Porsha out of her church.

Then, once Raven received the three hundred thousand from Porsha, she would pay D.C. as promised, but she would still get John to transfer the original two hundred thousand she'd already planned for—plus another three hundred. Because the more she thought about this, why shouldn't she get paid right along with D.C.? Why shouldn't she walk away with five hundred thousand dollars free and clear, so she could finally build her dream home? The house she wanted to construct would run anywhere from seven hundred fifty thousand to a million dollars, anyway, so a half million would make the perfect down payment.

Just thinking about the way this whole next month would play out got Raven excited, because not only would her debt to D.C. be paid in full—which meant she would no longer have to live in fear—but she would also be five hundred thousand dollars richer. It was so interesting how Porsha's money would be saving her life, and John's financial expertise would fatten her personal bank account like never before. The whole scheme was brilliant, and now Raven wasn't as sorry as she had been about D.C. showing up at Bible study last week. Because if he hadn't, there was a chance Raven might not have had the courage to blackmail Porsha. Well, maybe she still would have at some point, but she wouldn't have made an attempt this soon— not to mention she likely wouldn't have discovered a much easier way to oust Porsha and keep all the profit from the ministry for herself. Raven also wouldn't have risked losing Kane, which was exactly what she was doing by sleeping with John. Although, it was like she'd been thinking all along: She did love Kane, but he didn't take priority over her ministry. It wasn't like she was going to get caught with John, anyway. So once D.C. became history and Porsha did, too, Raven would end this charade of a relationship with John. He would certainly be hurt, because she could tell how in love with her he was, but he would have to move on and find someone else. What he needed was someone who was more noticeably on his level—a plain Jane, so to speak—and Raven would get back to being the powerful woman that Kane deserved. She would reap multiple rewards and become wealthier than ever. She would have everything she wanted.

Chapter 29

Porsha had been meeting with Michelle for the last fifteen minutes, and Michelle's attitude seemed worse than it was last week. Porsha had called and asked her to come to her office to review a few more documents for her women's ministry, but Michelle seemed totally put out by it.

"Okay, look, Michelle," Porsha said. "What's wrong?"

"Nothing."

"Well, then why do you seem so different?"

"I'm not."

"You're treating me very coldly, and it's never been like that with you and me before. We've always had a great relationship, and in all honesty, a good friendship. So please tell me what's really going on here."

Michelle sighed a bit louder than normal. "I'm just busy is all. I have a lot to do, and I also need to get ready for our staff meeting. Which is only an hour from now."

"Is your health okay?" Porsha asked.

"It's fine."

"Because if you're not feeling well or going through anything at all, you know you can tell me."

Michelle half nodded but seemed uninterested.

"Do you have any questions?" Porsha said.

"About what?"

"The e-blast schedule I need you to set up or the three handouts I need you to create. I also need the date and time included in both of this week's automated phone call announcements. And in the one the day before the first meeting as well."

"Everything will be taken care of."

Porsha wanted to ask her again what was bothering her, but finally she said, "Then that's all I have."

"I'll see you at the staff meeting," Michelle said, already on her way out the door.

Something wasn't right, and while Raven was the last person Porsha conversed with anymore, either at church or otherwise, she got up and went to go see her.

She walked down the corridor, just past Michelle's office, and knocked on Raven's door.

"Come in."

"Hey, you have a minute?" Porsha said, entering and shutting the door behind her.

"I'm getting ready for staff, but if it's important go ahead."

"This won't take long, and I'm just wondering if you've noticed something different about Michelle."

"Not really. Like what?"

"The way she's been acting. Almost like something's wrong or maybe she doesn't feel well."

Raven shook her head. "No, I haven't noticed anything like that. As a matter of fact, when I first got here this morning, she told me about this new store at one of the outlet malls. She went shopping there yesterday."

Porsha folded her arms. "Oh. Well, maybe she's just upset with me about something."

"Does she have a reason?"

"No."

"Did you ask her if something was wrong?"

"I did. Both last week and a few minutes ago. That's why I decided to come check with you."

"Well, I don't know what to tell you. Oh, and by the way, I watched that little message you gave on Sunday morning, and it wasn't bad. But it's like I told you last week, the more you do it, the better you'll be at it."

Porsha didn't even bother responding to Raven's demeaning comments and simply said, "I'll see you in the meeting."

Then she headed back toward her own office. Raven was being just as cold as Michelle was, and the only difference was that Raven acted as though Porsha was beneath her. Raven had been indirectly doing this kind of thing for a while, but now she didn't even try to hide it. She showed her true colors boldly and unapologetically, and she seemed to enjoy trying to make Porsha feel bad. But Porsha wouldn't let her do that. Not when she believed she was finally doing what God wanted her to do, and that her words were lifting people up. Raven was just upset because Porsha was now speaking before the congregation every single

Sunday versus only every now and then. She didn't like it, but until Porsha mapped out her exit and went to Raven to discuss it, she would continue sharing a short message with their parishioners as planned.

When Porsha arrived back at her desk, she smiled. She wasn't sure where they'd come from, but two dozen red roses quickly brightened her mood. She loved flowers, especially roses, but when she realized who they likely were from, her spirits dropped. She and Steve hadn't spoken since two days ago when he'd stormed out of her house, but she'd had a feeling he wouldn't be leaving things as is. She'd tried to explain her position as best as she could, but it had only made him angrier. He hadn't understood her decision, and to some degree, she doubted he ever would.

Porsha went around her desk and lifted the small envelope from the arrangement. She opened it and pulled out the card. Just as she'd thought, the roses were from Steve. It was a nice gesture, but he was going to have to find a way to get beyond this. Their affair was over, and although Porsha wasn't sure about a number of things evolving in her life right now, she was clear on this: She wouldn't sleep with Steve again, or with any other married man for as long as she lived.

Porsha slid the card back inside the envelope and sat in her chair. But as soon as she picked up her pen, her phone rang. As expected, Steve was calling her, and she didn't want to answer him. But she also knew that if she didn't, he'd either call her again or drop by her house, and she definitely didn't want that.

"Hello?"

"How are you?"

"I'm good. What about you?"

"How do you think, Porsha? I mean, this breakup is obviously pretty easy for you, but I haven't slept in two nights. I'm miserable, and I really need to see you."

"But we already talked about this. You know how I feel and that I can't see you anymore."

"Why, though? Why did you decide this now?"

"I haven't felt comfortable with our situation for a while, but this week I knew I couldn't continue being with you."

"And it's all because you've suddenly become this *godly* woman? No other reason?"

"You're saying that like it's a joke and you don't believe it, but God really has shown me how wrong I was to sleep with another woman's husband. I always knew it was wrong on my own, but now I know that God will never allow me to have real peace until I move on from our relationship. He also won't bless me with a husband."

"That's what this is really all about, isn't it? You want to be married."

"You've always known that, Steve, so please don't make it sound like you didn't."

"That's not what I'm saying. I'm just asking if this was your real reason for breaking up with me."

"Maybe partly, but it was mostly because I don't want to sleep with a married man anymore. I keep telling you that, but you're not hearing me."

"Well, what if I left my wife and got a divorce? Then what?"

"I don't think that's the answer."

"Why?"

"Because I realize now that if you did leave your wife and married me, I would always be waiting for you to have an affair. And there wouldn't be a single thing I could really say, not when I knew I deserved it."

"I wouldn't do that to you. You know I wouldn't."

"But you did it to Denene, Steve."

"That's because I don't love her, and to be honest, I don't think she loves me, either. She never questions me about anything. I can basically come and go as I please."

"But you loved her once upon a time. Am I right?"

"Yeah, but what does that have to do with anything?"

"It has to do with everything. Because just like you fell in love with her and then somehow stopped loving her, you could do the same thing to me."

"But I wouldn't. Things would be different with us. I would be faithful to you until death."

"That's easier said than done. But none of that matters now, anyway, because I don't want to be the reason you leave your wife and son."

"You say that today, but I can remember you asking me to leave them plenty of times."

"And I was wrong, I told you that on Sunday."

"Can we talk about this in person?"

"No, let's just move on with our lives."

"But you know that's not what I want."

"I'm sorry. I know you want me to say something different, but this really is it for me."

"Then I guess I'll talk to you later," he said, and hung up.

He hadn't even waited for her to say good-bye, so maybe this would be his last time calling her. Maybe he would think long and hard and do what she'd suggested to him on Sunday: seek professional counseling and work things out with his wife. Because if he did, maybe he would see that there was still hope for his marriage. Maybe he would fall in love with his wife all over again, and life would be good for them. That's what Porsha hoped for. That's what she would pray for tonight before going to bed.

Chapter 30

Kane still hadn't called Raven, but now he'd shown up at her home unannounced. Normally, she never cared if he dropped in without calling, but he was interrupting her Facebook Live preparation. D.C. had given her until midnight to complete the broadcast, and since it was already eight p.m., she wanted to get this over with.

"So I guess you're not mad at me anymore?" she said, sitting on the sofa in her family room.

Kane sat across from her in one of the chairs. "I'm still not okay with what you did. You're really wrong for this."

"What? Telling my story? Being honest about what happened to me?"

"That's not what I mean, and you know it. I'm talking about that video you recorded for the congregation. Because all that's going to do is make people accuse Pastor Black even more."

"I didn't share that video with the public. That was only played for our members."

"But baby, you know some of our members are going to tell family and friends outside of the church. It's guaranteed."

"Well, I can't be responsible for what everyone else does," she shot back. "And anyway, why are you so worried about a man who sent me to prison? A man who slept around on all three of his wives? You act like you care more about him than you do me."

"That's not true. Plus, you're talking about Pastor Black's past. He's very public about his terrible history, but he also regularly shares why and how he changed for the better. But even if he hadn't, no one should have to deal with these kinds of accusations. I told you that before, and now you've made things worse."

"How?"

"By giving more details about your rape and then alluding to the fact that you borrowed money from this *pastor*, and when you wouldn't pay him back he raped you. Well, everyone knows that you stole money from Pastor Black and then you went to prison."

Raven was getting tired of Kane grilling her the way he was. "Exactly. I said in the video that I *borrowed* money. So why would anyone think I was referring to my situation with Pastor Black?"

Kane shook his head as though he thought she was lying. "Your choice of words won't make a difference in some people's minds. All most folks care about is the idea that you couldn't pay back money you owed to a prominent pastor, and he raped you before you went to prison."

"Well, that's not my problem."

"Why couldn't you just say, 'I won't be identifying my predator, but I do want everyone to know that Reverend Curtis Black didn't do this to me'? One sentence was all it would've taken."

Raven knew she wasn't getting ready to clear Pastor Black's name out of the goodness of her heart, and that she was only doing it because D.C. was forcing her. But what a perfect opportunity she was being given to make it sound as though she were.

"Well, if you hadn't rushed in here being so self-righteous, I would've told you about the broadcast I'm doing tonight."

"Where?"

"On Facebook Live. I thought more about it, and I realized I was wrong. Just like you said."

"So you're actually going to say he didn't do this to you?"

"I am, and I'll admit something else. Even though I really was raped, a part of me was hoping that people would begin to think Pastor Black was my assaulter. Right or wrong, I still haven't gotten over the fact that he sent me to prison. I also saw this as a good way to get back at Dillon. So you were right about everything you said last week. You know, about me not having a great relationship with my ex-husband or his family. I wanted them to suffer for causing me all the pain they did."

Kane moved closer to the edge of the chair. "But sweetheart, you're a pastor. And you preach about forgiveness all the time. So why would you want to cause this kind of harm to someone you no longer have to deal with?"

"Because maybe I'm not perfect like you, Kane," she said matter-of-factly.

"I'm not perfect. Not even close. But lately you've been doing things that I don't understand. You don't seem to care who you hurt, and all you talk about is growing the ministry. Getting more members and online followers. Being the most well-known female pastor in the country. Making millions."

"And you have a problem with that?"

Kane glared at her. "I do, and I don't like the person you've become."

"Well, I don't know what to tell you. I mean, what's wrong with wanting to be successful? What's wrong with wanting to bring as many souls to the Kingdom as I can?"

"There's nothing wrong with that at all, but you seem to be more concerned about fame and money. I mean, if you ended up with fifty thousand local members, I wouldn't see anything wrong with that as long as you were doing things the way God wants you to. That this would be about *His* Kingdom and not yours."

Raven frowned. "Oh, so now you're judging me?"

"That's not what I'm trying to do."

"Well, it sounds to me like you're saying I'm not a good person. That I'm actually a sinful one."

"Well, as of late, you've been doing things I've never seen you do before, and I don't like it."

Raven heard everything he was saying, but she didn't have time for this. She also needed to review the script that she'd written for the broadcast again. Although, the more the wheels turned in her head, she wondered if maybe this spat they were having was working in her favor. Maybe it was giving her a chance to suggest a breakup between them. It would only be temporary, of course, but if she and Kane were to end things, she'd be able to spend all the time with John that was necessary. She could even make John believe that she and Kane had broken up for good, and that she belonged to him now. This brief split between Raven and Kane would also allow her the freedom she needed to handle Porsha and put all of this madness behind her. When it was over, Raven would beg Kane to come back to her and they would resume their relationship.

"So you're just going to keep staring at me?" Kane said. "Acting like this is no big deal?"

"To be honest, you've been doing things I don't like, either," she lied. "Asking me questions all the time and trying to tell me what to do. So maybe we should take a step back."

"You mean break up?"

"Call it whatever you want."

"I suggested that last week, so maybe we should. Especially if you're planning to continue down this selfish and vengeful journey you're on."

"Well, I'm always going to do me," she said in a callous tone. "And neither you nor any other man will ever change that. I won't be controlled by anyone. Not even the perfect Kane Alexander."

"Wow," he said, standing up, and Raven wondered if she'd gone too far. She could see how hurt he was, but that wasn't why she was doing this.

She almost took back some of her words, but he kept talking.

"You've really shown me a side of you tonight that I wasn't counting on. But it is what it is."

Raven wanted to rush over and hold him, but she had to be strong. She needed to get things in order, and this separation of theirs would allow her the chance to do it the right way. So instead, she watched Kane leave her house. She would miss being with him, but she knew these next four weeks would pass quickly. They wouldn't take long at all.

Raven had checked her hair and makeup one last time, and now she was sitting in her home office at her desk. She'd recited her message out loud a few different times, both earlier today and again when Kane had left, so she was definitely ready.

She now picked up her smartphone, set it in its upright cradle, and clicked on the Facebook icon. Then she took a deep breath and opened the video feature. She waited about two minutes, allowing folks to join in, and finally began.

"Good evening, everyone, and I hope you're doing well. I know it's a bit unusual for me to broadcast a message on a Tuesday night, especially since I already did my normal Monday recording yesterday. But after seeing more and more rumors here and on other social media sites, I had to do some soul-searching. Last week, I'd decided not to identify the man who raped me, because I didn't think it was necessary. I also didn't want to relive any more of this awful part of my past than I had to. But then, lots of folks began wondering who this person was, and it wasn't long before the majority of people began making assumptions. The name that came up more often than not was Reverend Curtis Black. At first, I didn't understand why, but after speaking with others I realize now that because I worked for him right before being sent to prison, it sort of sounded as though I was referring to him. But tonight, I want to clear up these vicious rumors once and for all. My ex-father-in-law, Reverend Curtis Black—pastor of Deliverance Outreach here in Mitchell, Illinois—did not rape me. Pastor Black hired me to be his chief financial officer when I was barely thirty years old, and he trusted me like I was family. I hadn't even met my ex-husband yet, but Pastor Black treated me and all his other employees exceptionally well. To my knowledge, not only did he never disrespect me or approach me in the wrong way, he also never did so with any other female employee. So while it is true that my marriage to his son ended in a very nasty divorce, Pastor Black had nothing to do with that. He was always kind to me, and sadly, I was the one who betrayed him when I was struggling with my gambling problem. But all of that is in the past, and that's where I want it to stay. So finally, I just want to thank all of you again for the outpouring of love and support that you've shown me. This has certainly been both a trying and a very eye-opening week, but with God's help I know I'm going to be fine. Thank you again, and know that my prayers are with you always," Raven said, smiling. "Good night, and God bless you."

She clicked the Stop button for the recording and breathed deeply again. If she'd been able to do things her way, she never would've spoken so highly of Pastor Black. But she also hadn't wanted to take a chance on D.C. claiming that she hadn't left Pastor Black "lookin' like a saint." Raven hated D.C., and getting rid of him a month from now wouldn't be soon enough. More important, she would never have to think about that lowlife thug again.

Chapter 31

*P*orsha couldn't have been happier. Fifty-two women had shown up for her first ministry meeting, and they all seemed just as excited as she was. Porsha was also elated to finally know, without a doubt, that God had called her to lead it. Actually, there had been a point when she'd been sure that He'd given her this assignment, but over the last few days she'd second-guessed herself. She'd done so because she was still fornicating. She'd stopped having an affair with Steve, but she was still sleeping with Dillon. She didn't want to but she also *did* want to, and she was having a hard time telling him no. It was difficult, and now she fully understood the scripture Mark 14:38, which talked about how the spirit was willing but the flesh was weak. In her heart and soul, she knew what she was doing was wrong, but when she and Dillon got together, she lost all control. She would try to tell herself that the last time truly *was* the last time, but then the next night she'd find herself in bed with him again.

So for this reason, she didn't see herself as the best

example, but she also knew her intentions for the ministry were sincere. She genuinely wanted to help other women—hopefully thousands at some point—and that had to count for something.

When everyone had settled into their seats, Porsha recited 1 John 4:7 as planned, and then she closed her eyes and prayed. When she finished, she smiled at the women. "Well, good evening, everyone."

"Good evening," they all replied, and Porsha loved that the ladies were of all ages. If she had to guess, she'd say they ranged anywhere from twenty to sixty.

"I was certainly hoping for a great turnout, but I never expected our first meeting to be so well attended. So thank you for taking time out of your busy schedules to support this," she said, pulling the cordless microphone from its holder and walking in front of the podium. "If you were here a couple of Sundays ago, then you heard me talk about why I thought this ministry was so important to create. But for those who weren't, I'll briefly share that information with you. To begin with, I mostly knew that the single women of this church needed a ministry that was designed just for them. We have our joint ministry for men and women, but that's not the same. So, I realized it was time we did something for women only. But even better than that, I know God called me to do this, and that's the most important thing about it. Plus, do we really want to talk about our monthly cycles or menopause with men in the room?"

Everyone laughed and chattered their opinions to one another.

"So again, I wanted us to have something for us. I wanted us to have one evening a month where we can come together and share our concerns. We can ask questions and find solutions to our problems," she said, walking over to a table next to the podium. There lay a stack of folders that contained three handouts, and now Porsha wished she'd asked Michelle to assist her. Although, with the way Michelle had been acting, she probably wouldn't have attended, anyway. The good news, however, was that Michelle had made sixty copies of each document, so there were more than enough.

Porsha walked to the far-left side of the room and gave a group of folders to the young woman sitting in the first seat in the front row. Then she did the same with the ladies who sat at the beginning of the two rows behind her. When they'd passed the folders down to the others and everyone had taken one, Porsha took the few extras and set them back on the table.

"There are three handouts inside. One explains our mission statement; the second is a contact form for you to fill out, just in case I need to communicate with you directly. And the third one has my office and cell phone numbers printed on it, along with my email address. So please feel free to use either at any time. My goal is to always have a certain topic to begin with, depending on what you all suggest for any given month. And I'll decide that topic based on the majority. You can email me your desired topic or leave a message at one of my numbers. But tonight, I'd like to make this more of an open forum where we can talk about anything we're currently dealing with or struggling with. I know it isn't always easy to discuss your problems in front of this many women—at least not until you all get to know each other a little better—but for those who do feel comfortable, I hope you will. I realize that some of you do know each other, but at some point, we'll begin having outings so that we can spend more time together."

The ladies seemed to be in agreement, so Porsha decided to break the ice with her own topic.

"I guess I'll go first. For me, as some of you heard me say two Sundays ago, I just want to find a good man who will love me as much as I love him. That's all I want, but for years I haven't been able to find someone like that. I have, of course, dated men who I was fully committed to, but they didn't feel the same. Or if they did, they couldn't keep it up for very long. They would claim they loved me, and then a few months later they would be gone," Porsha said, seeing many of the women nodding. "Although, I will admit," she continued, "that I haven't always dated men who were right for me. Sometimes I knew up front that I shouldn't get involved, but I did it anyway. Then, as expected, I ended up hurt and hoping once again to find someone to love me. But what I'm finally discovering now is that it can't be about what I want, it has to be about what God wants for me. He has to send me my soul mate, because He's really the only One who can. I say this because, let's face it, ladies, most of us probably haven't done that great of a job when it comes to choosing men. If we had, none of us would need to be here tonight."

They all laughed again.

"So, having said that, let me see by a show of hands how many women have never been married."

About 40 percent of the women raised their hands.

"And how many are divorced?"

Nearly 50 percent of the women put their hands up.

"And widowed?"

Now, the final three women raised their hands.

"It might seem interesting that the majority of the women here are divorced, but it just goes to show how so many women don't marry the man God has for them. It's the same as what I just described about myself with dating. But my hope is that this particular ministry will help turn things around for all of us."

Porsha walked closer to the front row.

"So now I'll give all of you a chance. And if you raise your hand, I'll bring the mic over to you. Also, please accept my apology for not having anyone here helping me and for not having more than one microphone. But as I said earlier, I just wasn't expecting so many of you to be here."

A twentysomething young woman raised her hand and stood up. "I don't have anything to share just yet, but I would love to help out next month if you need me."

"How very kind of you, and absolutely. What's your name?"

"Lisa Warren."

"Well, thank you, Lisa. I really appreciate it, and let's you and I get together when the meeting is over."

"Sounds good," she said, sitting back down.

Porsha scanned the room to see if anyone else wanted to speak.

A fortyish woman stood up, and Porsha walked the microphone over to her.

"Good evening," the woman said.

"Good evening," the ladies responded.

"My name is Tina Payne, and I first want to say how happy I am to be here tonight. So thank you, Minister Porsha, for making this happen for us."

Porsha smiled, but she also felt guilty again. Because the last thing she wanted was for these women to begin trusting her and confiding in her as a minister only to find out months down the road that she was a fraud. So even though she wouldn't break the news to them tonight, she was making a pact with herself right now. She would tell the entire congregation the truth before their next ministry meeting.

Porsha smiled. "You're quite welcome, Tina, and thank you for coming."

"So my problem is this," Tina said. "I'm forty-seven, but whenever I meet a man my age or even a little older, I find out pretty quickly that he wants a younger woman. And there was even a time when my oldest niece and I were out shopping, and a fifty-year-old man smiled and told her how beautiful she was. Then he asked her if she was married. I know he was fifty, because he was shopping for something to wear to his fiftieth birthday party. Oh, and in case you're wondering how old my niece is, she's only thirty."

"Oh my," Porsha said, and some of the other women snickered.

"I mean, so what are we as middle-aged women supposed to do? How are we going to find someone our age or even ten years older, if they're only looking for some sweet young thing? I don't mean any disrespect to our young ladies here tonight, but this is a real problem. I even have friends and coworkers who have shared similar stories with me."

Porsha agreed. "I've heard those stories as well, and I just don't understand some men. I think many of them get to a certain age, and they start acting as though they need to feel young again. And for whatever reason, they think a woman twenty years younger will do that for them."

"That's *exactly* what it is," another woman said. "I've had the same problem."

"It's definitely true," a thirtyish woman toward the front added. "I always have older men trying to talk to me. Which I have to say I don't mind at all, but it's very common."

Porsha realized she didn't really need the microphone, because the room was small enough for everyone to hear just fine. "This makes it very difficult for women who want to find men their age. But the good news is, your man is still out there. I really believe that, and we women just have to pray, ask God to help us, and then be patient. Because if the relationship isn't ordained by Him, it won't work out for us anyway."

"Thank you," Tina said, passing Porsha the microphone back.

"Anyone else?"

A woman who looked to be no more than twenty stood up. "Hi, my name is Jackie."

"Hi, Jackie," Porsha said.

"I'm a little nervous about saying this, but it's really bothering me so I just want to know your opinion."

"Go ahead," Porsha told her. "That's what this ministry is all about. Sharing and helping each other."

"Well, my parents taught me at a young age that it was wrong to have sex before marriage. But all the guys I meet expect me to do it. Then, when I tell them I can't, they want to know why. And I'm always honest about it. I tell them that it's a sin to fornicate."

"Good for you, Jackie," Porsha said, wishing she'd been as strong as this young lady during her college years, because that's when she'd lost her virginity. Not to mention, she'd been sleeping with men out of wedlock ever since.

"Well, I guess if you want to look at it that way," Jackie said. "I mean, I know living the way God wants us to live is the right thing to do, but it's also the reason I'm still single. Most guys just don't want to waste their time with a woman who isn't having sex with them. They're not willing to wait until marriage."

"Sweetheart, that's been true since the beginning of time," a woman who looked to be sixty said. "They want what they want, and if you don't give it to them, they disappear. Fast as a magician."

Even Jackie couldn't help laughing, and so did Porsha and the rest of the ladies.

"I am so sorry you're going through this," Porsha said, "but I think I speak for everyone by saying how proud we are of you."

All the ladies applauded.

"Because staying pure isn't the easiest thing for anyone to do," Porsha continued. "For a man or a woman."

"It's not," Jackie said. "And I have to constantly think about First Corinthians seven, nine. My mom taught it to me when I was twelve, and she told me to always meditate on it when I felt tempted. But I will say, there have been a few times when I didn't want to meditate on it, and I didn't want to focus on doing the right thing. I just wanted to do what all my girlfriends were doing with their boyfriends."

"I completely understand. But I also love that you brought this topic up, and that you had the courage to share your feelings about it. You're one of the youngest ladies in the room, if not *the* youngest, but we can all learn something from this. And if you don't mind, can you quote First Corinthians seven, nine for us? I'm sure many of us already know it, but I just think it would be good to hear it right now. And then for next month I'll include it on one of the handouts."

"Sure," Jackie said. "'But if they can't control themselves, they should go ahead and marry. It's better to marry than to burn with lust.'"

Porsha tried to keep a straight face, because as an assumed minister she knew this scripture should mean everything to her. She should be following God's Word as closely as she could, but she wasn't. Clearly He didn't expect anyone to be perfect, but when a person sinned, he or she was supposed to learn from it. Not commit the same sin all over again. And again. And again. That's not how Christians were meant to operate. This whole idea of sinning and repenting and never getting out of that same vicious cycle only led to trouble. It caused lots of uncertainty and unnecessary pain.

And Porsha should know because she was sleeping with Dillon every chance she got. But if a twenty-year-old could abstain, so could she. Dillon wouldn't like it, but he could either accept it or find someone else to sleep with. Because she couldn't keep doing this. Not anymore.

Chapter 32

Raven strolled into John's office and shut the door. Since it was Friday, she'd decided to dress down a bit and was wearing a thigh-length sleeveless blouse over a pair of dark-wash skinny jeans. Normally she dressed elegantly and professionally regardless of what day of the week it was, but now she was to the point where she did anything that might excite John. Over this last week, she'd seduced him in practically every way she knew how, and he'd loved every second of it. Raven had also successfully convinced him that she needed five hundred thousand dollars to oust Porsha instead of the original two.

She walked in front of his desk, leaned over it, and pecked him on his lips. Then she sat down in one of the chairs. "So how's everything going?"

"Very well. I've reviewed every account the church has, so now I just need to figure out which to transfer from. I also have to decide on the amounts, because not only do I not want to move five hundred at one time, I don't want to transfer more than fifty, either. But don't worry, everything will be fine."

Raven crossed her legs. "Good. Do you still think it'll take another couple of weeks or so?"

"Actually, no. More like a few days from now. Maybe even as early as next Tuesday or Wednesday."

"Really? That quick?"

"Yeah, and actually the sooner the better, because we have auditors coming in November."

This made Raven a little nervous. "That's only five months from now."

"Yeah, but your average income is about fifty thousand, so with you forgoing that for the next four months, we'll have the first two hundred paid back by October. That way, even if the auditors question the withdrawals and deposits, I'll have figured out a good explanation for the full amount by then."

Raven nodded like she was okay with what he was saying, but she wasn't. Yes, she'd told him she would pay all the money back; however, there was no way she was doing that. She was keeping that half million dollars he was embezzling, and when the time was right she would tell him. By then, he'd be so caught up with lust and the hope that they were going to be together forever, he would hurry to steal more money if she wanted him to.

"We should be good then," she said. "Everything will work just the way we planned it."

"It will."

"I really appreciate everything you're doing for me, because I know this isn't something you've done before."

"No, but when I told you that I would do anything for you, I meant it. Plus, I know you're only doing this to save the ministry."

"I am. I would never take hard-earned money from our members and online followers and not pay it back. Never."

John leaned back in his chair, staring at her.

"What's wrong?" she said.

"Nothing. Just admiring how beautiful you are and how much you love people. You're a good woman, and that's why I don't understand Kane. You know…why he slept with Porsha behind your back."

"Neither do I, but that's all in the past now."

"I still can't believe you confronted him and then broke up with him."

"Well, I did. He left me no choice, but everything happens for a reason."

"Why do you say that?"

"Because if he hadn't messed around on me, you and I wouldn't be together."

"This is true, but I'm still sorry that he hurt you the way he did."

Raven hunched her shoulders victim-style.

"And then there's Porsha," he said. "I can't believe her, either. It's bad enough that she slept with your ex-husband, but to sleep with someone else you cared about…that's major."

"Not everyone is your friend. Some women will do anything when it comes to getting a man."

"And you still haven't said anything to her?"

"No, and I'm not going to until my attorney sends over those legal documents. Then, once you transfer the money, I'm going to offer her a cashier's check in the amount of five hundred thousand dollars. This will be in exchange for her signing away all past, current, and future rights to NVCC and the overall ministry."

"Do you think she'll go down like that without a fight?"

"She will if she wants me to keep that video tucked away."

John shook his head, slightly chuckling. "I'm still stunned about that one."

"Actually, I'm being pretty nice, because I really don't have to give her a dime. But she did invest the initial money for me to start NVCC, and I'm just trying to do the right thing," Raven was sort of amazed herself at how easily and credibly she told lies. What was more astounding was the way John hung on her every word and believed everything she said. He would die if he knew the truth: that instead of offering Porsha a six-figure payout, Raven was going to blackmail her for three hundred thousand.

"Like I said, you're a good woman, and you'll be blessed for that."

"I definitely try to be, but all this betrayal and deceit comes with the territory. Pastors have a lot to deal with, but we have to forgive no matter what."

"I get that, but women like Porsha give women like you a very bad name. As it is, people are already leery about females being ministers and pastors."

"I know, but Porsha is who she is."

"Well, the good news is that she'll be out of here soon," John said. "You'll be able to pay her and call it a day."

"And I can't wait," she said, standing up. "Anyway, I'd better get back to my office so I can finish reviewing my sermon for Sunday."

John slid off his glasses, scooted his chair back, and walked around his desk. He pulled Raven into his arms and kissed her. "You have made me a very happy man, you know that?"

Raven looked up at him. "And you've made me a happy woman."

"Are you spending the night again?"

"I sure ammm," she sang.

"I hated for you to leave this morning, and now I wish I could wake up with you every day."

He was getting a little carried away, but Raven went along with his fantasy. "I know. Maybe in the future, though."

"You mean that?"

"Of course I do. Absolutely."

Raven had read through her sermon notes and made a few more revisions, and now she and Michelle were reviewing her upcoming travel schedule.

Michelle leaned toward Raven's desk. "Here's your event calendar for the remainder of the year. I'm sure you'll have other invites, but I don't think you should add on much more."

Raven scanned the document. "I agree. I purposely turned down everything for this month and next so I could enjoy the summer at home, but I didn't realize I'd said yes to so many fall engagements."

Michelle smiled. "Well, it's not like I didn't try to suggest otherwise."

Raven laughed. "I know, but I always think it'll be fine. Plus, I need the exposure."

"That's true, but you also need to find some balance between your travel, social media activity, and everything you do here at the church. We just need to figure out a better plan for you is all, and we will."

"You never cease to amaze me, and I truly appreciate you."

"Just trying to do my job. That's all."

"Well, as much as I hate to bring this up, it's time to handle that situation you and I talked about two weeks ago."

"You mean with Porsha?"

"Yes, and I finally figured out a way to get her out of here. And it won't be long, either. But because this whole plan is a bit complicated and unorthodox, the less you know the better."

"Okay, but just let me know if I can help."

"I will. My goal, though, is to keep you completely out of this. That way when Porsha is gone, your job won't be affected at all," Raven said, trying to convince Michelle that she was keeping her somewhat out of the loop as a way to protect her. But in reality, Raven was only hiding the details because she knew she was preparing to blackmail Porsha and also steal from the church, and she didn't want Michelle to know she was capable of such crimes.

Michelle didn't say anything, so Raven slightly changed the subject.

"So I hear a lot of women showed up last night for Porsha's new ministry. I saw one of our members at a coffee shop this morning, and she said her sister attended. She also said her sister couldn't wait for the next meeting."

Michelle set her notepad and pen on the edge of Raven's desk. "I saw a couple of comments on our web site, and I have to say, Porsha is very excited about this. It's the only thing she's had me working on for the last two weeks."

"Yeah, but if those women only knew who Porsha really was. If they knew about all those skeletons piled up in her closet, they wouldn't be so quick to support her."

"Well, just knowing that she's been smiling in my face all this time, knowing she doesn't like me, has really changed my feelings toward her. I have to force myself just to speak to her."

"I'm sorry that I even had to tell you about that, but you deserved to know," Raven said, and realized that this was the perfect moment to turn Michelle even further against Porsha. "And you also need to know this: When I was married to my ex-husband, she had an affair with him."

Michelle's eyes widened. "Please tell me you're kidding? Because if that's true, how did you become friends?"

"Because I have a huge heart, and even when people betray me I can't help forgiving them."

"Oh...my...goodness. How did you find out?"

"That's a long story, but just know that some people never change. And Porsha is one of them."

Michelle folded her arms. "And she calls herself a *minister*? She's fooling so many people. Innocent people right here at NVCC."

"Yeah, and I take full blame for that."

"Why? Because it's not like any of this is your fault."

"It sort of is, because I took money from her so I could start the ministry. Then I signed a lifetime financial agreement with her. I made a huge mistake, but it'll be fixed very soon."

"I sure hope so, because a woman like that shouldn't be here."

Michelle had lost all respect for Porsha, just like John had, and this was exactly what Raven had been hoping for. Not one but two NVCC staff members had turned on Porsha, and Porsha didn't even know it. This was only the beginning, though, and Raven wouldn't fully rest until she was gone. Permanently.

Chapter 33

D illon set two bags of food onto Porsha's granite-top island. Originally, he'd invited her out to a restaurant, but she just didn't think it was good for them to be seen in public yet. Maybe in the future, but certainly not before Porsha left NVCC and cut all ties with Raven. Plus, Steve had begun calling and leaving messages for her again this week, so she didn't want to take the chance of running into him, either. Especially since he'd called three to four times, both yesterday and the day before. On Monday and Tuesday he'd only tried to contact her once, but now the calls were coming more frequently and he left a message every time. But Porsha had deleted all of them without listening, and she was hoping he would finally leave her alone.

"Everything smells so good," she said.

"No one has better Italian than Gino's. Not in Mitchell, anyway."

Porsha lifted two house salads and two tiny foil-wrapped

loaves of bread from one bag, and two entrée containers from the other. "You're definitely right about that."

Dillon pulled a chair back and sat down, and Porsha removed the covers from their meals. Dillon had ordered chicken Florentine, and she'd gotten cheese ravioli with marinara sauce.

"You want anything to drink?" she asked, walking over to her stainless steel refrigerator.

"Just a bottle of water."

Porsha grabbed two of them and then sat across from Dillon. "You want to say grace?"

"I'll let you do it."

"Why do you always say that?"

"Because you're the minister."

"Yeah, but you used to be one, too. None of that matters, anyway, though. Anyone can say grace."

"Okay, fine," he agreed, reaching for her hand and closing his eyes. "Dear Heavenly Father, thank you for this time of fellowship and for the food we're about to receive. We ask that You let it serve as nourishment for our bodies, and we thank You for the people who prepared it. We ask these and all other blessings in Your Son Jesus's name. Amen."

"Amen," Porsha said, opening her eyes. "Now, was that so hard?"

"No, not at all."

"Well then, from now on we'll just take turns. Sometimes you'll do it, and sometimes I will."

"Fair enough," he said, forking out some of his chicken

and setting it on his plate. "So have you gotten any more feedback about your ministry meeting?"

"I did. Remember when I was telling you last night that one of the young women offered to help me?"

"Yep."

"Well, two others called me this afternoon to volunteer as well."

"That's great."

Porsha ate some of her buttered garlic bread. "I also received a voice message from a woman asking if we could talk about oral sex the next time."

Dillon raised his eyebrows. "Really? Did she say why?"

"She did. She wants to know if it's okay to have oral sex with your spouse or if it's a lustful sin. She said that when she was married, she never felt comfortable doing that with her husband, and it was one of the reasons he left her. And they didn't really have other problems."

"Well, I know everyone thinks differently, but can you blame him? I mean, when you're married you should be able to pleasure each other any way you want."

"Yeah, but I don't think a man should leave his wife just because she won't do everything he wants in bed. Marriage is a two-way street, and both parties should agree on their levels of intimacy."

"Maybe, but all I'm saying is that I don't believe it's a sin, and there's nothing wrong with it."

"I don't believe it's a sin, either—not if you're speaking about a husband and wife who took vows before God—but it's still a decision you have to make together. I mean, maybe all she needed was for him to be a little patient. But either way, I think it's too bad that they didn't sit down with a good Christian counselor and try to work things out."

Dillon drank some of his water. "Well, I know one thing. I would love to be a fly on the wall at your next meeting."

"It's definitely not the most comfortable subject to talk about, because some people will think like the woman who called me, and some will think like we do. But then, who are we to judge either of them, because we're fornicating every day now," she said, trying to build the courage to tell him that she'd made the decision to become abstinent.

Dillon looked at her and then ate more of his entrée, but he didn't acknowledge her comment.

Porsha bit a piece of her ravioli.

"So what's Raven up to these days?" he asked. "Trying to find a new prominent pastor to slander?"

"I hope not, and to be honest, I'm still shocked that she said so many great things about your dad. I know you guys wanted her to clear his name, but she went above and beyond."

"Yeah, which is why it's almost too good to be true. Raven never does anything without some ulterior motive. So I'm wondering what else she's up to."

"Let's just assume that she's done doing that kind of thing."

"Yeah, well, I'll say this again, and I'm going to keep saying it until you hear me: You need to be careful."

"We don't even really communicate anymore," Porsha

admitted to Dillon for the first time. "Only if we have to, but that's pretty much it."

"And why is that?"

"We just don't. Things are very different with us these days."

"And that's why you'd better start watching your back. Raven will stab you multiple times before you even realize it. She wasn't like that when we were married, but once she filed for divorce I saw a side of her that I never knew existed. She fights dirty, and she has no remorse behind it. I know having two affairs on her was wrong, but Raven doesn't like to lose at anything. And as much as I hate to bring this up, she still has that video of you and me."

"I know, but I try not to think about it. And I'm hoping that if she was going to use it, she would've done it already."

"I thought she was going to threaten me with it during our divorce proceedings, but you know why she didn't, right?"

"No, why?"

"Because you were her money source. You helped her get her ministry up and running, and she didn't want to make waves with you. So believe me when I tell you, that's the only reason the world hasn't seen you and me having sex."

"I hate that I ever made that video. It's one thing I would do over if I could."

"It's partly my fault, too, because I know you only did it when you found out about Taylor."

"Still, I wish I hadn't because if Raven ever sends that video to the wrong people, we will never live it down."

When they finished eating, Dillon leaned back in his chair, patting his stomach. "That was good."

"So was mine," Porsha said, standing and covering their leftovers.

Dillon got up, too, walked around the island, and pulled Porsha into his arms.

"What are you doing?" she said, smiling.

"You know what, and you also know what I want."

Porsha could already feel her flesh weakening. When she'd gotten home last night from the ministry meeting, Dillon had wanted to come over, but she'd explained how tired she was. He hadn't liked her response, but thankfully, he'd told her to get some rest and he would just see her this evening. But now, he was kissing her up and down her neck and caressing her body. He was driving her crazy.

"No, don't," she said, pressing her hands against his chest.

"Why? What's wrong?"

Porsha took a deep breath. "Dillon, I'm sorry, but we need to talk."

"Now? About what?"

"Let's just sit down."

"Whoa, this must be serious," he said as they sat across from each other.

"It is," she told him, remembering the talk she'd had with Steve last week—which hadn't gone very well. He hadn't been happy about her decision, and although her situation with Dillon was very different, she knew he wouldn't be happy, either. But all she could do was try.

"So I know we're trying to get our relationship back on track, and that we've been having a lot of sex."

"We've been making love," he quickly corrected her. "And there's a difference."

"Okay, I'll give you that. When I'm with you, it does feel like we're making love, but it's also wrong."

Dillon shook his head and dropped it backward, sighing. He was clearly annoyed.

"I know you don't like what I'm saying, but I don't want to keep committing a sin I feel guilty about."

"But baby, nobody's perfect. You know that, right?"

"I do know. But I'm still trying to be a better person, and I need you to be okay with that."

"I don't know what to say."

"Say you love me enough to be abstinent."

"That's a lot to ask."

"Are you saying you don't think fornicating is wrong?"

"Of course I know it's wrong. I told you I'm not the same person I used to be, and I've made a lot of changes. I don't do most of the things I used to do, but not being able to make love to you is a bit much."

"Well, if I'm going to lead a women's ministry, I need to do what's right. If I'm encouraging other single women to abstain, then I have to do it as well. I don't want to be a hypocrite."

Dillon looked at her. "So what does this mean exactly?"

"That we can't have sex."

"I know, but what *can* we do? Kiss? Caress each other? What?"

"As long as it doesn't go any further. Which means we should probably leave the caressing part out."

"So basically, kissing is it then?"

"I know you don't like this, and I'm sorry."

"We'll make it work."

"Are you sure? Because I don't want you to agree to something you can't keep up. I won't tolerate you messing around elsewhere."

"That's the least of my thoughts. I told you that I love you, and I meant that."

"I love you, too," she said before she could stop herself. Ever since they'd started seeing each other again, she'd purposely not told him because she was afraid of being hurt. "So now that we have an understanding about that, why don't you let me clear the food away. Then we can relax in the family room."

"We can do that."

Porsha got back up, but then she realized the food was still too warm to put in the refrigerator. So she gathered their plates and utensils and carried them over to the sink. But as she turned to look back at the island, Dillon stood close behind her and wrapped his arms around her waist. She hadn't even seen him get up.

He kissed her neck again, and she leaned away from him.

"Dillon, don't," she said.

Now he turned her around and pressed her more against the counter. "Baby, please. Just this one last time."

"No."

Dillon ignored her resistance and kissed her deeply on her lips—and she felt her body weakening again. Before long, she kissed him back and gave up trying to stop him. She knew she would hate herself when this was over, but she couldn't pretend she didn't want it. She still knew it was wrong, but the more Dillon kissed her and touched her, the more she lost self-control. She fell totally in sync with all that he was doing to her, and now they were headed upstairs to her bedroom. But this would be the last time. Until she got married.

Chapter 34

It was only six a.m., but Porsha was already up on her treadmill, crying a flood of tears and watching Pastor Gwyn Shepherd. She'd tried her best not to sleep with Dillon last night, and just as she'd thought, she sorely regretted that she had. After leaving the women's ministry meeting on Thursday, she'd decided to abstain from having sex, but just one day later she'd failed at it. She had allowed lust to outweigh her conscience and the stance she was trying to take against fornication. But this time, she'd extended her sin even further—she'd allowed Dillon to spend the night, and he was still upstairs, sleeping. This worried her, because if she didn't stop what she was doing, the next thing she knew they'd be living together. Shacking up as though there was nothing wrong with it and forgetting about what was important.

Porsha wiped her face with both hands and tried to settle down. Then she turned up the volume on the television. Not so loud that it would wake Dillon, but to a level where she could hear Gwyn's sermon over her treadmill.

"One of the toughest things Christian single men and women deal with is fornication," Gwyn said, and Porsha knew she hadn't turned on the television by mistake. She also knew that whenever God gave you what you needed—*when* you needed it—coincidence had nothing to do with it. Everything with God was always on purpose and timely.

Gwyn swiped her tablet screen and then looked out at her audience. "This is the reason I love James, chapter four, verses seven through ten, which says, 'So humble yourselves before God. Resist the devil, and he will flee from you. Come close to God, and God will come close to you. Wash your hands, you sinners; purify your hearts, for your loyalty is divided between God and the world. Let there be tears for what you have done. Let there be sorrow and deep grief. Let there be sadness instead of laughter, and gloom instead of joy. Humble yourselves before the Lord, and he will lift you up in honor.'

"This passage says everything. It outlines the struggle of trying to do right but ultimately doing wrong. Then, when we're talking about sex before marriage, sometimes men can feel weaker when it comes to abstaining, and women have to set the example. You have to stick to your values and uphold your decision. Keep your promise to God. Because let's face it, He didn't create His Ten Commandments just for the sake of doing so. He created them so we would abide by them. And, of course, when we don't, there can be a serious price to pay—especially when you commit a sin and you know it's a sin, yet you continue doing it anyway. You end up reaping what you sow in one way or another. Plus, there's something else you need to remember. If a man truly loves you and respects your wishes about not having sex before marriage, he won't keep pressuring you about it. He won't ask you to do something that goes against your Christian beliefs."

Porsha heard everything Gwyn was saying and felt as though her spirit was being renewed with every word. Yes, she'd backslid again with Dillon last night, but no more. She was so much better than that. And her mind was made up about something else: She couldn't put off confessing to the congregation about her selfish and ungodly reasons for becoming a minister.

Porsha raised the incline on her treadmill, feeling energized and hopeful. Then, surprisingly, her doorbell rang. She frowned because rarely did anyone drop by unannounced this early on a Saturday morning. But maybe it was one of her neighbors and something was wrong.

So she muted her television, paused her workout program, and went to the front door. But when she looked through the frosted-glass window, she saw Steve. He saw her, too, and she thought she would pass out.

He beat on her door multiple times and rang her bell like an unruly child. "Open up this door, Porsha!"

Porsha slowly backed away, praying he would leave. But he didn't.

"I knew this was the reason you started acting like you didn't want me anymore. Now, open up this door!"

Porsha moved closer to one of the entryway walls, still wishing he would go away.

"And I know you...got all my...messages," he said, slurring his words and staggering. "I know you did, but now you're laying up with some...new man. Open up! Open this door, so I can see who this nobody is. Why don't you...let me see the competition?"

Porsha had never known him to drink so much as wine, but he was completely intoxicated.

Steve rang the bell again—repeatedly—and slammed his fist against the door.

Porsha stepped back into the entryway. "Steve, please go home. I'm begging you."

"Why? So you can keep disrespecting me with another man? You're my woman."

"I'm not, Steve, and you know it. Now, please leave."

Steve punched the door again. "You're nothing but a lying whore...pretending to be all God-fearing. And you... call yourself...a minister. Please."

Porsha heard Dillon rushing down the stairs, and she closed her eyes with worry. This was the very thing she'd been afraid of, and she wished Steve had left when she'd asked him.

"Who's out there keeping up all that commotion?" he said. "This early in the morning?"

Porsha couldn't speak even if she wanted to. Because not only hadn't she wanted Dillon and Steve to meet, she also hadn't wanted Dillon finding out that she'd been seeing a married man. Dillon already knew she'd slept with him when he'd been married to Raven, but she still didn't want him knowing she'd continued doing that kind of thing. She was so embarrassed.

"Baby, who is that?" Dillon asked again.

"Oh, so there he is!" Steve said. "And maybe since your little whore won't let me in, you will."

Dillon brushed past Porsha and reached for the door-knob.

But she grabbed him by his arm with both hands. "Dillon, please don't."

"Why? Who is it? The guy you told me you were seeing?"

Porsha just stared at him, because even though she'd broken up with Steve, she'd never mentioned that to Dillon. She'd simply wanted to forget about that whole relationship. But now here he was, bright and early, causing a scene for her and her neighbors.

"Look," Dillon said, "I'm either opening the door and dealing with this fool, or I'm calling the police."

"No," Porsha pleaded. "Maybe he'll just leave on his own."

"Baby, he's drunk. Can't you see that? And he's obviously not happy about you having another man in here. So trust me, he's not going anywhere."

"You trick-whore," Steve yelled. "After I went to my wife this week and asked for a divorce, this is how you do me? This is how you treat me...when you kept claiming you loved me?"

Dillon looked at Porsha, seemingly unfazed by what Steve had just said, and reached for the doorknob again.

But Porsha stopped him—again. "Let's just go into the family room. Because eventually he'll get in his car and leave."

"And what if he doesn't?"

"He will," she said, silently praying that she was right and leading Dillon down the hallway.

But the next thing they heard was a loud crash and glass shattering in the living room. And when they rushed in there, they saw a large landscaping rock that Steve had likely taken from Porsha's yard. Porsha and Dillon now hurried to the front door, but Steve was already getting in his car and starting it up. Within seconds he sped off, and Porsha was relieved. Until they heard another crash and saw that Steve had slammed his car into a stop sign.

Dillon looked at Porsha. "That's it. I'm calling the police, whether you like it or not. Before this fool kills somebody."

Porsha didn't even bother arguing with him, because she knew it had to be done. Steve was highly intoxicated and driving around like he was sober. He was a total mess, and he had to be stopped. Not later today or tomorrow, but now.

Chapter 35

aven could still see the excitement on Porsha's face, and it made her sick. This morning, they'd all attended their usual weekly staff meeting, and Porsha hadn't hesitated to share how successfully *her* first ministry meeting had gone. She'd talked about the number of women who'd shown up and how they were already looking forward to next month. Raven hadn't smiled, asked any questions, or commented, and all Porsha's great *news* had done was make Raven want to kick her out of NVCC even faster. And thanks to John, she would be able to confront Porsha tomorrow.

This one thought alone tickled Raven with joy, because everything was finally going to be hers. Keeping the money that John had transferred to her this afternoon was major in itself, but now Porsha's fifty-thousand-dollar-per-month cut would be hers as well—which meant that for the first time in Raven's life, she would know what it felt like to earn seven figures. Her annual income would rise to

$1.2 million, and with as popular as she was becoming, she would soon earn far more than that.

Raven had been very smart about the way she'd run the ministry, and all her hard work was paying off. This also meant that she could now resume her romance with Kane. She knew it wouldn't be easy, but in a matter of days Kane would give in. He would come back to her the way he always had.

Raven curled up on her sofa and dialed his number.

"Hello?" he answered.

"Hi. How are you?"

"Okay, I guess."

Raven waited for him to say more, but he didn't.

"So I'm sure you're a little surprised to hear from me," she said.

"Actually, I am."

"Have you missed me?"

"Not really."

"Not even a little?"

"Raven, what is it you want?"

She tried to think of something better to say, but she couldn't. "You're still upset, aren't you?"

"Why are you asking me stupid questions?"

"I'm just trying to talk to you. Trying to call a truce."

"Why? You have time for me now? You want sex? What?"

"That's not fair, and you know it. I was wrong. I admit that, but I'm also sorry about what happened. I never should've acted the way I did."

"But you do this all the time. If you don't get your way or

I disagree with something you're doing, you go off. Or like this time, you break up with me."

"I know, and again, I'm sorry. Sometimes I don't think rationally, and I lose it. Running a church is hard enough, but running an entire ministry is very stressful. You know that, Kane. You've always known it."

"Yeah, but ministry or not, I'm not going to let you treat me any way you want. I'm also never going to be your yes man. I won't stand idly by, watching you do awful things to people."

Raven wished he would get off his soapbox and just get over it. "I'm not asking you to do that. I'm just trying to explain why I do some of the things I do."

"Well, that's not good enough anymore. I need something different in a woman."

Raven wondered how long it was going to take for him to get beyond this. "Are you saying you want someone else?"

"Right now, I just want to be left alone."

"Why are you so bitter? I made a mistake, Kane. That's all."

"You're always making mistakes, and then you expect me to forgive you and be happy. Well, I've told you before how I'm getting tired of that. And I meant it."

"Baby, you're scaring me," she told him, realizing now that it was time she said whatever he needed to hear. "Please don't tell me that in just two weeks, you've fallen out of love with me. That you've decided you're done with me for good. Please tell me that's not true."

"I've just had enough. I don't like this roller coaster ride we're on, and I want off."

"What can I do to change your mind?"

"Go on with your life. Find someone who you really love and care about. Continue to do you."

Raven knew he was purposely reminding her of what she'd said to him the last time she saw him. That she was always going to do *her*. And she'd be lying if she said that anyone would ever be more important than she was to herself. But she also didn't want to lose Kane. She loved him — as much as she could love another person — and she wanted them to work things out.

"But what if I don't want that?" she said. "What if I don't want to find someone else? What if I only want you?"

"Then you'll just have to get over it."

At first Raven had thought he would eventually soften up, but he was sounding as though their breakup was permanent.

"I'll do anything," she pleaded. "Anything at all."

Kane laughed, but she could tell he was being cynical. "Your dramatics aren't going to cut it this time. I'm really done with you, Raven."

Gosh, he wasn't budging, and this was so unlike him. Maybe they'd broken up and gotten back together more times than she'd realized, and Kane was at his limit. "What if I worked really hard to prove to you how much I love you? What if I show you that I can really change for the better?"

"Look, I just got home from work about an hour ago,

and I haven't eaten. So we'll have to do this another time."

Raven swung her feet to the floor. "Baby, please. I really mean it. I'll do whatever you want."

"You know what? I believe you, because you've done it before. But you can't keep it up. You do things, I forgive you, you become the most loving woman in the world, and then you go back to being the same old selfish Raven. You do that because, sweetheart, it's just who you are."

"But I can change. What if we get counseling and then get married?"

Kane laughed again. "You're really reaching this time, aren't you?"

"No, I'm serious. I mean, this all started because you wanted me to tell everyone that Pastor Black didn't rape me. And I did, Kane. I did what you wanted."

"Yeah, but only when you got good and ready. I also wonder why you suddenly came down with a huge case of niceness."

"So you don't think my message was sincere? You think I did this because I had to?"

"I don't know anything. Who's to say?"

Raven shook her head and burst into tears. She didn't want to cry right now, but she couldn't stop herself. "Why are you doing this?"

"Because I deserve better."

"And I can give you that. I didn't realize things were this bad, but I promise you I can fix them."

"I have to go."

"Well...can I at least call you later?"

"If you want, but I probably won't answer. I have an early day tomorrow."

"Kane, it's only ten after six."

"And?"

"Okay, fine. I'll call you, and if you answer you answer. But I'm not giving up."

"That's up to you. I'll talk to you later."

"Good-bye, baby," she said, and set her phone on the large square leather ottoman in front of her.

This call with Kane hadn't gone nearly the way she'd hoped. Sure, she'd expected some resistance, but not a full refusal to reconcile. He'd been angry and disappointed with her before, but never like this. He sounded so burned out from all that had transpired in their relationship. Raven knew things hadn't been perfect, but for the first time, she realized how miserable she'd made Kane. He'd loved her and treated her better than any woman could hope for, but she'd never fully appreciated it. Now she was on the verge of losing him for good. Or at least that's what it seemed like, because Raven would never let that happen. She wasn't a quitter, and she would keep at him until he took her back. She would love him the way he wanted her to, and she would finally marry him. All she had to do was finalize things with Porsha, hire a few new staff members, and focus on Kane. Then all would be well and Kane would be happy. She would be happy, too.

Raven went upstairs and washed her face and then toned and moisturized it. But for some reason, she thought about

John and wanted to double check with him about that transfer. So she dialed his number.

"Hey, baby," he said.

"Hey, how's it going?"

"Just missing you. Wishing you were here or that I was over there."

"I know, but I'm really tired and I need to prepare my mind for tomorrow."

"Well, everything is all set."

"You really stepped up for me, John, and I'll never forget it. You went completely out on a limb to help me, and I'm truly grateful."

"I would do it again if it meant preserving the ministry."

"You're a sweetheart."

"Yeah, I know," he said, laughing. "But how do you plan on handling this? Are you going to call Porsha at home tomorrow evening or meet with her before then at the church?"

"I'm doing it face-to-face. That way I can explain my separation offer, and she'll know I'm serious."

"I hope she agrees to it, signs everything, and leaves without drama."

"Don't worry. She will. Because having that video floating around for everyone to see would ruin her," Raven said, but then a thought surfaced, one that gave her a bit of pause. If for some reason Porsha did pass on her offer, Raven would have to think twice about actually releasing that video to the media because Dillon also starred in the performance. And if she crossed Dillon again, he would rush to get new revenge.

But truthfully, she wasn't worried about that happening, because Porsha *would* sign the agreement and give Raven the three hundred thousand dollars she was demanding. She would bring her a cashier's check, and that would be it. End of story. End of everything.

Chapter 36

Four days had passed, yet the fiasco from Saturday still upset Porsha. She hadn't seen it coming, and while Steve had never been fine with ending their relationship, Porsha was shocked about his getting stone drunk and then showing up at her house. Worse, he'd become indignant and destructive and had broken her window. But what bothered her more was the fact that he'd called her a whore three separate times. He'd turned into someone she hadn't known, and she'd wondered if he would ever leave. But sadly, when he had, he'd crashed his vehicle, had gotten arrested, and had been charged with a DUI. After Dillon had called 911, he and Porsha had watched the police pull up, handcuff Steve, and take him away. It had proven to be a pitiful sight, and now Porsha regretted not answering his calls last week. Maybe if she had, she would've been able to reason with him—make him see that their breaking up had been best for everyone involved. Maybe if she'd listened to even one of his messages, she might've heard the desperation in his voice. There was a chance that if she'd called him back, maybe they could have talked things through, and Steve never would have gotten drunk and gone driving at all.

But either way, the disaster on Saturday had opened her eyes, and she now knew for sure that Gwyn Shepherd had been right. When a person didn't abide by God's rules, there was a serious price he or she ended up paying. In Porsha's case, she'd helped ruin another woman's marriage—causing her husband to ask her for a divorce—and Porsha would have to live with that reality forever. In her heart of hearts, though, she hoped that Steve and his wife would find their way back to each other and fall more in love than they'd ever imagined.

Porsha tried to settle her thoughts so she could concentrate on a few ministry items she was working on. But as soon as she did, she heard knocking.

"Yes?" she said.

Raven walked in with a folder full of documents and closed the door behind her. Normally she would have asked Porsha if she was busy or had a minute, but not today.

Porsha sat up straight but didn't say anything.

Raven sat down without being asked. "So here's the deal. This agreement of ours isn't working anymore."

"Meaning?"

"This so-called partnership. It has to end."

Porsha crossed her arms. "And how do you expect that to happen? You paying me out?"

Raven slid the folder across Porsha's desk. "No, honey, quite the opposite."

Porsha opened it and scanned the first few pages. "This states that I'd be signing away all claims to New Vision Ministries, Inc., and all its entities."

"Exactly. All you need to do is sign each of the signature pages, and Michelle can notarize them."

Porsha half smiled. "Surely you don't expect me to walk away with nothing."

Raven's eyes turned cold. "I do, and you will."

Porsha just looked at her, and although she'd already made up her mind to leave the ministry at some point, she hadn't expected this. Raven had actually gone behind her back and had legal papers drawn up. It was true that only days ago Porsha had decided that if walking away from the ministry meant losing all her financial benefits, it wouldn't change her mind. Because in all honesty, she didn't care about the money as much as she did about distancing herself from Raven. But seeing these documents made this much more real, and she was appalled by Raven's audacity.

"Have you forgotten how you started this ministry?" Porsha asked her.

"I know exactly how."

"Then you must know that I'll need to be paid something."

"That's not going to happen, but let me tell you what is. You're going to sign those documents and bring me a cashier's check in the amount of three hundred thousand dollars."

Porsha laughed at her, but deep down she already knew

where this conversation was going. She knew Raven was planning to blackmail her. Porsha and Dillon had both wondered if this day would come, but they'd never discussed it until last Friday. Now Raven was doing exactly what they'd hoped she wouldn't.

Porsha tried to mask her shaken spirit. "So let me get this right. You're asking *me* to leave with no payout, and you want me to give *you* three hundred thousand dollars?"

"I'm not asking anything. I'm telling you."

"Well, that's not going to happen," Porsha said, still trying to disguise how panicked she was.

"It will, and I'll expect my money by Friday. That gives you two days and plenty of time to get it," Raven said, standing up. "And if you don't, that porn video of you and Dillon will go viral in a matter of minutes."

Porsha didn't bother saying another word, and Raven walked out of her office just as calmly as she'd strolled in. She held her head very high, and she seemed almost proud about what she was doing. She was as evil as Dillon had claimed, and Porsha had to call him now to warn him. She had to fill him in and try to figure out how they were going to stop his ex-wife.

Porsha left the church right away and hurried over to Dillon's. She'd known this sex video of theirs might come back to haunt them one day, but she hadn't thought it would be this afternoon. She also hadn't expected Raven to literally try to oust her from the ministry with no claim to anything. Porsha hadn't read all of the documents or even the first few of them thoroughly, but Raven had already confirmed that Porsha would leave with nothing. After all she'd done for Raven, this was the thanks she got. Although, the truth about the evolution of their friendship couldn't be ignored. Porsha was guilty of sleeping with Dillon, and it had been a miracle that Raven had forgiven her. But Porsha also knew that her money had been Raven's motivator. She hadn't cared about Porsha's affair with Dillon, not once she'd discovered that Porsha could help her get what she needed. It took money to start a church—at least on the level Raven had wanted to—and Porsha had willingly invested every cent. Porsha had thought she was making up for the affair she'd had with Dillon, and that Raven was being sincere about their friendship. But over the last year, and more noticeably over the last month, Raven had changed. She almost seemed to despise Porsha, and now Porsha wondered if Raven had told Michelle something awful about her. Then, yesterday during the staff meeting, Porsha had noticed that John had barely spoken to her as well. Which was strange, because he was one of the kindest, most decent men she knew.

When Porsha pulled into Dillon's driveway, she got out and walked up to his door.

He opened it immediately and hugged her.

Porsha wasn't sure why, but as she lay in Dillon's arms, she wanted to cry. Finally, she did and she knew it was because all her past sins were being exposed, and it was time to pay the consequences.

They sat down on the sofa, and Dillon shook his head in

disgust. "I knew it was only a matter of time. I told you how that witch was."

"I know, but I'm the one who gave her that disc in the first place. I never, ever should've done that."

"Baby, please just stop. I know you wish you could change that, but you can't. So now we just have to stand up to Raven."

"How?"

"We have to call her bluff."

"And take the chance of her leaking that video everywhere? No, Dillon, I just don't want that."

"So you'd rather let her swindle you out of three hundred thousand dollars? Isn't that the amount you told me on the phone?"

"It's not like I have a choice."

"You do have a choice."

"Well, unless you know something I don't then I'm withdrawing the money in the morning. She gave me until Friday, but I'm taking care of this as soon as possible."

"No, you're not. You have to give me a chance to figure this out. Handle it another way."

"What can you do?"

"You just have to trust me."

"And what if you don't come up with anything?"

"Then you can pay her the money. But at least give me until Friday afternoon. Just forty-eight hours."

"I don't know."

Dillon pulled her close and kissed her on her forehead. "It'll be fine. It has to be."

Porsha didn't like taking a chance on what Dillon *might* be able to do. She wanted guarantees. She wanted to know for sure that this threat would go away.

"I really just want to end this."

"I know you do, but have you thought about what else could happen?"

"Such as?"

"Who's to say that Raven still won't leak the video? Because even if you ask her for it, you can bet she has other copies."

Actually, Porsha had thought about that very thing, but it wasn't as though she could do anything about it.

"What a nightmare," she finally said.

"I know, but we'll get through this. That I can promise you."

"These have been some of the worst few days of my life. First that disaster with Steve and now this."

"It's been interesting for sure, but like I just said, we'll get through this. You're my girl, and I'm with you all the way."

Porsha turned toward him. "Are you sure?"

"Of course I am."

"Even with us not having sex? Because I'm really serious about that, Dillon."

He sighed. "I won't lie, that's going to be hard. But I won't ask you to do something you don't feel comfortable with anymore."

"Well, if you don't think you'll be able to deal with it, you need to be honest. That way, we can go our separate ways."

"That's not happening. I really do love you, Porsha, and I know you love me. So that's that. Plus, just as soon as I can get you to trust me again, we'll be getting married, anyway."

"Yeah, okay, Dillon."

"You think I'm joking, but I'm dead serious. I've already told my dad about us, and when this Raven drama gets straightened out I want you to meet him. And the rest of my family."

Porsha gazed into his eyes. "You're serious, aren't you?"

"I've never been more serious about anything. My past isn't pretty, but I'm not the person I used to be. I know I keep telling you that, but it's true. I did some awful things to my brother and my father, but all I wanted was for them to love me. I wanted to be accepted and treated like the rest of my siblings."

"I get that, and I'm glad you finally know what that feels like. There's nothing like having a close family, and there's not a day that goes by when I don't wish my parents were here. My mom and dad were my world, and sometimes I feel completely lost without them," Porsha said, tearing up. "It's so hard."

"Well, with my mom dying when I was a baby I never got to know her, but I loved my aunt who raised me with all my heart. I think about her all the time, and I'll never stop missing her."

Porsha tried to stop herself, but she laid her head against Dillon's chest and bawled. She knew that things wouldn't always be this bad for her, so she prayed for God to give her strength in the meantime. That way even if Dillon couldn't fix this thing with Raven, Porsha would tell her to do what she had to. Because at this very moment, Porsha had decided that she would much rather get this over with now, versus waiting to see if Raven might try to blackmail her again years down the road. So no, she wouldn't pay her three hundred thousand dollars. She would stop trying to cover up her deepest secrets and would face her consequences. It was the only way to handle this blackmail scheme — that is, unless Dillon came through with another alternative.

Chapter 37

Raven replayed the horrified look on Porsha's face and laughed out loud. Even with all of Porsha's millions, Raven had brought her to her knees. Of course, Porsha had tried to act as though she wasn't fazed by Raven's demands, but Raven knew she was scared solid. She'd been caught terribly off guard, and Raven had enjoyed seeing her squirm. That was what she got, though, for sleeping with Dillon behind Raven's back and then thinking she could make decisions about NVCC. If Raven had said it once, she'd said it ten thousand times: New Vision Christian Center and New Vision Ministries, Inc., belonged to her and only her. Sharing any control or decision-making wasn't an option, but Porsha obviously hadn't gotten that memo because she'd begun incorporating whatever she wanted. But that was okay, because Raven had figured out a genius way to fix her for good. Porsha would pay that money, pack her office up, and never show her face at NVCC again. And if it was possible, Raven would make sure she never used the name Daughters of Ruth again, either.

Yes, the whole single women's ministry idea had been all Porsha's, but she'd started that ministry at Raven's church. So Raven felt as though she owned it. But she also knew that names of churches and titles couldn't be copyrighted, so there was no sense thinking about it.

If she could, though, she would ruin Porsha to the point where no church would have her; something that would be easy to accomplish if she released that video. But it was like she'd already concluded before, starting a new war with Dillon and his family wasn't worth it. Although, if she wanted she could probably find a good film editor who could shadow Dillon's face and show only Porsha's. But instead, Raven would be nice and have mercy on her—if she paid that three hundred thousand dollars and signed every single one of those documents.

Raven wrapped her hair up with a silk scarf and climbed into bed. It was only nine o'clock, but she'd showered and slipped on her pajamas an hour ago. Part of her had hoped she might be able to go see Kane, but when she'd called him earlier he hadn't picked up. He also hadn't answered when she'd phoned him back last night.

But now she tried him again.

"Yeah?" he finally said after four rings.

"Is that how you answer the phone now?"

"Raven, why are you calling me?"

"I told you yesterday. I'm not giving up."

"Well, I wish you would."

"Kane, every couple has problems."

"Yeah, but not these kind. And if they do, more power

to them. Because I'm not living like this for the rest of my life."

"Like what?"

"With a woman who only cares about herself. What she can get. Who she can use. How much fame she can drum up. And let's not forget, how much money she can accumulate."

"Why are you being so cruel?"

"I'm not. I'm being real."

"But that's not who I am. I mean, I do want to grow the ministry to the highest level it can be, but I'm not selfish."

"Yeah, you keep right on thinking that. And anyway, what part of growing the ministry do you think is most important? Or do you even think about things like that?"

"I don't get what you mean."

"Just what I said."

"You're confusing me, and what's with all these crazy questions?"

"They're not crazy. I just want to know how much your growing the ministry has to do with people. Like for example, are you really doing this to help God's children? Are you really concerned about souls being saved? Or do you only care about the tithes and offering contributions they give?"

Raven's mouth flew open. "Wow. Just wow. Is that really what you think of me?"

"Why can't you just answer my questions?"

"Because they don't make sense. They're foolish and uncalled for."

"Yeah, well, I'm sure they are—to you, anyway. And to be honest, your lack of response says everything. It shows exactly how self-centered you are."

Raven had never heard Kane use such a nasty tone with her before, and for the first time, she had a feeling that this truly was the end for them.

"Maybe I should give you some space and call you in a few days," she said.

"Don't bother."

"Do you hate me that much?"

"I do."

"Why?"

"Because this whole time you and I have been together, I never cheated on you once."

Raven squinted her eyes. "Yeah, and I've never cheated on you, either."

"Really?"

"Yeah, really," she said, wondering what he knew.

"So I guess you've been spending all that time at John's for no reason? Ever since you and I had that big blow-up."

Raven tried to conjure a quick lie, but nothing came out.

"Yeah, that's right. I followed you to his house one evening, and then I drove by there again on a few other days close to midnight—and your car was still there. So don't even try to deny it. Don't say anything. Just make this your last time calling me. And if you call me again, I'm blocking your number."

"Oh my God, Kane—" she said, attempting to explain.

But he hung up before she could finish her sentence.

Raven closed her eyes and covered them with her hands. How had she let something like this happen? And been so careless? She'd spent so much time giving John what he wanted in the bedroom so he could transfer that money to her that she hadn't covered her tracks. But to be honest, she hadn't worried about Kane following her because he wasn't that kind of man. He was mature and confident, and he never resorted to anything petty. He certainly had never spied on her before or even acted as if he wanted to. Until now.

Still, it was shocking, and she knew she had to end things with John quickly and carefully. She'd planned on doing that anyway, but she'd also decided that at the very least, she'd be able to keep him on as her CFO. But that whole idea had become null and void a few minutes ago. The more she thought about it, too, John had become just a little too obsessed with her. He even acted as though he thought they might get married someday. So she definitely had to let him go. Not just because of what Kane had found out but for many reasons. Raven would give him fifty thousand dollars of the money he was embezzling for services rendered, though, because he'd certainly earned it.

She also wanted to double check with John again about their overall plan, making sure everything was set to go. John had assured her that it was, but she just wanted to confirm with him one last time. So she called him. But after a few rings, the call went to his voice mail. She didn't bother leaving a message, though, because she knew he would call her back within minutes. He always did.

Raven still had another call to make, however, which actually was the most important one of all. So she dialed D.C. Interestingly enough, his phone rang and went to voice mail, too, so she hung up. She'd been hoping to tell him that she would bring him his money by the end of next week, which was a little sooner than expected. But now she would just wait and call him again when Porsha delivered that cashier's check. Raven was also happy to be paying D.C. a lot earlier than planned, so she could finally sleep normally again. In fact, she sort of wished D.C. had been willing to take a cashier's check himself, because then she could have paid him immediately. She knew he didn't operate that way because of the paper trail aspect, but it certainly would've been easier than having to withdraw so much cash. But nonetheless, all would soon be well, and Raven would be able to get back to the great life she was creating.

The kind of life that most people only dreamed about.

Chapter 38

*F*riday was finally here, and Raven was glad to know that this was the last day Porsha would step foot inside NVCC. She also couldn't help thinking about all the money she would soon have, which was the reason she'd spent most of the morning searching online for lots that could house at least a seven-thousand-square-foot home. Many were located about a half hour from the church, and actually, she liked that idea. Right now, she lived only about fifteen minutes away, but she didn't like the fact that some of her members knew exactly where she resided. None of them stopped over unless she'd asked them to do something church-related, but she also didn't want them simply driving by whenever they wanted. Because who was to say that there wouldn't come a time when she had certain visitors she didn't want them to see? Some things just weren't everyone else's business, and she wanted to protect her privacy. It was the reason, too, that she was leaning more toward building a gated property, because that would ensure the best kind of seclusion.

As the morning continued, Raven became more and more excited because everything in her life was about to change for the better. She would actually be earning a minimum of one hundred thousand dollars per month. It was sort of hard to fathom, because she still remembered how thrilled she'd been when Pastor Black had hired her a long time ago and paid her just over seventy per year. But now she was on her way to earning what he did. In fact, if it hadn't been for all the books he'd written and the millions of copies that had been sold, she would soon earn more than him. But that was okay, because Raven was doing fine where she was and she had no complaints.

She looked at her watch and wondered what time Porsha would be showing up with those documents and that cashier's check. It was already half past eleven, and Raven hoped she wasn't planning to wait until the end of the day. Especially since Raven wanted to deposit the money right away and then write checks to twelve other accounts. She'd purposely opened all of them at different banks, because even though it wasn't common for anyone to withdraw twenty-five thousand dollars in cash at one time, Raven didn't have a choice. D.C. had forced her into mob-like territory, and she had to see this thing to the finish. She would literally have to visit one bank after another...twelve...different...times. But the good news was that it would all be over very soon. Then, this morning, she'd also gone to the bank that John had transferred the five hundred thousand dollars to. She did trust John not to double-cross and steal from her, but to be safe, she'd withdrawn the money and split it equally into two new money market accounts.

Raven sat at her desk for another half hour but started to feel a bit nervous. Partly because she still hadn't heard from Porsha, and partly because she hoped John had covered all of his tracks the way he'd told her. She certainly trusted his intelligence, but last night, when she'd gone over to sleep with him one last time—because he'd called, begging her like never before—he'd seemed more concerned about sex than he had about the money transfer. He'd also seemed a little nervous, and she hoped he wasn't allowing fear to get the best of him. Because after all, before Raven had coaxed him into embezzling the money, John had been a straight-laced, by-the-book financial guy. He'd always followed the law and had never placed the church or Raven at any risk when it came to the federal government.

But maybe she was just paranoid, and John was fine. Still, she called his office to check on him. But he didn't answer. So she left hers and walked down there to see him. When she looked through his doorway, though, she noticed that his lights weren't even on. It was unusual for him not to be in yet, but maybe he had an outside appointment. So Raven went back to her office and closed the door.

But only five minutes after she sat down, Michelle hurried in. "I don't know how to tell you this, Pastor, but Porsha and Dillon are here. They're waiting to see you."

"Together?"

"Yes."

"Did they say why?"

"No."

Raven tried to think fast, because she hadn't planned on Dillon finding out about her conversation with Porsha. She also wouldn't have expected Porsha to contact Dillon about anything. But all this showed was just how desperate Porsha was in terms of trying not to sign those documents and pay the money Raven was demanding.

Raven wasn't afraid of them, though. "Send them in."

When Michelle turned and left, Raven walked around to the front of her desk, sat on the edge of it, and folded her arms.

Finally, Porsha and Dillon entered.

"What's with the sitting-on-the-desk thing?" Dillon said, shutting the door. "Some kind of power move?"

Raven hated Dillon, and she was irritated already. "What is it you want? Why are you here?"

He glared at her. "Well, first of all, Porsha's not signing away her rights to anything or paying you any money."

Raven smirked. "Really? Well, if she doesn't then that porn video of yours will become the most-watched sensation on the Internet."

"No, I don't think so," he said. "And I'll tell you something else. Not only will you never try to blackmail Porsha again, but you won't be blackmailing anyone."

Raven tightened her face. "Dillon, just get out, okay? And Porsha, I suggest you hand over my money and those documents."

Porsha stared at her but never said a word.

Dillon pointed his finger at Raven. "I told you I wasn't playing with you, and I meant that. You messed with me the whole time our divorce proceedings went on, but now it's payback time."

Porsha turned her head abruptly and looked at him. She acted as though Dillon was catching her off guard, too.

"Yeah, yeah, yeah, Dillon," Raven spat. "Whatever you say."

Dillon smiled at her. "You think you're the smartest person alive, when really you're one of the stupidest women I've ever met. And because you were bold enough to steal all that money from my dad when you worked for him, I knew you would steal again if you had to. Especially if D.C. put some real pressure on you. And not thirty thousand dollars' worth, either, but ten times more than that amount. I knew if he demanded that kind of money, you would find a way to steal it from your own church. But I also knew you would never do it yourself, because you didn't want to go back to prison."

Raven's body went numb, and she had to hold on to the edge of her desk with both hands to steady herself.

Dillon smirked at her again. "Yeah, I'll bet you're taking me serious now, aren't you?"

Raven looked at Porsha, wishing she would say something—anything—but she was as stunned as Raven.

"But just like D.C. put the pressure on you, he put even more pressure on that John character."

"What are you talking about?" Raven asked, trying to make sense of what Dillon had done.

"You slept with him again last night, didn't you?" Dillon asked, but his question sounded more like a statement.

Raven swallowed hard, trying to relax her breathing.

"Don't even bother trying to answer that," he said, "because I already know you did. And I have the video footage to prove it."

Porsha covered her mouth with both hands.

Dillon walked closer to Raven, staring her down, but his cynical smile was gone. "So if you even think about leaking that video to anyone, I'll be leaking yours...Pastor Raven."

Raven couldn't speak if she wanted to, so she just watched him turn and walk away.

"Baby, let's go," he told Porsha.

But before they could open the door to leave, a small group of men and women barged in. Raven didn't even have to ask who they were, because she knew they were FBI agents. She knew John had betrayed her, and that life as she knew it was over. Worse, as Dillon and Porsha exited Raven's office, Dillon glanced back at her. He never said a word, but the snide look on his face spoke volumes. It said everything.

Chapter 39

D illon, what happened?" Porsha yelled. "What did you do?"

"I took care of things just like I said I would. You can't play with somebody like Raven. You have to deal with her like the enemy she is or suffer the consequences."

Dillon drove out of the church parking lot, and Porsha was still trying to figure out how Dillon had exposed Raven to the FBI.

"Why didn't you tell me what was going on?" she asked. "Why didn't you prepare me?"

"Because I didn't want you involved. I just wanted to protect you from Raven. I wanted to stop her from ever trying to blackmail either one of us again."

"I get that, Dillon, but why was the FBI there?"

"Because I called them."

"Why? And is that the reason you made a copy of those documents Raven gave me?"

Dillon pulled up to the stoplight and looked at her. "Baby, I really don't want to give you any more details. Just know that Raven will never bother you again. She's going back to prison, and that'll be the end of it."

"How did you know she was going to steal money from the church?" she asked.

"I just did. I used to be married to Raven, remember? I know how she thinks and what fuels her criminal side. I also hired a private investigator to follow her."

"You what? When?"

"Sweetheart, I'm begging you. Please let this be."

"No, Dillon, I want to know and I want to know now."

"I hired him months ago, but it wasn't until these last couple of weeks that he saw Raven spending a lot of time at your CFO's house. Then he learned that she was staying overnight sometimes."

As Dillon drove through the intersection, Porsha looked straight ahead. Raven had actually been sleeping with *John?* And used him to steal money for her? Porsha knew Raven was capable of a lot of things, but this wasn't something she'd expected.

"Well, who is this D.C. person, and what does he have to do with any of this?" she asked.

"You're just not going to stop, are you?"

"No, and if you don't want to answer my questions, you can just drop me off at home and leave."

"D.C. is the loan shark that you've heard Raven talking about in her sermons. You know, when she shares about how she worked for one and stole from him."

"Yeah, and?"

"Well, D.C. is also one of my brother-in-law's best

friends. And even though D.C.'s profession isn't legal, he still loves and respects my dad, too. He always has."

"Are you saying that Levi and your dad asked D.C. to do this?"

"No, neither one of them know anything about this. But when Raven made those rape accusations and got all those rumors started about my dad, I knew it was time to stop her. So I called D.C., told him what was up, and we came up with a plan. And like I said earlier, I knew it would only be a matter of time before she figured out a way to steal money. I also knew her CFO would be the best person to help her."

"Is that why she cleared your dad's name?"

"Yep. D.C. told her he would give her more time to pay, if she did."

"And Raven was that afraid of D.C.?"

Dillon looked at Porsha again. "Yeah, and everyone else had better be afraid of him, too. Because D.C. means what he says, and Raven knows his history. When she worked for him, she saw what happened to people who owed him money but didn't pay."

"This is crazy," Porsha said.

"Maybe, but it was very necessary."

"But how did you guys make John turn on Raven?"

"It wasn't like it was all that hard. D.C. just waited for him to get home and then went inside his garage. And pointed a gun to his head. After that, they went into his house, and D.C. told him how everything was going to play out. And that if he did what he was told, D.C. would let him live. That was two nights ago, and then before daylight yesterday morning, some of D.C.'s boys went over and set up a hidden video camera in John's bedroom."

"Poor John," Porsha said, because he'd always been such a nice guy. Porsha was sure he still was, but it was just that he'd gotten caught up with Raven.

"He'll be fine," Dillon said. "I mean, I'm sorry D.C. had to scare him the way he did, but it was the only way to get him to make that video and turn over all of Raven's and the church's financial information. He met with the FBI early this morning."

"Will he be charged with anything?"

"Not at all. They've already promised him full immunity. Although I will say this: When you told me that Raven was blackmailing you for the same amount that D.C. had told her she owed him, I thought maybe she hadn't stolen *any* money from the church. I thought she was just planning to get it from you. But then when D.C. asked John what Raven was up to, he told everything. That gun D.C. was holding made all the difference."

"So Raven was going to get money from me, *and* she had John stealing from the church?"

"Yep, and I'm not shocked about it at all. I tried to tell you who Raven was and that you couldn't trust her."

"Yeah, you did, and you were right. But that's not my biggest worry right now."

"Then what is?"

"That I still can't trust you, either."

Dillon frowned and looked at her and then turned his attention back to the road. "Why?"

"Because you had a private investigator following Raven, and you didn't tell me. Then, when I told you some guy had shown up at Bible study and Raven had gotten all nervous about it, you acted like you didn't know who I was talking about. But that was D.C., wasn't it?"

"Baby, I already told you that I didn't want to involve you in this. D.C. is a professional criminal, and the less you know about him the better."

"But you still lied to me."

"Not because I wanted to."

"But you did, and you never thought twice about it."

"You're taking this the wrong way."

"Really? Because it sounds to me like you're still the same ol' Dillon, trying to get revenge on your ex-wife."

Dillon stopped at another light. "So would you have rather I just sat back and let her take three hundred thousand dollars from you? Or what if she'd still leaked that video?"

"But you know she's a felon."

"Yeah, that's kinda my point. Raven is capable of doing anything."

"And it doesn't bother you that you're sending her back to prison?"

"Are you saying she shouldn't be punished for stealing money from your church members? Because that's exactly who that money belongs to."

"No, I'm not. I just hate that things turned out the way they did. That you used a hardened criminal to threaten John's life, and that you have no remorse about the revenge you just got on Raven."

"I won't even lie. I don't."

"Then it's like I said, you're the same ol' Dillon."

"You just don't see how serious this is. The kind of damage Raven was getting ready to cause. Not just to the church, but to you and me, too. And I wasn't going to lie down and take that. I wasn't letting her get away with it."

Porsha turned toward the passenger window and didn't say anything else for the rest of their drive. What a day this had been, and she was burdened with so many emotions. On the one hand, she was glad Raven had been caught—both for trying to blackmail her and for embezzling money from the church. But on the other, she was hurt by Dillon's lies and deceit. She loved him, but what if the next time someone crossed him, he called D.C. to handle it? So she just didn't know what to think or how to take this. She wanted to believe that Dillon had only called D.C. because there had been no other way to stop Raven. But what if his sole motive had been to get back at Raven for taking half of his money during the divorce? He'd also had to pay her half of the equity from their house. Or what if he was still upset about his church burning to the ground while Raven's church had been thriving since she'd founded it? Raven had never stopped believing that Dillon was responsible for that fire, either, and now, sadly, Porsha wondered the same thing. So much so that she wanted to cry because in her heart, she knew Dillon still wasn't living his life right—at least not as much as he claimed. And Porsha couldn't spend the rest of her days wondering what he might do next. It was just too much to deal with and too much to take on. Porsha wished things could be different because she did believe he loved her, but she knew it was time to slow down the rekindling of their relationship. If they could somehow work things out and build from there that would be great, but if they couldn't, she would accept that outcome as well. Because in the end, she just wanted to be happy and live in peace. Joy and no drama was all she wanted from now on.

Chapter 40

*P*orsha finished praying one last time, picked up her message notes, and left her office. It was Sunday morning, and although two days had passed since Raven had been arrested, Porsha was still stunned. So much had happened in such a very short period of time, and now Porsha had to face the congregation for more reasons than she'd planned. She'd already decided that today would be the day she would officially resign as associate minister, but she hadn't expected Raven to be locked up and waiting to be arraigned in court tomorrow. Porsha also hadn't known until speaking with an attorney friend of hers yesterday that repeat felony offenders faced up to twenty years in prison. So she couldn't help wondering why Raven had thought it was okay to steal money from a church again.

Everything had changed in a matter of days, but Porsha was trusting God to give her the words He wanted her to say this morning. She knew most of the parishioners were still in shock from seeing both local and national media coverage, so her hope was to try to console and reassure them that all would be well. And while she'd known that all the gory details would eventually be exposed, she wasn't happy about Dillon leaking everything as quickly as he could through social media. The news outlets, of course, reported on Raven's embezzlement charges and her attempt to blackmail "her associate minister, Porsha Harrington," but Dillon had made sure that everyone had also learned about Raven's affair with her CFO.

As she walked farther down the corridor leading to the sanctuary, Kane walked toward her. Ever since Porsha and Raven had begun talking less and less, Porsha hadn't spoken to Kane much, either. They said hello to each other on Sunday mornings and also at Bible study, but that was it.

As he walked closer, he smiled and so did Porsha. Then they hugged.

"I am so sorry," he said. "Sorry that Raven tried to blackmail you, and that you've now been left to clean up her mess."

"I know, but it has to be done. And I'm sorry, too. Because I know how much you loved her."

"Yeah, well she obviously didn't love me. If she had, she wouldn't have started sleeping around on me the way she did."

"I really am sorry," Porsha said, reiterating her sentiments.

"None of that is your fault, but I just wanted to let you know that I still plan on being a member here and my prayers are with you."

"I really appreciate that," she said, knowing that he had no clue that she was stepping down from her position.

"Well," he said, "I'd better try to go find a seat because needless to say, *everyone* is here today. Probably some people who aren't even members."

"I'm sure that's true, and I sort of expected it."

Kane hugged her again and opened the door leading into the sanctuary. He waited for her to enter, and then he continued up the far left aisle of the church.

Porsha walked across the front row and into the pulpit. When she stepped behind the podium, she smiled as much as she could, but it was hard seeing so many hurt, somber faces. Still, she began with 1 John 4:7, the way she had the last few Sundays.

"'Beloved, let us love one another, for love is from God, and whoever loves has been born of God and knows God.'"

There were a few *Amen*s and nods of agreement, but not nearly as many as she was used to hearing and seeing.

Still, she continued. "I have spent the last couple of days trying to figure out the best way to speak to all of you this morning, but first, I just want to say how sorry I am for everything. You all have supported this ministry to the fullest, some of you since the very beginning, and I know this is not how you expected things to turn out. When any of us decides to join a church, we do it because we love the message of the senior pastor and the overall atmosphere of the congregation. We also do it because we want our senior pastor to be very knowledgeable in the Word, to be loving and compassionate toward all people, and to have the utmost integrity. But unfortunately, not all pastors, or even associate ministers for that matter, do things the way they should.

Many say one thing while standing in the pulpit on Sunday and then do something totally different when they leave the church. This is certainly not what God wants from his pastors and ministers, but sadly, this is sometimes the reality. They either start out with good intentions and go astray, or we discover that they never meant any good in the first place.

"And the reason I know this to be true is because for two years I have served as your associate minister when I've known all along that God never called me in that manner. He never called me to be a pulpit minister to preach His Word or to use that title to earn money."

Some people raised their eyebrows, while others locked eyes with the person sitting next to them in shock. Worse than that, some showed a feeling of disgust.

"I know my confession is only adding to the pain you're already dealing with, but I just couldn't go another week without telling the truth. Raven is the founder of this church and the general ministry, but I completely funded the start-up and saw it as a business investment. I then earned the same monthly income that she did. And while I don't want to judge Raven's heart, I also don't believe either of us ever chose the positions we did because of our love for God. I mean, I do love God with all my heart, but what I'm saying is that this wasn't the reason I decided to become a minister. I did it because of what I knew the financial benefits would be. And I am so very sorry for that. You didn't deserve to be lied to and treated this way, and I will spend the rest of my life regretting what Raven and I did," she said as tears filled her eyes. "But my hope is that you will somehow find it in your heart to forgive me. I know it might take a very long time, but my prayer is that my future actions will eventually prove just how sincere I am and how much I love all of you.

"But before I take my seat, I would just like to share a few words of encouragement," she said, gazing into as many faces as she could. NVCC had a capacity of 1,500, and not only was every seat taken, but some folks were standing across the back. "The Bible says that many are called but few are chosen, and as you can see, Raven and I called ourselves but we were not chosen by God. We also allowed money to become too much of a priority, and money should never be a deciding factor when a person enters ministry. The other thing that I want to share is that not everyone is chosen or destined to be a pulpit minister. There are many different ways to have a ministry, and I think that's where so many people lose their way. They don't realize that nursing home ministry, hospital ministry, bereavement ministry, jail ministry, shelter ministry, and so many others are very much needed. God has a calling for every single one of our lives, but just know that you don't have to become a pastor or start your own church to do that. I also want to encourage you to keep your faith in God and to focus on your own personal relationship with Him. Because Lord knows, it is sometimes very easy to start worshiping and praising another human being, more so than we worship and praise God Himself. And as most of you know, Deuteronomy five, seven says very clearly, 'You shall have no other gods before me.' And that's exactly what He means. So I hope you will continue to pray and diligently read your Word, because God's Word is what will sustain you. I also hope you will begin praying for God to bless NVCC with a pastor who has been called and chosen by Him, because this is what will make all the difference here.

"And finally, I want you to know that I spent all of yesterday calculating every single dime that I've collected from this church over the last couple of years. And as a result," she said, picking up a sealed envelope and showing it to the congregation, "I've written a check to NVCC for the full amount. I know this doesn't make up for the pain I've caused you, but I still know that it's the right thing for me to do. The church will, of course, be hiring another CFO, but I will still be giving this payment to one of the other lead staff members to deposit. It is the very least I can do, and again, I am truly sorry for everything. And with that said, please know that I love you, and that you will continue to be in my daily prayers. Always."

She smiled again, and this time tears rolled down her face. But to her surprise, Kane stood up, slowly but firmly clapping his hands together. Then, a few more members got up and did the same thing. Soon, nearly everyone was standing and applauding, and as she stepped down from the pulpit, one person after another hugged her, thanked her, and told her that all would be well—including Michelle. This made Porsha cry even more, and although she was embarrassed and encumbered with guilt, she felt relieved. This morning, she'd been sure she'd have to leave

NVCC and find another church, but now she didn't think so. And if they would allow her to remain a member, she would do all she could to help them find a pastor who *was* called and chosen by God to minister. Porsha would also dedicate all her time to her Daughters of Ruth ministry and do exactly what Raven had tried to force her to do last week: sign away all her financial rights to New Vision Christian Center and New Vision Ministries, Inc. She would do it happily and willingly, because this was a new day for her. A whole new life. And she thanked God for allowing her another chance to get things right. She thanked Him for his love, mercy, and grace, because that was all she truly needed. It was all anyone would ever need if they trusted God. And that truth alone gave her hope—and made her smile.

Acknowledgments

As always, I thank my dear Heavenly Father for everything. You have blessed my life in more ways than I can count, and I am forever grateful.

Thank you to my dear Will for being the amazing husband and man you are and for loving me and supporting me in such a wonderful way. Thank you for everything, and I love you with all my heart, mind, and soul.

Many, many thanks and all my love to: my brothers, Willie Stapleton, Jr. (and April) and Michael Stapleton (and Marilyn); my stepson, daughter-in-law, and grandsons, Trenod Vines-Roby, Latasha Vines, Alex Lamont Knight, and Trenod Vines, Jr.; all my nieces, nephews, aunts, uncles, and cousins: Tennins, Ballards, Stapletons, Lawsons, Youngs, Beasleys, Haleys, Greens, Robys, Garys, Shannons, and Normans; to my first cousin and fellow author, Patricia Haley-Glass (and Jeffrey), my best friends, Kelli Tunson Bullard (and Brian) and Lori Whitaker Thurman (and Ulysses), and my cousin, Janell Francine Green; our pastor: Pastor K. Edward Copeland, Mrs. Starla Copeland, and the entire New Zion Missionary

Baptist Church family; and my spiritual mom, Dr. Betty Price and the entire Price family.

To my publishing attorney, Ken Norwick; Beth de Guzman, Maddie Caldwell, Linda Duggins, Elizabeth Connor, Stephanie Sirabian, Kallie Shimek, Genevieve Kim, and everyone else at Grand Central Publishing; my freelance team: Pam Walker-Williams and Ella Curry; to every bookseller who sells my work, every newspaper, radio station, TV station, magazine, web site, and blog that promotes my work, and to every book club that continually chooses my work as your monthly selection. Thanks a million to all of you.

Finally, to the best readers in the world—thank you for supporting me for so many years and for making my writing career possible. I love you dearly.

Much love and God bless you always,

Kimberla Lawson Roby

Email: kim@kimroby.com
Facebook.com/kimberlalawsonroby
Twitter.com/KimberlaLRoby
Instagram.com/kimberlalawsonroby
Periscope.com/kimberlalawsonroby

Reading Group Guide
for
Sin of a Woman
by
Kimberla Lawson Roby

Discussion Questions

1. Dillon claims that he has changed for the better. While there are hints that he has indeed moved on from his adulterous and vengeful ways, there are also indications that he may not have changed as much as he thinks he has. Do you believe he's really changed? What do you think will happen between Dillon and Porsha?

2. Porsha feels compelled to make a few changes in her life, but she initially has difficulty following through on doing the right thing. What are some reasons people might find it difficult to do the right thing? What are some practical things we can do to help ourselves follow through on our convictions?

3. Raven's social media channels become one of the main avenues through which she manipulates her congrega-

tion. In what ways do you think social media can be a pitfall for leaders? In what ways do you think it can be helpful? Should the boundaries in social media use be different for authority figures? If so, in what ways?

4. Raven's ministry grows tremendously despite the fact that she lacks a genuine desire to adhere to the Bible's teachings or to help other people. What do you think were the main factors in the church's growth? Do you think it's possible to detect corruption within religious organizations? If so, what are some things you would try to look for?

5. Porsha begins a women's ministry called Daughters of Ruth (exclusively for single women), which was met with positive reception. Would you want to join a men's or women's ministry? If yes, what are some of the issues that you would want to discuss?

6. Porsha undergoes a radical change of heart, even though nothing in her circumstances had drastically changed. What do you believe were the factors that brought about this change in attitude and perspective? Have you ever had an experience in which you felt like you had to change your habits and/or general direction in life? If so, please share.

7. Raven blackmails Porsha by threatening to release Por-

sha and Dillon's sex tape. If you were Porsha, what would you do? If you had known what Dillon was planning, would you have agreed to use D.C. to threaten Raven the way he did? Do you agree with how Dillon handled the situation?

8. Porsha steps down from the pulpit because she knows that it is not her calling to be a minister. Why do you think some people choose professions or lifestyles that are not in line with their passions, talents, and purpose? How important do you think it is to live according to your calling? Do you feel that you are doing so? Please share why or why not.

9. New Vision Ministries is hit with shocking and very disappointing news about its leaders. If you were a member of the congregation, what would you do? Would you forgive either Porsha or Raven and stay at New Vision Ministries? Or would you leave and find another church?

10. Porsha has made many friends and enemies due to her vast wealth, and at times it can be difficult to differentiate between the two. All Porsha wants is to live in peace without drama, so what are some things that Porsha can do to prevent drama from happening to her again? How can she be more discerning with people who may be using her for her wealth?

11. Raven is arrested, criminally charged, and will likely go back to prison. Do you think that this experience will teach Raven a lesson, or will it only fuel her desire to seek revenge against Dillon?

12. This novel is full of characters, especially leaders, whose outward titles and appearances do not match their inner private lives. Do you think that leaders should be held more accountable for this inconsistency? If you saw an inconsistency in one of your leaders, what would you do?

Q&A with
Kimberla Lawson Roby

Sin of a Woman is your fourteenth Curtis Black novel. When you were writing the first one, *Casting the First Stone*, were you already thinking of turning it into a series?

No, and this is likely the most unknown truth about the series overall. When I wrote *Casting the First Stone*, which was my third novel, it was never my plan to write a sequel or a series. This was the reason I went on to write standalones for my fourth and fifth books. But at the same time, I continued hearing from many readers, either by email or at book signing events, asking when "the next Reverend Curtis Black book" would be released. Finally, my literary agent encouraged me to give my readers what they were asking for, and I'm so glad I did.

Once you were set on continuing with Curtis Black, did you come up with a road map for a few books? Or did you figure things out book by book?

Originally, I'd thought that I would only write a trilogy, but once *Too Much of a Good Thing* and *The Best-Kept Secret* were released, I received more requests from readers than I had before, asking when the next book in the series would be available. So from there, I decided I would continue, but with every book I've written in the series, I've not known what the next story would entail until it was time for me to sit down and write a short synopsis.

The first three books were written from Curtis Black's point of view. But the next one, *Love & Lies*, was written from two women's points of view. Tell us how that came about.

After writing the third book in the series, *The Best-Kept Secret*, readers were excited about the fact that Curtis had finally met his match with his third wife, Charlotte. So I decided that it might be interesting to write *Love & Lies* from Charlotte's point of view as well as from the point of view of her best friend, Janine. I wanted to focus this particular book on the women in the series and their thoughts about their various relationship struggles.

The books teem with real-life issues—infidelity, greed, sibling rivalry, mental illness, and so much more—and you don't gloss over them. Why have you chosen to tackle such difficult topics?

When I self-published my first novel, *Behind Closed Doors* (not in the series), what I heard from readers more often than not was that the reason they'd enjoyed reading it was because they could relate their own lives to those of the two main characters. Then, for those readers who couldn't relate personally, they stated that they knew friends or family members who had experienced similar trials and obstacles. So from that point on, I decided that I would always try my best to write about real-life issues and particularly those that are somewhat taboo or controversial. Or if the real-life issues I write about don't fall into either of those two categories, they are usually issues that I feel passionate about and don't believe we as human beings talk about enough. I try to focus on issues that tend to be discussed privately, even though so many people would be helped if they were discussed more often and openly.

You have a flair for creating characters readers love to hate. Do you find them easier or more interesting to write than characters who are good?

That's a very good question, and strangely, it's one I haven't thought a lot about. On the one hand, I do think it's easier and more interesting to write about highly flawed characters who commit one sin after another, because you have lots of latitude when it comes to plotting the terrible actions of those characters. But on the other, it's also easy to write about characters who try to do the right thing, because even though no one is perfect, good characters represent positive and pleasant scenarios. It's really enjoyable for me when I get to write about characters who consciously treat others the way they want to be treated.

In the case of some of Curtis Black's children, the apple didn't fall far from the tree. How do you decide if what's in store for them is come-uppance or redemption?

Whenever a child grows up with a parent who makes many bad choices and hurts a number of people, there's a chance that some or all of those children will follow the same path. But for some reason, Matthew has always had a big heart and noticeable compassion for others. So for him, instead of receiving come-uppance, he tends to end up hurt by the people he loves. For Alicia and Dillon, the two of them have made many bad choices, but to some degree, they've each experienced both come-uppance and redemption. Then there's the youngest daughter, Curtina, who will soon enter her teen years and will, no doubt, become a handful for her parents.

Name your top three favorite characters and why.

Tanya (Curtis's first wife), as she is the ideal wife and mother from the very beginning.

Matthew (Curtis's second son), because he genuinely cares about everyone and tries to live a decent, respectable life.

Curtis, because as bad of a person as he was, he has now completely turned his life around for the better and he's remained that way for years. I love the fact that he is proof that anyone can change if he or she wants to.

Curtis Black has evolved a lot over the course of the series. When you think about all he's gone through and where he's at right now in his life, is there anything that you hadn't anticipated in the beginning?

When it comes to Curtis, I've known for a very long time that he would become a true man of God, a faithful husband and an upstanding father. It is true that he always loved his children deeply, no matter what, but I also wanted him to become a great example for them. In the end, my ultimate goal was to have him do all the good things he spoke about on Sundays from the pulpit.

You interact a lot with your fans on your tours and on social media. Have you noticed if your readers' attitudes

toward Curtis Black and his family have changed over the years?

Yes, they definitely have. Early on, most readers could barely stand Curtis Black, and some openly stated how they hated him. But as time continued on, they began to tolerate him, and ultimately many readers began to like the new man he's become. In contrast, however, many readers can still barely stand Charlotte, and they want her to get what they believe she has coming to her.

Can you look into your crystal ball and give us a hint of what's coming up for the Black family?

There will likely be new problems that evolve with one of the children in the Black family, and of course, Curtis and Charlotte will be very much affected by them.